T0304565

'Totally gripping... A sympathetic protagonist in Emily, fabulously toxic characters in the repellant Scarmado family, a tense, claustrophobic setting and a sense of mystery from the start all add up to a compelling locked room thriller.'
HARRIET TYCE

'Glamorous and atmospheric with a cast of brilliantly untrustworthy characters.'
CATHERINE COOPER

'Deadly glamour on the high seas.'
ERIN KELLY

'A thrilling read that will whisk you away into treacherous waters!'
LESLEY KARA

'Wild! I gulped down the gripping twists and turns of this murderous *Succession* at sea thriller like fine champagne. Loved it.'
ANGELA CLARKE

'Agatha Christie meets *Succession*... A compulsive drama.'
JO FURNISS

'A perfect holiday read but with teeth! Incisive, thrilling and crammed full of deliciously toxic family nastiness.'
KATE SIMANTS

'Secrets and lies of the rich and privileged – this book is twisty, it's devious, it's fun.'
SAM HOLLAND

'I was gripped from start to finish, so much so I missed an afternoon's work because I *had* to find out how it ended. A complex, fast-paced locked room thriller sprinkled with all the glamour and mystery of the super rich.'
SE LYNES

'Such a cleverly constructed tale about the secrets families and friends keep. I tore through it in two sittings.'
ROBERT SCRAGG

'A superbly crafted mystery... beautifully charts a course between classic whodunnit and white-knuckle thriller.'
DOMINIC NOLAN

'Layered full of suspense and intrigue, with a cast straight out of *Succession*.'
CAMERON WARD

'The perfect mix of glamour, intrigue, danger and excitement... Tons of twists and turns kept me guessing until the final pages, which I did not see coming!'
POLLY PHILLIPS

'I adored this *Succession*-style thriller... Told with haunting flashbacks and a fascinating cast of characters orbiting a charismatic and mysterious patriarch... Beautifully written and utterly gripping.'
HEATHER CRITCHLOW

'High glamour, grit and suspense – a perfect locked room mystery with an enviable setting.'
NIKI MACKAY

FIVE NIGHTS

RACHEL WOLF

An Aries Book

First published in the UK in 2024 by Head of Zeus,
part of Bloomsbury Publishing Plc

Copyright © Rachel Wolf, 2024

The moral right of Rachel Wolf to be identified
as the author of this work has been asserted in accordance with
the Copyright, Designs and Patents Act of 1988.

All rights reserved. No part of this publication may be reproduced,
stored in a retrieval system, or transmitted in any form or by any means,
electronic, mechanical, photocopying, recording, or otherwise,
without the prior permission of both the copyright owner
and the above publisher of this book.

This is a work of fiction. All characters, organizations, and events
portrayed in this novel are either products of the author's
imagination or are used fictitiously.

9 7 5 3 1 2 4 6 8

A catalogue record for this book is available from the British Library.

ISBN (PB): 9781803287829
ISBN (E): 9781803287782

Cover design: Emma Rogers

Typeset by Siliconchips Services Ltd UK

Printed and bound in Great Britain by
CPI Group (UK) Ltd, Croydon CR0 4YY

Head of Zeus
First Floor East
5–8 Hardwick Street
London EC1R 4RG

WWW.HEADOFZEUS.COM

For Jack and James

PROLOGUE

The invitation had landed on the doormat with the bills, pizza take-away fliers and the reminder that the car tax was coming. Amongst all the flimsy envelopes, it stood out: crisp, thick, ivory. Expensive – a luxury cruise leaving soon. The promise of an escape to somewhere else. Somewhere better. I knew before I picked it up who it would be from, even though it had been three years since I'd seen her.

Will you go? Dad had said as I dropped the post on the kitchen table. I'd shaken my head, flicked the kettle on for coffee, trying to stop my hands from shaking.

Belle had got in touch. I think I'd thought, deep down, that she was gone for good.

The text arrived, only moments later. I read it, feeling the ground shift slightly. Things were going to change and I wasn't sure I was ready:

Please come, Em. I need you. The cabin's all paid for. The ship is incredible. Portsmouth to New York. I'll book an airline ticket for you to fly home. First Class. Please, Em. Come x

I thought of Belle and me three years ago, crewing on yachts in big oceans under the hot sun. Those images are sticky and bright, and I'd tried to wipe them away. To forget what I'd done. The whole thing. But no matter how much I try to refocus, I think they'll always be glued behind my eyes as a reminder of how great we had it, for a while.

Now, at twenty-eight, my best friend had married Sir Mattia Scarmardo, the billionaire, and I'd fled home to Dad.

I'll go if you don't, Dad had said, and grinned as he'd shaken cornflakes into a bowl, standing on the old lino of the kitchen floor.

I'd looked out into the fenced garden through the kitchen window, looked at the hazy, remembered figures of Belle and me, at the bottom of the green square of grass, playing in a blow-up paddling pool when summer arrived and our town had lit BBQs and people had lain out on rugs behind their houses, flat and pink, turning pinker.

Once upon a time, I'd have bitten your hand off to leave it all behind. I'd been desperate to see beyond our back garden. Desperate to find the big wide world. Not now.

Despite being terrified, despite wanting to let the past sleep, of course I'd go, in the end. I would go despite knowing I shouldn't. Despite knowing Belle and I were broken. I owed it to Belle. I owe her more than five nights. I owed it to try and become us again.

Would I have gone if I'd had a glimmer of how badly it would all turn out?

We'll cope, Dad had said. *Go on, love. You work too hard. You haven't had a holiday in years.*

I'd done nothing about it all day, pushing the invite out of my mind. But when I'd kissed Finn good night, and stroked his brow, I'd watched him sleep and realised that Dad was right. They would be OK. He's almost three now. Dad could easily look after him. I couldn't hide behind him anymore.

I owed Belle. For her to reach out, she must need me. After what I did, I couldn't refuse. There was a time when we lived like we were glued together.

Paddling pools, school holidays, growing up side by side. On our eighth birthday, we copied a blood brothers pact from an old movie using Dad's penknife, and Belle spent two days in bed on antibiotics. The site of her cut swelled up angry and red. Blood sisters.

I couldn't refuse.

So after I'd locked up for the night, I'd packed a bag and wondered how, in my cheap clothes and cheap shoes, I could slot into a luxury cruise.

I had no idea what was coming.

DAY ONE

1

The port is busy. A line of passengers look up at the new ship gleaming white under the heat-wave sun, one of the hottest Junes on record for Portsmouth. The sea is blue and stretches out flat, not a ripple in sight.

I've been talking to the couple in front of me for a few minutes now as the line inches forward. The woman must be in her late fifties; she wears a huge hat, blue and bright, and she has gold hoop earrings and bright-red lipstick. She's as shiny as the new ship.

She smiles at me. 'Is it your first cruise, dear? Emily, you said your name was?'

'Yes, Emily. First time as a passenger. I like your hat,' I say.

She beams, touching it as she replies, 'It's new. I've heard the Scarmardo family themselves will be on board.' She speaks in an awed whisper.

I open my mouth to comment when the husband says, 'Well, they do own the bloody ship! It's the first voyage! Why he went into ships I have no idea. Don't like his washing machines much myself. He sells billions of them but they're always breaking down. Cheap, but you get what you pay for. I hope he builds these things a bit better.'

We all look up. Beautiful. So huge I can barely breathe.

'Wow,' I say, and the woman nods in agreement.

In my bag, I have the crisp, white invitation. And I have the note that arrived in the post the day after. Covered with thick black marker pen, it read: STAY AWAY FROM THE SHIP. I KNOW WHAT YOU DID. No name. A warning from someone who wished to stay anonymous.

I'd thrown up after reading it. The guilt suddenly as fresh as it had been three years ago. I'd felt sick and hollow all day.

Someone knew.

That decided it. The warning hadn't put me off coming. If anything, it had made up my mind. I might be terrified to see Belle again, but if someone knows, then I can't run from that.

Coming has meant ripping myself from the safety of my life with Dad and Finn. I'm still not fully healed, even three years later. I'm not ready to go forward, or to look back. My life has become predictable and stable. It was what I needed after the horror of the yacht. Maybe this jolt out of my routine of work and looking after Finn and Dad is what I need, even if I'm not prepared.

I have to find out who else knows the truth, our secret.

I should have called Belle, but I'd put it off. After three years, I need to see her face to face. There's too much to say.

I promise myself again I will keep Finn safe – he's all mine. Someone is threatening me, and I need to sort it out to secure our future.

'You're very pretty,' the woman says, and I snap back to reality and smile.

'Thank you.'

She digs me with her elbow. 'You know the eldest son, Jimmi, is single?'

For the first time in a while I laugh but the woman is still speaking. Her eyes widen and she grins, digging me again. 'I might get a selfie.'

'Don't go anywhere near them! They're all awful. More money than sense.' The husband twists the top from a Coke bottle and it fizzes down his arm. 'That Mattia Scarmardo looks pretty heartless to me. You know his first wife drowned on their

8

private beach? So sad – but then he up and marries again in five minutes, to someone half his age. His new wife is younger than his oldest son! I'm only here because you talked me into it. I hope we don't see those bloody immoral kids – all fast cars, too much money and booze.' The man takes a drink from his Coke bottle and wriggles in his shirt. 'This new material you got me is itchy.'

The wife starts talking almost before he finishes, ignoring the grumpiness of her husband. 'Well, I for one can't wait to see them! All five of the children are going to be on board. The youngest – Chloe – she's in this magazine, look.' The woman's hat brim flaps as she scrabbles in the blue-and-white striped tote bag hanging off her arm. 'Here!' Pulling it out, she opens it to a double-page spread and there, Chloe Scarmardo, twenty-one years old, looks out at us. Dark roots, bleached, bobbed hair, purple streaks, gold necklaces hanging low over a pink vest top.

'She can't sing for toffee. Pressure's on for her now, though. I heard a rumour Mattia Scarmardo is delaying retiring. That new wife of his must want his coffers properly stocked. Means the kids might not inherit the company this year like he announced they would. All that inheritance withheld.' The husband shakes his head. 'I wonder what she sees in her *billionaire* husband? Certainly, not his age. He's almost seventy, isn't he?'

'Oh my gosh, he's only sixty-four, and he's very handsome. She's very beautiful, though. Belle, she's called, isn't she?' The woman looks to me for confirmation and I nod.

I have no idea if the Belle I knew is the Belle I'll see today. How much can someone really change? And she's married into everything that reminds me of why I ran back home. I still have bruises from three years ago. Scabs I keep picking at. This week could open them up with one swipe. To step back into the past, to confront the possibility that someone other than Belle knows what we did. What I did. There's part of the story the world knows, and part only we know. And now maybe someone else.

I need to do this.

I want to tell this friendly woman in the hat that I know Belle, that she can be the kindest person you'd ever meet. That she'd once stood in front of me in the playground, when the whole football team had been laughing at my unbranded trainers in PE, and she'd shouted them all down and made them apologise. I want to tell them that I can't believe Belle married just for money. She's so much more than that. I want to say that if Belle married because she feels like she needs a place of safety, then it's my doing. I want to say all of this, but I don't, because what good would it do now? I need to save it for later. I need to say it to Belle, and there's nothing this couple in the shiny hat and the itchy shirt would do with the guilt I carry. I'm here to put that right.

'Oh honestly, you're being such a downer,' the wife says, eyes rolling at her husband. 'Now, don't go embarrassing me if we meet them. Lordy!' She clutches her hand to her chest. 'Look at those cars. I bet they're all inside!'

'That's one way to arrive,' I say as a line of black SUVs with tinted windows pull up, the heat of the day making them shimmer. Drivers leap out and open doors as ship crew rush to open the red rope that leads to the VIP entrance.

Out climb the family that the whole world knows: the Scarmardos. The eldest exits first.

'Oh, Jimmi is so handsome, isn't he? Even better in the flesh! And a bit mysterious. You never see him with anyone on his arm – not for years. He's worth a fortune; he's got his own business in Italy.' The wife clutches my arm excitedly.

I look over at him. Tall and dark. They all wear sunglasses. Aloof. 'I'll keep that in mind,' I say, smiling.

'There's that Xander,' the woman purses her lips. 'Whatever you do, do not go anywhere near him. A new girlfriend every week. Oh my God, there's his twin, Lila! She's the brains apparently. Never smiles though.'

Both tall with short, cropped, blond hair and olive skin, the twins are striking. Jimmi lifts his hand but not his arm, half waving at the line of passengers. Some shout his name, wave excitedly.

The doors to the second car open up, and Chloe climbs out. Jimmi kisses her and she heads immediately to the line of passengers, already leaning in for selfies.

'That one's Ben, but they call him Bean,' the husband next to me says, drinking his Coke. 'I think because he's small. Not as good-looking.'

I smile at the husband, who is clearly up to date on the Scarmardos, despite his attempts to appear disinterested. I wonder if he reads his wife's magazines when she's not looking.

We look at the brother who follows Chloe out. He's shorter – must be about five foot eight. Unlike Lila and Xander, he has mousy hair and is very pale. Even the huge sunglasses he wears don't make him seem any bigger.

'I heard they call him that because he's allergic to baked beans,' his wife says.

'My God, woman, the things you read!' The husband splutters Coke down his nose and I bite back a laugh.

The last car door opens and out climbs Mattia Scarmardo. Even the husband next to me stands a little straighter at seeing him. Born in the North East of England to an Italian taxi driver father and his mum a cleaner from Newcastle, Sir Mattia Scarmardo had set up an electrical production company at the age of sixteen that is now worth billions. He was knighted a few years ago. The last yacht Belle and I crewed was owned by his company, but I'd never met him in the flesh, only ever seen him in magazines.

'You know what they say about him,' the husband says, lowering his voice as though the family can hear. 'That he sees with a microscope and a telescope all at the same time. He sees where things are going, and nobody ever slips a detail passed him.' He sniffs. 'I'm a bit the same, myself.'

Jimmi Scarmardo greets his father, and after ducking his head to look in the back of the car, he turns to the line of passengers, where I'm standing. I wonder if Belle is in there. He points in answer to something and nods. Then he strides over, heading straight for me.

'Oh. My. Actual. God.' The wife clutches my arm. 'Is he really coming towards us?'

All eyes look in our direction.

He's now only a few metres away, and he's even taller this close. He takes off his sunglasses and smiles – more mouth than eyes – and looks straight at me.

'He's looking at you. I think I'm going to faint,' the wife whispers. Her fingers are still dug into my arm.

'Emily!' Jimmi says, as though he says this every day. Like he's known me for years, he kisses both my cheeks and lifts up my bags.

It's clear Jimmi Scarmardo doesn't know who I am.

'Jimmi,' I say, with all the cheeriness I can muster as I flinch a little when his face comes close to mine. Belle must have asked him to come and get me. She must have pointed me out. I wonder why she didn't come herself.

The flattening heat hits me afresh for a second, and I square my shoulders. I've got this.

I feel myself flush. Nerves like tiny pins prickle all over, and my mouth is dry. My feet won't lift. The card is burning a hole in my bag. *I KNOW WHAT YOU DID.*

People raise their phones my way, a swivel of interest.

'Belle can't wait to see you. Let's go!' Jimmi turns and walks towards the roped-off VIP line, where crew stand waiting.

'Who is she? Who have we been talking to?' I hear the husband say as I force myself to race after Jimmi, aware that the entire line of passengers is staring at me. My cheeks burn. A man with an old Blur t-shirt, grey hair and a press pass round his neck lifts a camera and points it straight at me.

There are almost three thousand passengers boarding today.

All eyes right now are on us. After years of keeping to myself, I am vulnerable again.

Why did I say I'd come? What have I done?

2

I follow Jimmi up the gangway and onto the ship; music plays and there are crew members dancing, holding trays of champagne for all of the passengers as they board. Whether this is usual or an inaugural cruise gesture, the sheer glamour of the whole thing is like another world.

'Hey! Ready for the cruise of your *life*?' sings out a dancing crew member, spinning as he flashes the biggest smile.

I laugh as I lift a glass and take a big swallow.

'Just come to me,' the smiling crew member shouts, 'if you need anything! But I doubt you will; this ship is the best there is!'

Jimmi walks slightly ahead. I don't know whether he makes no effort at conversation to move through the communal areas quickly, or whether he just can't be bothered. I feel a buzz of anticipation at seeing Belle again, but the beauty of the ship is a distraction. It doesn't give me any space for doubts.

I slow to take it all in. We pass through a huge lounge area, with brightly coloured coffee tables and slick chairs; the Scarmardo green – like sunlit grass – races around the ship in lights and colour. The scale of the whole thing is out of this world. A few passengers are already on board, drinking champagne. No one is moving to their cabin. There is sparkle everywhere. Glass shines, and I see a bright aquarium running up the centre of the ship, showcasing multi-coloured fish, vines and lights. The mood in this huge lounge is high. It spreads over two levels, with spiral stairs leading down to an even wider lounge area. A group of performers dance at the other side of the bar. The party has already started.

Details about the ship had come with the itinerary: eleven restaurants, four pools, a spa, a basketball court, casino, nightclub, arcade, basket swings which arc out over the sea. Adults only. This ship is more than a holiday; it's a lifestyle choice, a bucket list. I think of the couple I'd been talking to in the queue – the big, blue hat and the itchy shirt. I imagine their delight with this energy and vibe. The wife will love it.

There is still the crush in my chest at the thought of seeing Belle again, but I shake it off for a second more to enjoy the music, the bubbles, the atmosphere. After soggy tents and caravans dripping with condensation, this holiday is like walking into how the other half live. I could get used to it. I feel the tiniest spark of desire for something else. A better life. It used to burn like a fire in me. Maybe it had never gone out and has been quietly smouldering for three years.

I see Jimmi heading away and I run to keep up with him. I just catch him as he stops to speak to Xander and Lila, waiting by the lifts. He nods to me as I arrive. I'm uneasy that Belle didn't come to greet me – the rest of the family must already be on board. Why would she leave it to Jimmi? What does it mean?

'Who is *she*?' Xander says, looking me up and down, then turning back to his siblings.

I grip the champagne I'd been handed. I open my mouth to reply but then realise he's not actually speaking *to* me.

Jimmi presses the lift button. He hasn't spoken to me since we were outside either. I wish Belle was here. Maybe she's as tense about the meeting as me. Maybe she's in her cabin, waiting to see me, feeling nervous too.

'She's Belle's friend,' Lila says.

'Hello,' I say, brightly, to garner some reaction, but they ignore me completely.

'Hello?' I say again, but not one of them turns. I put out my hand to Xander, who is the nearest. 'I'm Emily.'

'Do we have to be nice to her?' Xander says to Lila, standing barely three foot away, ignoring me flat, and I laugh out loud. Jimmi gives me half a distracted smile, looking at his phone.

'I'll take you to Belle in a bit,' he says, as though I'd asked, as he looks at his screen.

I'm standing, waiting for a lift, with Jimmi, Lila and Xander Scarmardo, which is the closest I've been to people I've only ever seen in magazines. Is it going to be like this all week? I bite my tongue. *Stay quiet.* They're Belle's new family, so there's no need to piss them off. I need to watch them. I don't know what's going on with Belle, but if I'm going to fix us, there's no point winding up her new family before I even say hello.

Belle would have told me a few years ago that I'm the hot-head. I'm the lit match. I've changed somewhere along the way. I'm more measured. That girl is like a fragment; she's a ghost.

'Ignore them.' A voice to my left makes me turn. 'I'm Ben.'

'Bean,' Xander says. 'At some point you need to start introducing yourself with your real name.' He sounds bored.

Bean replies, 'Finished in court with your speeding fines, Xander? Or was it a drugs charge, or maybe drink driving? I almost thought you were going to miss the launch. But you wouldn't want to disappoint dearest Daddy again, would you?' Bean lifts an eyebrow, turning to me. 'You said your name's Emily? Nice to meet you.'

'Hi,' I say.

Xander is still ignoring me, and rolls his eyes at Bean, saying, 'Well, at least one of us actually manages to have some fun. Anyway, just a load of bullshit. Why are we here, again?' Xander drains his champagne glass. 'Five nights on a boat. With a load of civilians. Surely cruises are for the newly wed or over-fed? Christ, I don't think I'm going to leave the cabin.'

'Please don't. The only thing that would make this better is knowing you'll be out of sight,' Bean says. 'Back in Dad's good books yet?'

'Did someone say something? No? No one?' Xander says, staring over Bean's head.

Jimmi glances at his phone. 'Dad says if he hears Xander swear once on the ship, he's cutting his allowance for another month. You know how much he wants this to succeed. He has to be a model citizen. So play nice, Xander.' The lift counts down to our floor. God, this ship is huge.

For the first time since meeting me in the queue, Jimmi looks at me directly, nodding towards the lift. 'I'll take you to your room.'

Belle. I'll see her soon. My pulse races. I wish she'd met me herself. The waiting is worse now I'm on board.

'He's right, play nice,' Lila says to Xander. 'The company's money is holding this together. Remember how utterly fucked we are if it fails. It's just one trip.' She hasn't lifted her head from her phone. She's taller than me, and she wears a silky summer dress, which looks simple but is cut too well to have come off the peg.

'The bloody *Belle*,' Bean says. 'Did you see her name on the side of the ship?'

'Didn't you know?' Xander says. 'Keep up. Can you imagine her not having her name on the side? The boat was Belle's idea, after all. We're here by royal command.'

I ignore the comment about Belle and store it for later. It's interesting that Lila seems so tense about the company and money. I thought the Scarmardos were loaded.

Still, no one even glances in my direction. I wonder if they care that I listen to all this. They clearly don't care if I relay it to Belle. I'm not surprised she needs my help if this is her new family.

'Well like it or not, it has to succeed. So put some effort in this week,' Lila says, her head staring down as she swipes at something on the screen. 'We need to keep the company from burning down.' Her phone buzzes and she swears. 'Jimmi, we'll need to do a call with the investors. They've still not committed and are threatening to pull some of the funding. Meet me in my cabin in ten?' She steps away from the lift, talking on her phone through some hidden blue-tooth device, her London vowels switching to perfect Italian. Her voice and perfume fades quickly.

'Emily, shall we go?' Jimmi asks me as the lift slides open. Business-like, he holds the door open with his arm, half glancing at his phone. I don't know if he's very distracted or just rude.

I don't mind either way. The less he gives me, the less I need to hand over. I don't want them knowing anything about me, Finn or Dad. I'm here for Belle, but to them I'll be invisible.

As though he can read my thoughts, his head tilts as he looks at me, studies me.

'I can find my cabin. I've got—' I hold up a wrist band that apparently opens everything I need. 'I know the number.' I make sure I greet the indifference with the same tone; I need to blend in.

Xander is clearly bored, saying, 'Oh, leave her. The butlers will be on the deck when we finally get there; they'll look after her. I'm assuming if she's Belle's friend, Dad will have rolled out the red carpet.'

'You're being rude again, Xander,' Bean says.

'There's that niggling noise. Did someone say something? Such a whine in my ear,' Xander says, stepping past me, into the lift. He elbows Bean out of the way. 'I hope this cabin is big. I'm not used to cattle class like you, Bean.'

I move forward, but from beside me, Bean charges in, shoulder dropped, and pushes Xander up against the mirrored wall. Xander smashes against the glass, then pulls out of Bean's hold, and spins his arm around his back.

Xander is a good six inches taller than Bean and much broader.

Bean yelps, swears, and I watch as the lift door begins to close, rebounding against Jimmi's arm. I wonder if I should just ditch them now and take the stairs. The shift from the public harmony to this private in-fighting is too quick. Bean swears again, pulls forward and lands a blow, but Xander grabs his arm and twists it up behind his back.

Jimmi doesn't even glance their way. He still has his arm on the lift door, and he looks deep in thought, watching his phone closely.

This can't be the first time the brothers have fought.

Bean elbows Xander in the stomach, grabs him from behind and holds him in a choke hold. Xander thumps Bean in the stomach, then leans down over Bean and bites his hand.

I glance around but there's no one else here. I imagine they'd pull it back quickly if there were passengers nearby. Public harmony, private fighting.

Jimmi gestures to me, as though his siblings' behaviour is entirely normal and something to be ignored. 'Come on. You'll want to get to your room before all the passengers arrive. There's a welcome speech in the bar soon, so we'll have to be ready.' He sounds impatient.

I want to ask what's so interesting on his phone, and what did Lila mean about the company needing money.

I want to ask Xander if he read the magazine expose last month, and was it true he spent thousands on a bag of icing sugar he bought in the loos of some swanky LA bar?

I want to ask why Belle hasn't come to find me yet.

I line up all these questions for later, when I get used to the rocking of the ship, and remember that nothing is ever as stable as it seems.

Xander finally releases Bean from the headlock he'd slipped him in, and Bean rubs his neck, red-faced. His sunglasses have fallen from his head and are caught on his shirt. One of the arms is twisted as it hangs. No one gives them a second glance. Hundreds of pounds gone in a blink. I feel sick.

'Ignore them,' Jimmi says, nodding to his brothers. He finally seems to realise that watching the fight unfold must be unnerving. 'I told Dad I'd look after you. Belle's asked if you'll visit her cabin once you're cleaned up.'

I step forward, instinctively pulling away from Jimmi slightly as I walk past him. I stand with the now quiet brothers. As Jimmi walks in and the doors begin to close, Bean lands another blow on Xander, who side steps into me. Partly as a reflex, and partly because I want to, I lift my elbow. As he falls against me, I deliver a sharp blow to his ribs which makes him double over. Since the attack on the yacht three years ago, I've taken self-defence courses, I work out in the gym. I can look after myself. But I fake a shocked expression and a stumble.

'Watch it!' he shouts, scowling at me.

Jimmi speaks sharply, 'It's you who needs to watch it, Xander. You fell into her. Are you okay, Emily?'

'Yes, I'm fine. Just a surprise. So sorry, did I catch you?' I say to Xander, and I'm pleased to have finally garnered some response. I watch him touch his ribs gingerly, and Jimmi half smiles at me, looking concerned, his eyes on me for a few seconds.

The doubt I'd tried to keep from my face about being here must be luminous as Jimmi says, 'Your butler will show you where Belle's cabin is. Dad won't be there; he's busy with the ship. It will just be Belle.' His half a smile widens. 'You'll meet the wolf later.'

3

I catch my breath as I explore my cabin. It has more floor space than our house. Two reception rooms and a guest bathroom, a private balcony with an enormous hot tub and an outdoor sofa suite – I'm given a tour by the butler: a tanned woman about my age, with short, dark hair, a smile neat and smooth like her uniform. She is impeccably clean, even the uniform is cut better than the clothes I wear.

'Let me know what kind of coffee or tea you like in the morning. Any special requests, you can text or call me on this number. Let me know if you need your hot tub filled or cocktails to the room. I've arranged a massage for you in a few days, to try out the spa. Call me any time, night or day, with any requests.' She hands me her card, still smiling. It's not wavered once, like she's been trained not to drop it. She holds it as carefully as a tray of drinks. 'My name is Mirka.' Her voice has a touch of an accent, something close to European, and the whole thing feels wildly glamorous.

I take the card, feeling railroaded with luxury. I'm pleased she's repeated her name; when she said *butler* earlier, I'd heard nothing else.

I manage, 'Thanks.' *Do I tip? How much?*

Instead, I grip the card she's given me like it holds me up and I will her to vanish so I can go and see Belle.

'Oh, and this was under your door. A note.' She hands me an

envelope with my cabin marked on the front before leaving; a quick nod, the scent of lemon hanging in the cabin.

It suddenly hits me that I'm about to see Belle for the first time in three years. We'd gone from inseparable to not speaking overnight. I thought she'd still be angry, but her text had sounded forgiving: *Please, Em. Please come. I need you.*

Here, with all the bright lights of the cabin, the ship, Belle's lavish lifestyle, I see how far I have retreated in the last three years. Belle's name is on the side of this ship, and mine is on the mortgage of our tiny house.

I'd missed Belle like I'd had a limb sliced off, but I'd learnt to ignore it. I'd put that part of my life in the past. I needed to build a steady future for Finn. I visit the gym, I go to work, I take Finn to the park.

I'm nervous about disturbing all of that – that someone who knows what I did could undo all the work I've put into stabilising life for Finn.

But I couldn't let Belle down. Not twice.

At some point, I suppose I'd known I'd face her again.

I grew up next door to Belle Myrtle. She was there on my first day of nursery; there when my mum died when I was ten. There when my dad lost his job as a builder after being injured and I went to school in charity-shop clothes and to the foodbank at the weekend. Her parents both worked in the office at the local factory where Dad finally started work again, and we all lived in a housing estate near the industrial park.

She asked her dad to find me a job at the factory once I was sixteen, during the holidays, earning money for cinema trips and then, later, for a Saturday night out. We bought cheap nail polish and applied it to each other. We gave ourselves highlights with lemon juice in the summer and stole the fancy white wine from her mum's fridge, which we'd drink under covers on sleepovers while answering the quizzes in teen magazines about what kind of boy we should be with, learnt lyrics to our favourite songs.

She was there for every crush, my first date, to discuss my first kiss. *Tongues? No tongues?*

She was there when we plotted our escape. We would leave this town with its decaying hope fallen beside the empty crisp packets that blew up against the concrete seawall. The cold sand, dotted with beer cans and broken glass. We were going to conquer the world.

Her parents were killed in a car crash the day after our university graduation. They'd been driving home. So, once all the paperwork was signed, and the funeral was over, raw and loaded with grief and student debt, we put aside plans for world domination and instead got onto boats aged twenty-one, and decided to see the world by working our way round it, by crewing for the holidaying rich. Up before dawn to prepare breakfast, to wash down the deck. The Indian Ocean, the Caribbean, the Mediterranean, the Aegean Sea, the Java Sea.

It had been magic.

Then there was that one day.

I shake my head out of the memory, and text Dad and Finn, taking a photo of the bed to include with the message. I think of Finn jumping up and down on it shouting, '*Again! Again!*' with his pink cheeks and red t-rex who is dragged everywhere. I wish he was here, but I wouldn't risk putting him in the path of any danger. And someone is threatening me. This trip isn't about relaxing.

My bedroom is like a palace! Wish you were here. Will let you know when I get to New York xx

I press send but I'm not sure it goes through – the reception is wobbly. I'd said I'd be in contact to let them know I'd arrived.

Enjoy yourself, love, Dad had said. *Don't be on the phone. We're fine. Bring back lots of chocolate. Do they make sticks of rock in New York?*

There's open champagne on my ultra-modern coffee table,

which fizzes up my nose as I take a sip and wander outside, staring up at the sun. The day is baking and I feel its burn quickly.

I slide open the envelope, blank on the outside, expecting maybe a note from Belle, an itinerary, or information on dinner.

The fizz in me dies.

White card. Black marker pen. No name.

THE SHIP LEAVES PORT 7 P.M. TONIGHT
GET OFF WHILE YOU CAN

4

'Emily!'
     Belle opens the door and there's a second of hesitation before she hurls herself at me.

Her arms tighten around my shoulders, and the worry I'd felt at seeing her is crushed and vanishes. I hug her tight and quick.

Belle: energy which bursts out of her like fireworks, determined, dry witted – so funny she could spin anything for laughs. Raw. Vulnerable. My other half. The better half of me. Three years has been an age, but right now it feels like no time at all.

'I'm so sorry, I'm so sorry,' I say into her hair, and her arms pull tighter still.

'No – fuck that. We aren't doing that. No raking over the past.'

My throat hurts with tears that threaten in that raw, raspy way.

'Come.' Belle pulls me down into her ring of sofas. Her room is almost identical to mine. I've been given the fanciest type of cabin, clearly.

There is open champagne on her coffee table too, and she pours me a glass. I almost take her hand, but I take the champagne instead. I think of when I used to grip her fingers tightly on the way to school when we were four years old, or unsteady on heels after a night out. The same height as me, she's thinner now, as I am. Long, dark hair where I'm blonde. I know her face better than I know my own, and I search it for clues, for the truth of where we are now. What we've become.

After all the anticipation of seeing her again, I feel both strangely at home, and also utterly displaced. I struggle for some normality.

'Mrs Scarmardo,' I say, and I lift my glass. 'How did *that* happen?'

She clinks my glass, and I take in the diamonds in her ears and the rose-gold watch, discreet and sparkly, the new air of authority. 'You must have read the papers. I met him at a charity event, not long after his first wife died. I was speaking about what happened – being a hostage, what it was like.' She shrugs a little. 'He was there to put right what went wrong on his own boat. It was love at first sight.'

'Really?' I laugh, noting how she glosses over *what happened* as though she'd lost her car keys. I think of the violence of that morning. The days of waiting to hear if she was alive. We haven't even touched on that yet and I feel like until we do, I can't relax. 'You mean his billion-dollar empire meant nothing to you?' I aim at light teasing, but my delivery is off.

Belle lifts a hand. The intimacy of a second ago dissipates like smoke. 'I get it. Everyone wants to believe I'm a gold-digger. Especially his satanic children. You know one of them leaked a photo to the press of me coming out of Cartier laden with bags? Everything I'd bought that day were gifts for *their* Christmas presents – and they knew it. But they'll stoop to anything to get a rise out of me.' She talks tough, but I notice that her skin looks pale and she's very thin. Beneath the diamonds and fancy clothes, on closer inspection, she seems to be disappearing before my eyes.

'You know that's not what I mean,' I say, floundering. 'I'm glad you found each other. He's a lucky man.' I take a deep breath. I have to ask her. 'But, Belle, look. We have to talk about what happened. I haven't seen you in three years, and your invitation came so out of the blue, and I just want to say—'

'No, Emily. Sorry, but I haven't got the strength for emotional re-hashings. You're sorry, I'm sorry.' She waves her hand, and this gesture is new. 'But can we start afresh? We've known each other for too long. And I need you, Em. I've always needed you, of course, but I especially need you now. More than ever. Give me a minute to explain. So, no difficult questions, at least not tonight.' The authority slips to a plea, and she ends with a megawatt smile and a laugh. That smile was one of the reasons she'd shone so brightly back home.

I bite back the questions I want to ask. I mustn't show irritation. Of course I will have to work at the friendship, and we'll talk about it eventually. We'll have to. But I'd forgotten this about Belle: that she was able to cut straight through anything to get to the next scene. I focus on everything. I obsess.

'OK,' I smile despite myself. She doesn't want to look backwards, and maybe that's for the best. 'God, I've missed you. No tough questions. But *this*…' I gesture to the cabin. 'You have to tell me, what's it like being constantly surrounded by all of it?'

Her shoulders drop a fraction; she must have been holding them high. 'It's crazy. Totally crazy.' She takes a swig of the champagne then puts it down. 'There. I said I'd have one swallow with you, then nothing. I've been off the booze for two years now.'

I look at her again – it's more than her just being pale and skinnier. Her eyes are dull. Her hair is pulled off her face but it looks thinner.

'Belle, are you ill?' I put my glass down.

'Not ill, no. I'm pregnant.'

5

Belle takes me into the cavernous bathroom, with its expensive soaps and scent of wealth. She pulls out a drawer, filled with boxes with the unmistakeable blue logo on the front.

If we're going to talk babies, can I tell Belle about Finn? No. I need to find out who is sending these notes before I trust anyone with that. Even Belle.

'You brought all these with you?'

'This last year I've been doing about six a day on a good day,' she says, staring at the drawer. 'I shouldn't have talked Mattia into building a ship, I should have told him to invest in pregnancy tests.'

'Oh, Belle!' I reach for her hand now. 'Have you been trying long?'

'Trying?' She laughs without humour. 'I have a window; a *condition*. And it all happened with Mattia so fast – it was like I blinked. And he's been...' Her head disappears into her hands. 'Oh, Em, he's been amazing. Ignore all the press. That man is one in a million. I don't know what you know. What you think. I don't care, not right now. We've had so many rounds of IVF. I've been pumped with drugs, needles, I take my temperature, I do these diets.' She waves her hand at stacks of glass bottles covered with names of vitamins and supplements. 'A few days ago, one was positive.'

'Belle!'

She bites her lip.

'Not getting too excited. I'm still doing the tests. I check all the time. At the weekend, I'd left the positive test in the bathroom at our London house, to show Mattia, and it disappeared.'

'What?'

'We'd had a family lunch on Sunday – a pre-cruise thing. Mattia likes to assemble the family when they're all in the same city. One of them snooped, took the test. So one of them knows I'm pregnant. Maybe all of them.' She waves her hand again – dismissing it. 'I can't think of that now. But since I've been with Mattia, they've been watching me. They hate me. And they'll hate this more. This is why I need you. I'm sure one of them is planning something. Mattia has suggested we announce early, but I'm scared – of what will happen, what they might do.'

I think of the notes and shake my head. I feel sick. What are we up against? I go to ask her what else there is to know – there's clearly more – but I hold myself back, try to let her tell it in her own time. I think of the fight in the lift – how things became physical quickly. Would they be violent with Belle?

Her voice falls to a whisper. 'And they hate me. All of them. Even Jimmi and Chloe. I get it. We married within six months of Viola dying, and they blame me. It was her dying that made Mattia look back over his life and decide to change, but they think it's me. This ship – he's trying to build something beautiful that will last. He's trying to bring some fun into our lives. He's reinvigorated. Life has bitten into him. But they all blame me. When he retires, they will inherit their fortunes and their share in the business. They'll be rich, independent. Now he's considering delaying his retirement, they blame me for stretching out their dependence. But they're rich enough – they just can't see it. They could make their own money. Be their own people.'

'Surely they'll get over that?' I lift a hair that has fallen on her face and tuck it behind her ear. 'Surely they'll come round?'

It's fear I see in her eyes. 'They can be vipers. Mattia said that since she died, they're the angriest people. Be warned. They will explode. If – *if, if, if* – it sticks, then they will have to deal with it.'

She pauses. 'I worry how far they could go. They tried to warn me off, before the marriage. One of them offered me money. Five million dollars. My price to fuck off. They didn't approach me directly – had a lawyer do it – so I still don't know which one it was.'

'No!'

'It's their inheritance. They're so protective of their father, the company, his wealth. To bring another heir into the mix, it's like I'm vying with them.' Her hand goes to her stomach.

'But—'

'Watch them, Em, they'll sneak off later, go into my room, run through my clothes, my jewellery. I worry—'

She stops, and across her face drifts a shadow.

'Go on.'

'I think,' she says slowly. 'I think one of them might be trying to…' She stops again. 'I was in the car recently, driving out of London. The wheel was loose. I was lucky – someone flashed me and I stopped. But…'

'Belle!' I feel sick. I think again of the two threatening notes, now stuffed in my toilet bag. If her stepchildren are plotting against her, could one of them know what we did? What I did? Have they dug up details I'd hoped were buried forever to use against us? I doubt they care about me, but if they know what happened, they could use it against Belle. I'd be collateral damage.

I open my mouth to tell her about the notes, but I find myself closing it again. She has enough on her plate. I'll tell her later. This will just scare her more.

Waving her hand, she changes tack. Pulling out her earrings, she finds some bigger ones, puts them in. 'Oh, it probably came loose on its own.' She swings her head and I feel like she stopped talking before she'd finished. 'Look, Mattia gave me these on our wedding day. Not too shabby, right?'

She'd talks in a lighter tone, a deliberate shift.

Whatever she'd almost said hangs between us. The old me would have forced it out of her.

But then, nothing's like it used to be.

6

I dress for dinner as the sun lowers over the very edge of the ocean, and the blue of the sky meets the blue of the sea like an embrace. I wonder if there's unity everywhere if I'd just let myself see it.

Then I pull myself together. This isn't some meditative retreat. I think of Belle and her thinning face. Her fears that her stepchildren are waging war against her: *vipers*.

On my way to my cabin, once I'd left Belle, I'd gone to the deck and watched the shores of Portsmouth recede. Past the Spinnaker Tower, past the rest of the, much smaller, boats. Once the coastline was too small to make out any details, and land looked like a toy village, I'd looked the other way. Ocean. Just miles and miles of ocean. Blue as far as the eye can see.

There's no turning back now.

I fasten a chain round my neck as there's a knock on the door.

'A pre-dinner cocktail.' Mirka stands at the door as I open it, smiling again. 'Can I help with anything?'

'No, thank you. Am I late?'

She shakes her head. 'Sir Mattia is expecting everyone in the champagne bar for the speech at eight thirty p.m. Then there will be a trip to the top deck by the pool, and dinner will be set up on his balcony.' She slips away after I take the drink, which is pale pink and fizzes quietly.

As she leaves, I'm sure I see Bean disappearing round the corner of the corridor outside my room. I wait for a second. If it was him, he's not coming back. Why is he hanging round my cabin? Could he have been the one who slipped that second note under my door?

Uncertainty is beginning to turn to fear. It's settling itself like dust on my skin, and I keep brushing it off, but I'm jumpy.

I need to focus on tonight. Be there for Belle. Help her. I need to find out who's sending the notes, and I need to keep an eye on the siblings, one of whom has gone to great lengths to try and persuade Belle to walk away. And that was before another heir was introduced into the mix. Once Belle's pregnancy is announced, what does that do to the stakes?

I look at myself in the full-length mirror. Belle had thrust a dress in my hands and a small bag with jewellery. *Wear these. You'll look amazing. Keep them. Don't thank me. It's just part of the ticket for the trip.*

Prada.

I shine tonight.

I've taken time with my hair. The dress is from someone else's life – a world away from cheap suits and instant coffee. I look better than I've looked in years, possibly ever. I've even taken time with my make-up.

Crewing on boats and mixing with millionaire passengers for all those years had taught us a lot – including how to enter a room and talk to everyone in under five minutes while saying nothing at all. I can fake holding my own with the Scarmardos for a night; they're so self-interested, I doubt they'll see through me. Maybe they won't see me at all.

I suddenly miss Dad and Finn so fiercely, I stare at my phone, but I don't let myself ring home. We'd agreed I was not to, but also, there's no way Dad would understand this. He knows who Belle is married to, but he's got no concept of this kind of living. *Are you having a nice time?* He'd ask, and I'd say yes. *Is the food nice? What's the weather like?*

I pull out the two cards, stiff amongst the toiletries.

I KNOW WHAT YOU DID.

And the second:

GET OFF WHILE YOU CAN.

I look at the clock in my cabin: 20:15. I feel a shiver of fear, but I refuse to be intimidated by the rich and entitled, especially now I know Belle needs me. It's my do-over. I can put right all my wrongs this week. I snap a photo of the notes then, carefully, I shred them with nail scissors and sweep the pieces into the bathroom bin.

I put perfume on, look at myself in the mirror.

I hold my breath, stand taller. It might have been three years, but I know how to move around money. I'm wearing armour in Belle's dress. I lift my chin.

Vipers have nothing on me.

7

VIOLA

Three years earlier, Sicily

Maybe not everyone has a moment when they know their life really began. Maybe some people grow slowly, and mature steadily, lifting upwards in a curve. Maybe they can never place a finger on when they first felt as though they flew.

There's one clear moment for me, though. A look. A flash across the room.

My first look from Mattia. The catch of my breath.

La mia vita, I remember thinking. *It has begun.*

I was young. Eighteen. We were away for the whole summer. It was hot that day, the sun had soaked all the way through my skin, making me heavy, my limbs leaden. It was all I could do to climb from the towel on the beach and head in for lunch. Papa insisted on eating in the cool dining room. He hated the sun. He went outside before eleven and after four, focusing summer days around a siesta like it was an immovable point. On holiday we ate a late lunch at three, once he had risen and was refreshed, ready for the rest of the day.

I was heading inside, after using those cold-water jet showers to rinse on the beach, and I pulled on a summer dress over my bikini. I remember thinking, suffocating, *la mia piccola vita*: my tiny life. When would I see the world?

All this beauty around me, all these people, laying in their expensive clothes, drinks, food at the click of the fingers, but how did it really feel to be alive? I wanted to burn a little – to strive. I was beginning to realise that with our family's money, life was easy for me – too easy. We had been studying the classics, and I was dream deep in the desires of the gods, their ambition, their *lust*.

The hotel we went to each year was in Sicily, set in a cove, a huge villa, stately and old. And I had just put down a book on Persephone, abducted by Hades so close to here. I had barely kissed a boy, and the idea of the passions of the gods…I knew nothing about anything. Looking back, I dreamt in short hand, in what I thought of as big ideas, love and death – and I understood neither. My daydreams were about a love as strong as death. I dreamt of a hazy future like a vivid but incomprehensible tangle of emotion.

I wanted to *feel*.

Papa liked it here, liked the deference; they knew who he was. His status as a successful businessman, head of his own empire, was well known. The area was private – tall cliffs, which were difficult to climb. It was overlooked by nothing but an old abandoned shepherds' hut that was almost impossible to reach.

Doors were opened for me when I headed inside. I was ushered to the table where Mama and Papa sat, amongst all the other guests seated for lunch.

The windows were tall near the table and looked out over the beach; the sun threw its rays away from us and I gazed out over the bronzing bodies, all that skin on display, and the sea stretched so flat and blue it could have been coloured glass.

As I lifted my wine glass, my small world pressed so hard, I was dizzy.

Some of my friends were working in bars for the summer, or had gone overseas. My father, with all his standing, all his money, offered me the five-star hotel we had always stayed at, and when I had begged to work in the bar near home in Bologna with my best friend, he had shaken his head quickly, smiling, and waving his hand in the air. 'You wait for your life to begin, but it will not begin in a bar! Come, enjoy the beach!'

It was an instruction, but I was used to Papa issuing invitations like decrees. No one ever refused Papa.

The food arrived at the table and I looked out over the flat, blue glass, the yellow sand. I didn't even know what I was looking for.

I was ripe – I was so ready to be granted my big wishes for excitement and love, it was laughable how little I questioned Mattia, how easily I gave myself away to him in exchange for imagined passions.

And so, when he looked at me, across the room, I was lost.

A few years older than I was then. Into his twenties and already a force in the room, power in his eyes. He looked over at me, slowly, and I felt his gaze on me, my bare arms, my thin dress.

I stared at him for only a few seconds, and he picked up his wine and walked towards our table.

'This is that young businessman,' Papa said as he walked towards us.

My tongue stuck to the roof of my mouth as Mama replied, 'The one who wants to buy your factories?'

I barely registered their exchange as I watched him walk towards us. For I knew he was coming for me.

He was tall, dark hair, dark eyes. He walked with confidence. He smiled at Papa as he sat down, and barely looked at me. But as he sank into the next chair, his foot found mine, and as it pressed gently against me, my heart beat quickly. My stomach turned over and a tiny fire was lit.

I felt naked.

'Mattia Scarmardo,' he said to me. And as Papa began an introduction to which I didn't listen, he leant forward and offered me his cheeks in a greeting. I knew I was coloured red from foot upwards. He smelt of an evening sea and a fire on the beach. A touch of smoke, of warmed sand.

Mattia joined us for the whole meal. After wine, after dessert, I had barely spoken a word, and Papa looked at the clock and said he and Mama would be ready to take a sail into the harbour soon. Mattia offered them the use of his boat – it would be ready for them if they would like to meet him.

It was agreed.

And Viola, he said, turning to me. *Would you like to walk with me now, to see the boat? We can meet up with your parents soon enough. Give them a chance to collect their things?*

And this was how I walked down the path through the cliffs and rocks with him – Mattia Scarmardo – for the first time, feeling his arm almost touching mine. As we turned the rocky path corner, down to the private moorings, he turned to me, asked for my permission to speak.

'Of course,' I said, trying to sound dignified.

And he took a step towards me, didn't touch me. He spoke so quietly, so intently: 'You must forgive me, but I have fallen in love with you. I need you to know it. I saw you across the room, and you took my heart.'

And then he held out his hand for me, so I wouldn't trip on the steps.

I knew it immediately. And in my youth, what I see now as lust, I knew then was love. Love became death. If I did not sleep with him, then I would die. If I did not become his, my life was over.

Looking back, I realise *of course* he knew who my father was, that I was the only child of the wealthy, renowned businessman, a man with factories and money to spare.

Was it me? Was it my father? I didn't think about why he crossed the room. Not until much, much later.

We were married within months. I held out for him on that holiday as long as I could, but, almost inevitably, I lay naked on the warm sand with him only a matter of nights after we met. Does he remember? How I lay beneath the stars and thought of the romance of the gods, and I gave myself over to every touch, every kiss?

I never questioned his absolute mastery of his craft. How he knew so exactly what he was doing, so expert in every touch. I never thought of him touching another.

Maybe if he hadn't been so practised, I would have questioned it more.

Of course, looking back, I know now that the first time is often a stumble, a slow let down. It takes time to learn how to give pleasure – to know how to touch. To dare to be pleased.

That first time with him, he made it easy. I didn't have to think about inhibitions – he touched me gently, asked me quietly.

He let himself go when I was already flying.

I lay open and naked, my back against the warm sand and I screamed his name on the beach in the dark, and afterwards I spoke of love without fear, because he had already professed his, and I really believed I had begun to live.

Love and death. This is my story of my life; from my first love until my death.

La mia vita, the life of Viola Scarmardo. I find myself drifting back to these memories, under the hot sun, the week of our trip to Sicily. I am now a grown woman, fifty-seven years old, a wife, a mother of five children

Maybe I can already sense what I do not know for sure, that in the next three days, I will die.

I sit in that same hotel – my first anniversary present, our private villa now. The secluded beach, surrounded by rocks, overlooked by the haunted shepherds' hut; the long windows, our private harbour. We have this week together. Our anniversary. Our thirty-eighth.

From love to death.

I am already short on time.

I had better tell my tale quickly.

8

'You look amazing,' Belle says as I meet her by the lifts on our deck.

'I was going to say the same to you.' On the tip of my tongue is *no creases* but it feels too early. I'm not sure we're really back to where we used to be.

'No creases,' she whispers, and then I know it's really OK between us. We used to say it before a night out. No tight hugging until later. Watch the make-up. Watch the clothes. When all we worried about was looking good. I feel a stab of envy for who we were.

Whoever we are now, we've slipped quickly into our old selves. So quickly it's both strange and not strange at all.

As the doors slide open, Belle slides her arm through mine. 'I'm nervous about tonight.'

I glance at her, seeing her brow tense.

'Mattia is going to make some kind of statement. He's been vague on details but he said the press will expect it. It might be to do with Jimmi. He used to be the biggest playboy there was, then when Viola died – or maybe even before that, I remember Mattia saying it was months before that.' She shrugs. 'It ground to a halt. No more women, no fast cars.' She lowers her voice. 'Mattia's quite old-fashioned about the role of the father – the idea of a legacy. The first born, heir apparent. And Jimmi is the image of Mattia. I think Mattia was always hoping he'd pull himself together. He's got a halo so bright Lila would blow it off with a rocket if she could.' She pauses. 'I'm scared of what they could do if they don't like what they hear.' She slides her hand over her stomach.

'We've got this,' I say, squeezing her hand, not sure if I believe it myself. 'I'm here. If the family start getting heavy, we'll just say fuck you very much for your kind words, then we'll head back to my cabin for a night of movies, PJs and chocolate.'

Belle laughs. 'I knew I needed you here. I can always rely on you.'

I feel a stab of guilt. There was a time when she couldn't rely on me. And we haven't talked about it yet. I wonder how straightforward a statement this is from Belle. But I can't worry about that tonight.

We approach the door to the champagne bar and someone with an earpiece, wearing a dinner jacket, nods at us and opens the doors.

The air in the room is strung tight. The crowd are polished and in their finery. Some are clearly press, some special guests. I see the family over in a corner, tall, slick and expensive. Crew move discreetly through the champagne bar with drinks on trays, piano music plays from somewhere. It's busy. Belle heads to the corner, which is separated from the rest of the room, occupied by the Scarmardo children. She moves like a pro – it's a Belle I've not seen before. She lands air kisses, accepts some applause. She worked rooms well when we were yachting, but the attention was never on her as it now. It lights her up. I can't take my eyes off her.

She's the wife of the owner, and she rises to the role. Of course her name is on the ship. The hollowed-out Belle of earlier this afternoon is hidden beneath a layer of expertly applied make-up and a killer blow dry. She is flawless.

The hum of chatter and the electricity of celebrity. Hot bodies and cold champagne.

Eyes swivel our way as we walk in and head towards the Scarmardos. Some smile, a few take photos. Belle glides me through it all.

'A selection have been invited to this,' she whispers. 'Investors, press, certain influencers.'

As she pauses to greet and be greeted, I hang back and take in the room, hungry for details. Everyone wants to say hello to Belle. I feel eyes on me and I stand taller. It's confusing, all the attention. I fly so low under the radar in my office job, it's good to feel seen again. And I look good tonight. But then the threatening notes must have come from someone in this room. There's a difference between being seen and being exposed.

'This is my friend, Emily,' Belle introduces me to anyone who stares at me long enough. A group clamour round us and someone leans forward to shake my hand, someone else writes my name down.

'How long have you known Belle?' a voice to my left asks, the man with the grey hair in the Blur t-shirt who holds a camera and wears a press pass. I remember him from outside. He speaks gently, and fades into the room quickly as Belle leads me away before I can answer.

'Well, you look different.' Bean hands me a drink and looks me up and down. 'Much more five-star. Great dress.'

'I guess you're not looking at me through the red mist,' I say, glancing over at Xander. 'Unless you're about to start punching your brother in the next five minutes?'

I throw a fake punch with one hand and raise an eyebrow at him.

To give him his due, he looks sheepish. 'Sorry about that.'

'What a way to say hello.' I let him off, smiling at him as I say, 'The dress is Prada. No getting blood on it though, OK?'

He laughs.

I need the family on side if I'm going to work out what's going on. Bean's the only one who's looked my way so far since I arrived.

'Good evening.' I hear a voice resonate through the speakers in the bar. We all turn to see someone I don't recognise introduce Mattia to the microphone.

'Thanks for the champagne,' I say to Bean, taking the drink he's offering me and swallowing a gulp for strength. Belle is nervous about the family's reaction to whatever Mattia is going to say. I tense up, and I feel Bean do the same next to me. I glance at him and see a tiny frown crease into his brow.

'We'll need more drinks soon.' He lifts two from a passing tray and hands another to me. 'Here. Drinking your way through these things is the best advice I can give.' His eyes fall on Belle, who has picked up a glass of water. 'No drinks for Belle?'

I ignore his question and watch Mattia.

'Welcome,' Mattia says. 'Two years in the shipyard and here we are! And all in time to celebrate the birthday of my wife, my muse. The beautiful Belle!'

Applause begins, then everyone in the room turns our way. Belle blows Mattia a kiss. I take in his tan, his silver hair. He radiates. Even without the microphone I think his voice would fill a room; it's not loud – it's just big. Commanding. Like the rest of him. His eyes are on Belle and there is no questioning his adoration. He glows when he looks at her.

I'm nervous to meet him. Not only because of the rumours: that he's a workaholic, a tyrant, a bully, that he's had affairs. More than just gossip about him, I want to know his tells, try and work out his strengths, his weaknesses. To get to know the man my best friend married. I've swotted up and watched interviews of him – his northern vowels mixing with an Italian lilt. His voice is like everything he does: distinct, intent.

What I know of him is how fierce he is, determination running over his face like a bloodline. He has a house in Newcastle, London, New York; villas in Italy, the south of France. But it's not just what he's amassed – the global electrical company – he emits authority, success.

If I'm honest with myself, I've been fascinated since she married him. Of all the families she could have ended up with, I still can't believe it's this one. I'd thought about reaching out to her, but it had been impossible. I'd seen the news along with everyone else. Read the magazines with her picture on the front. It had been like watching a newly discovered twin I'd never met. Certain mannerisms in the way she held herself had cut me to the bone with familiarity. But then there was the newness of her – of who she is now. *Mrs Scarmardo* is someone so far off my radar, she may as well live on another planet. Now that the new Mrs Scarmardo is Belle, it's both familiar and unfamiliar all at once. It will take some getting used to.

Mattia has changed too. Since his wife died and he married Belle, he's slipped out of the media a little. I've seen pictures of him and Belle, but they're through a long lens. On a boat, on a beach. Even his clothes look different. The suits – the fitted, slick look has switched to a more laidback appearance. Leisure wear for the rich.

Now this ship. Belle had said it was about fun, that life had bitten into him. His legacy is changing. Is he changing *for* Belle? *Because* of Belle? And what do his children think about that?

So far, his speech has been an ode to Belle and the new ship. But the press are waiting. They know something's coming.

Bean is tense beside me, and I glance at the others. They all watch their father without blinking.

'A hundred grand he does it,' Xander says, but it's quiet and I only just catch the words, the anger.

I watch Mattia, spellbound.

'It's been no secret that I am due to retire. I know my children are all ready to take the reins, and they've been waiting patiently for me so far.' Mattia gestures to where we stand, and there is some laughter in the room.

'However, with this ship, I feel responsible. We have launched a new venture, a new child, ready to make her way across the seas. We don't send our children off to school and feel our job is done, and in this too, I am eager to be around for this vessel, as huge and magnificent as she is. I'd like to take this opportunity to confirm we have two more ships planned in the next two years.' Applause breaks out, and Bean downs the rest of his glass.

'Here we go,' Xander mutters behind me, and Jimmi says, 'Not now. Hold it together.'

'Moreover,' Mattia is still talking, 'I feel like the proud father – I've decided to stay on until they're all launched. My children will not mind waiting. They're eager to pursue their own ventures, to make their own mark. I'm proud of all my children and their independence, and today, I'm proud of all my ships! Now, eat, drink, enjoy your cruise. We are the future of the seas!'

Cameras start flashing, and there is applause in the room.

Beside me I feel Bean's anger rather than see it. His breath comes quick and fast, and he is stiff. So far, he's seemed the most normal out of all of them, but he's still a Scarmardo, I remind myself.

'What the fuck?' Xander curses behind me. '*Our own fucking ventures? Independence?* Is that some coded message? Are we supposed to run out and start our own business now to prove ourselves worthy?' But when I look he is beaming and clapping. A frozen smile on his face.

Chloe is blanched as she claps furiously, and Jimmi rests his arm around her shoulders, apparently casually. I hear Bean mutter and the only words I pick out are *shit*, and *fan*.

The cameras turn on us, stood in our corner of the room, and for a second, I am blinded.

Bean lifts his glass towards his father, as though in a toast, and I can see that the effort to appear supportive must be killing him, yet they are all practised. Slick.

Smiling, Bean turns to me as though nothing has happened, but his mouth is tight when he speaks and the crease in his brow has deepened. 'Do you know everyone?'

I focus on his question, half nodding, trying to do as Bean seems to be and maintain a party poker face. I'm not sure whether to comment on Mattia's announcement.

Bean continues, 'That's Xander and Lila, the twins. Jimmi is over there with Chloe. I don't think you were properly introduced earlier.'

He stands close and speaks quietly. The press turns from us as Mattia begins to circulate.

'So what do we do on a luxury cruise?' I say, grasping at something to say, and aiming all my charm at Bean as I watch Belle talk to Lila, who wears a floor-length white dress that hugs without being tight. Olive skin, dark make-up. Everyone is behaving perfectly normally, as though the shockwave of a minute ago is already forgotten. It's unsettling.

'Well, I wasn't looking forward to it. But it's looking up.' He smiles, then shrugs. 'It cost enough. We may as well enjoy it. I could pop round to your cabin at some point, talk you through the highlights.' Bean looks at me then colours slightly – or maybe it's just the light. I have a flash of Bean outside my cabin – was he looking for me? He must be used to a million beautiful girls hurling themselves at him. He might be smaller, less good-looking than his brothers, but he still walks around with a wallet bigger than a car.

I never hurl myself at anyone, but I am disproportionally grateful for him talking to me. However, the notes aren't far from my thoughts. The fact that I might be exposed.

I might not have found my feet on this ship yet. But I have a public mask too.

These siblings can move from smiling to anger in a blink – and so I can.

'Well, here's to a celebration,' I say. 'I haven't seen Belle for years.' I give him my fake-confident smile, and clink my glass to his. 'To a great week.'

He grins and cocks his head to one side. 'Why is that? Why haven't you seen her? You weren't at the wedding. I don't think Belle had anyone there. It was just family. What's with crawling out of the woodwork now?'

I open my mouth, stung by the sudden edge in Bean's tone, but I'm saved from answering because Mattia Scarmardo is crossing the room with his eyes on me.

'Dad – this is Emily,' Bean says, which doesn't slow his father one inch. Mattia touches Bean's shoulder as he passes, full of smiles, and he opens his arms to me. Before I know it, I'm swept up in three kisses and a confidence tsunami.

'Emily! I've been desperate to meet you! Come. I see you have a drink. When I said Belle must bring someone, you were the only name she would give me.' He looks at me, intense and serious. 'We couldn't be happier to have you.'

He smiles, taller than me but not by much, dressed in a shirt and pale trousers. The attention of the room has followed him. I wonder if the *we* is a message to the family. Their eyes are all on me now.

Lila stares at me, expressionless. Even Jimmi is watching me, and Xander – so dismissive earlier – looks me up and down more slowly.

I'm x-rayed. A blue light passing quickly through me.

'Emily, you're so beautiful! It's like you and Belle have been cut from the same cloth.' He stands back and beams at me, and it seems that everything I've ever read about Mattia Scarmardo's charisma is spot on.

I open my mouth and he holds his hand in the air. 'Now you must call me Mattia. Please.'

'It's so kind of you to invite me.'

'Well, I'm just sorry we didn't meet earlier. And it's the least I could do. I should have done more. I have so much to apologise for.' He looks at me intently. He must be referencing three years ago, and I feel my stomach clench.

Hold it, I think, *just hold it together. They're all listening. They're all watching. Stand tall.*

He takes my free hand in both of his. 'Can you forgive me? It will take a lifetime to apologise to Belle, to make up for what she went through. But you went through it too. I should have had security on the boat in case of such an attack. It is my greatest regret.'

'Sir? The press...' a voice slips in and a woman with a green earpiece is talking to Mattia, leaning in slightly, discreet but insistent.

A flick of his wrist to request she wait, and the woman with the earpiece flinches the tiniest fraction. It's a practised retreat. A well-worn move. I pull back from him, taking my lead from her. There is no expression on her face, she holds herself carefully. Upright and watchful.

I also wonder why she flinched, whether Mattia's charm is real, or simply a guise. I log this for later.

'There's no way you could have known what would happen,' I say, trying to let him off the hook while shutting him down. 'We were unlucky. That's all.' As I speak, I'm reminded of the fact I haven't spoken to Belle about the attack since it happened.

'Excuse me,' Mattia says, pressing my hand warmly and still smiling at me. 'I must circulate quickly before we retire to dinner. Belle?'

Belle nods to the family to indicate I should stay with them as Mattia leads her into the bar.

I get a flash of what life must be like for Belle. To have these eyes on you all the time. Everyone a rival.

I catch Xander staring straight through me.

I've got this, I think. And I just pray that's true as he approaches.

'I'm Xander.' Tall with dark eyes, bright blond hair – the mirror of his twin – Xander pushes Bean aside. 'My turn to talk to our guest, little Bean.'

'Fuck off, Xander.' Bean's voice is quiet and his smile is fixed and in position. He forces his way back next to me, and for a second, I feel both of them up close, the zip of energy between them. There's clearly something behind the fight of earlier.

The effect of Mattia's attention on me has been quick.

Xander takes a step closer and stamps on Bean's foot. 'So sorry!' he says, and Bean stumbles, red-faced and cursing. These brothers are like children.

'We met earlier. How's the rib?' I ask.

'Oh, yes!' He looks the tiniest bit sheepish for a second, rubbing his rib quickly, which gives me a buzz of satisfaction. 'Well, Emily. Aren't I the lucky one, here with our honoured guest,' Xander says, moving on quickly as he leans in a little, but speaks loud enough for Bean to hear. 'I think little Bean must have developed a bit of a crush on you. Running to your side like a puppy. But you're far too good-looking for a little bean.'

Bean scowls. 'Watch out, Emily. Xander only has three girlfriends this week, so he's got a spare spot.'

'Play nice,' Jimmi says, his voice low, a warning. 'We're not done here yet.'

Jimmi is only an arm's length away. Chloe has stopped talking to him and is looking at me.

Xander says, 'What, Jimmi, you mean you don't want me to mention the fact that Daddy dearest has just announced to the world that he's not retiring yet? First, he delays when he meets the delightful Belle, but tells us he'll retire once the ship is launched. We'll inherit the company, run it, finally grow it into everything we've been promised since day fucking one. Now we're all stuck back on his purse strings – and does the ever-so-delightful Belle have a hand on them first? Shall I not mention that?'

'Xander.' The warning in Jimmi's voice is both quiet and fierce.

'We all know you're in his good books.' Xander leans close to Jimmi. 'Our *own ventures* – does that mean he's splitting the wolf pack? Has he promised it all to you?'

'Xander,' Lila warns.

At her bidding, he grabs another passing drink and turns back to me. 'That's a good outfit. Is it a hunting dress?'

'What?'

'Are you here on the hunt? Like Belle? She hunted my father down very successfully.' He swallows half the contents of his glass. 'Is that what they taught you at your little state school? You and Belle? How to fish?'

He's smiling as he says it. I keep my tone measured as I say, 'Belle loves your father. I've never her seen like this with a man.'

'Well, you've seen her for the last few hours, so you must be an expert. Here I was thinking you hadn't seen her for years. Now, remind me, Emily, why exactly is that?'

I'm saved from answering as Chloe steps forward. Does she smell blood? She puts one arm around me and pulls me in briefly. The brothers part for her, her smile wide. 'I'm Chloe! I've wanted to meet you all day. You're very pretty. Like, in a really authentic way.'

'So are you. I like your songs,' I say, although I don't really. She seems much younger than her age. I'd read she dropped out of university to launch a career as a singer. But degrees are what you do to get a job. When you're worth billions, they can just be a hobby, I suppose.

'I'm pleased you're here,' Chloe whispers. 'I feel sorry for Belle. Everyone's angry with Daddy for changing his mind. For putting so much of the company money into the ship. It's much easier to blame her than to blame him. And I guess she's being true to herself, you know?' She puts her hand on my arm and whispers again, 'I think you can help us be friends with her. I think she'd like that. I've been manifesting a family healing week. I think you coming is part of that.'

I smile. Chloe is cleverer than the vulnerable waif her PR make her out to be. And she's exactly right. A healing week is what Belle needs. She'll need all the friends she can get if the news about the baby breaks.

Chloe puts down a glass on a passing tray and picks up another. For all her words, she's drinking quickly, and I see her glance at Belle across the room with a look that could freeze the sun. Do they all lie when they speak? The layers of smiling covering a simmering rage makes my head swirl. I feel sick.

'A photo!' Mattia says, appearing out of nowhere with Belle, and even Lila smiles, almost mechanically. The family assemble, slick and rehearsed, as a photographer steps up.

I try to step back but Belle pulls my hand. 'Stay!'

Behind me, Bean elbows Xander as they line up and I hear him say, 'Back off, Xander. I'm not joking. Step the fuck away, I know you—'

'Jealousy turns you green for real, Bean,' Xander says. 'What, you think if I stepped aside then she'd come running? Bouncy Bean, chasing after a new toy, like it hasn't got a mind of its own.'

Mattia glances back and with a look Xander appears contrite. 'Sorry,' he mouths to his father.

'What is it with Bean and Xander?' I whisper to Belle as we all adjust our poses and smile again for more photos.

'I don't know. They had a fight a while ago. Mattia's had enough of it,' Belle replies.

Beside me, Jimmi puts his arm around Chloe. He speaks quietly but I hear him say, 'If the festival stuff is in trouble, I can sort something. I know you've been relying on the inheritance arriving.'

'Oh my god, Jimmi, don't fuss! I can do some things on my own, you know!' Chloe gives a dismissive wave, which I recognise as Belle's new gesture. Then the photographer asks us all to raise our glasses in a toast for one final photograph.

'If you mention it one more time, I'll hurt you for real,' I hear Bean say to Xander, his voice dense with anger.

'Smile!' The final click and flash, and Mattia exits, all of us following, falling in line quickly like he plays the pipe.

We're almost out of the bar when one of the press, the same one I'd seen earlier with the Blur t-shirt, the gentle voice and the camera, shouts, 'Chloe, tell us about the festival – is it all set to go ahead? I heard some rumours there's trouble with funding?'

Chloe is in front of me and I see the back of her neck flush red. She carries on and after a nod from Mattia to some crew who walk alongside us, I turn back to see the man in question flanked and escorted out. It all happens quickly.

'Get him off.' Mattia speaks quietly to the woman with the green earpiece from earlier. 'I don't want any of us bothered.'

'The ship has left port,' she says, looking worried, but he looks at her again closely. I don't see his face, but I see her reaction. She pulls herself up short, wipes the expression from her face and nods quickly, saying, 'Sorry, sir, I'll sort it, of course.'

I run over the man's question to Chloe in my head – it hadn't been aggressive, had it? It reminds me of how easily I could fall foul of this family.

Jimmi slips his arm through Chloe's, and he drops a kiss on her head. There's a rush of cooler air in the corridor and, after the heat of the bar, my ears ring and my head aches.

'A visit to the evening pool party, then dinner,' Belle says, standing close. I can smell Xander's scent and I feel Bean's eyes on me again.

My head spins. I can't pick an ally from the group, other than Belle. The evening stretches like an obstacle course, spiked with booby traps.

I need to stay alert. As the woman with the green earpiece said, the ship has left port. There's no turning round now.

9

The light on the pool deck is neon green, not quite a Scarmardo green but close enough; music so loud it's in my bones, comes up from my feet. The party is soaring. Three years ago, this would have been exactly my scene.

The pool is huge – much bigger than I was expecting. There are hot tubs all around the deck, and palm trees dotted between the bars. Like the rest of the ship, it's slick and expensive. Passengers throng everywhere. There's a VIP bar on the deck above, and people lean over. I guess they're looking for the family.

'You need a drink?' Belle passes me something luminous in a tall glass and Xander, slightly ahead, carries two. We stand in a roped-off area outside the stairway. It's slightly raised, above the steps that lead down to the pool.

'Our hosts!' the DJ shouts and the crowd roars. People are dancing; Mattia lifts one arm to wave, drapes the other around Belle. This must be part of the showcasing of the family – welcoming the first guests. He nods to Xander.

As though it's all rehearsed, Xander downs one of the drinks and passes the glass to Lila who rolls her eyes so quickly I wonder if she did it at all. Xander heads forward, towards the pool, raising his arms above his head. The crowd starts screaming and clapping as Xander pirouettes. Clearly in his element.

I watch Xander dance towards the edge of the pool; he tips the other drink up and downs it, lifting the glass high as the DJ whoops, then Xander holds the glass upside down over his head.

Bean sips his drink and stares straight ahead.

Xander now faces the pool and makes windmills with his arms, then brings his hands together, and motions as though to dive in.

The crowd scream, and a strobe light flashes in zigzags around the pool.

Xander hands the glass to someone, and Bean says, 'Here we go,' almost managing to sound bored, but there's a bitterness which gives him away.

The crowd chant now: 'Jump! Jump!'

Rolling his shoulders, Xander offers up one last spin on the spot, and then runs at the pool. Almost at the edge, he leaps upwards, and flips in the air, turning a full summersault, before wrapping his arms around his legs and landing with a splash in the centre of the pool.

Graceful. A perfect 10.

Water splashes everywhere and the buzz intensifies. Xander emerges in the water, arms aloft.

'We're done,' Mattia says to Jimmi, while clapping his hands. 'Dinner.' Whatever instructions Mattia has given Xander have clearly been executed.

The family pull quickly out of the crowd, but all eyes are still on Xander, who is pulling himself up from the pool to clamouring hands.

'Will Xander come too?' I ask Bean as we walk quickly, and we are down the stairs before I finish the question. The whole performance choreographed and I've barely caught my breath as we're on the move again.

'In a bit. He'll clean up first. Dad likes to parade him, let him set the tone if it's a party. So much press approval hangs on the first night. We're here to ensure it succeeds.'

'Wouldn't it be a success anyway, even without you all? I mean, it's pretty special.' I wave my arm. 'All this.'

Bean pauses to let me pass first in the corridor. We're almost at their cabin. All the VIP cabins are on the higher levels of the ship, at a vantage point over the sea. He looks at me and raises his eyebrows. 'Don't you know? I thought Belle would have told you. It's all on the ship. All of it. He's borrowed against the company to fund the cruise line. Millions, probably billions. If it doesn't work, then that's it. If it meets the targets, then great – another asset and we're richer than ever. A raging success. But the investors who looked so certain are wobbling; if the bank calls in the loans early, or we don't meet the targets, then it's game over. Scarmardo sinkage. And no floating back up. That's why we've all been summoned. Best PR foot forward. No fuck-ups. Or else.'

He tilts his head. 'I thought you'd know this. I thought that's why you might be here. So why *are* you here?'

'What?' I shake my head. 'Belle invited—'

'None of us have been allowed to bring anyone. Lila's fiancée is at home. Chloe's boyfriend is in New York. Uncle Marcus is unwell, apparently, and he's like a second father. Strict instructions. Our family only. And you.' He cocks his head to the side. 'What's so special about you, Emily? We all want to know.'

I remember again that, as friendly as Bean may seem, I can't trust anyone. They're all Scarmardos. He looks at me with questions, and the crease is back on his brow. Has it all been about lulling me into a false sense of security? They're all so tense, and me being here has clearly wound everything up.

I must be on my guard.

10

I suddenly need a minute on my own. My head spins from all the attention, the change of locations, all the smiling.

'I'll just grab my lipstick,' I say to Bean, and duck down the corridor towards my cabin. I wait until I've turned a corner and check the corridor is empty, looking left and right.

Then I lean back against the wall and take a gulp of air.

Bean asks an excellent question. Why *has* Mattia allowed me to come? If it's an all or nothing PR trip, why me? Surely Belle hasn't told him about being scared of his children. Is there some other reason? I think of Mattia three years ago. What happened on his yacht, the attack. If anyone could find out what really happened, then I guess he could. Did he send me the notes? Did he want me here to keep an eye on me? Punish me?

Belle had said the Scarmardos were out to get her and that could include me. They certainly don't seem to like her much. Only Chloe has said anything nice about her. But what else are they capable of? It *must* be one of them who sent me the notes – Mattia or one of his children. How at risk is Belle? Is it more than leaked photos? I think of the fight in the lift, of the crease in Bean's brow. There's a simmering rage in the family.

I wait until all the questions in my brain stop screaming and I try to think logically. I think of Xander's remark about hunting, of Bean's remark about how much the ships cost, about me crawling out of the woodwork.

I pull out the lipstick from my bag and reapply. The sugar

from the champagne races the adrenaline in my veins and my head spins.

I need to speak to Belle.

There's a sound in the corridor behind me and I pull myself up from my slouch and turn.

No one.

I must stay calm. I think of Bean disappearing past my cabin earlier – has he come to check on me now? If so, why does he keep hiding?

I take a breath, touching my cheeks as the heat in them recedes. I check my watch. I've only been gone five minutes. I take a step along the corridor and plan to circle round back to their cabin when I hear a cough. I stop to turn this time and wait. 'Hello?'

No one there, no answer. But, again, I think of the notes I'd received. Part of my brain has labelled them as nothing but an empty threat – something to warn me away. But I remember now what a punch I'd felt when I'd first read them.

What if they're more than that?

I need to get back to the dinner. I turn the corner and pass a door marked 'Staff Only', and I find myself walking faster, my heart rate speeding up again.

There's another sound, and my hands start shaking. I try to move even faster, but the heels I wear, the dress, are not conducive to running. I wonder, what if I—

I feel a hand grab at my neck and pull me backwards. I briefly see the ceiling. A flash of the lights, a picture on the wall.

Then I'm shoved into somewhere dark. I hear a click before I can even scream, and I'm trembling; my fingers reach out for anything familiar.

'Help!' I say, but it's no louder than a whisper, and my hands find walls all around.

I'm trapped.

The air is thick and I'm afraid – but small spaces themselves have never frightened me. The bunk beds on the yachts had seen to that. I lived in windowless spaces, slept, dreamt in them. I'm frightened because things have escalated. I hadn't really believed the notes before.

Now I'm terrified.

My phone. I can call Belle.

Pulling it out from my handbag in the dark, I drop it, and reach around. Kneeling, I find it, and tap the screen, feeling calmer as it lights up.

No signal.

The dark is hot, and I panic about air. I throw the flat of my hand against the door once more, striking it as I shout, 'Hello? Help!'

I wait for a few minutes. There's nothing. I force myself to breathe deeply – of course there's enough air in here. I just need to calm down.

Since the boat three years ago, I've taken stock. Learnt how to defend myself. Taken lessons in how to stay calm in stressful situations. But my mind races with dark thoughts: where am I? Someone's cabin? Who has locked me in?

I let the voices of tutors from all the self-defence courses I've taken in draughty town halls and windowless work-out rooms drift in. They all talk about trying to stay calm. *Breathe.*

So I breathe. I close my eyes. In for six counts, hold the breath for six counts, exhale.

Again. Then I do it again.

I feel tears at the corners of my eyes and I see Finn's face, chocolate around his mouth and his fist holding a Thomas the Tank Engine truck, worn at the edges and paint chipped from all the baths it had taken with him.

In for six. Hold for six.

I'm on the ship with three thousand people. I will be found. There's no way I'll die of thirst over the next four days.

In for six.

I open my eyes and bang again on the door.

Why would I have been locked in? I wish to God I'd taken the notes more seriously and not strayed away from the family. But then they could be behind this.

Have I seen something I shouldn't, something that I haven't registered? Do I pose a threat to someone? Or is it just about what happened three years ago – do they want to leave Belle defenceless to try to use it against her? I was warned not to come. Now I'm here, they want me out of the way.

There's a sharp whack on my head and I scream, throwing my arms up for protection as I kneel on the floor.

I bang repeatedly on the door from a crouch and get nowhere; my throat is tight and a sharp pain behind my eyes feels like it might split my head in two.

I force myself to keep breathing. My phone torch – I flick it on and look around. A bottle. It must have been what hit me – it's sticky. It smells of the spa body wash in my shower. There's a crack down one side. It must have split when it fell. My flailing and banging must have unsettled things.

Groping around me, trying to find anything useful on shelves, all I can feel are piles of stock. This must be a store cupboard.

Moving the phone around, trying to focus the light, I find a bucket and a mop.

I have no idea how long I've been in here. I look at my phone but I can't remember now what time my watch had said it was. My head aches.

I'm on my own. I just have to focus. It feels like I've been in here for hours, but it could be minutes.

I pick up the bucket, and swing it at the door. Then I do it again.

Trying to stay calm, I breathe in for the six then hit the door. I keep this up until my arms feel as though they'll fall off.

Finally, I hear a voice. 'Is someone in there?'

'Yes! Hello!'

'Hang on, it's locked. I'll be back in a sec.'

The time stretches, but finally there is a key in the lock and the door opens to Mirka and the man in the Blur t-shirt.

'Emily! What happened?' Mirka is kind but I see the key in her hand and I wonder who else has keys to the locks on this boat. I feel suspicious of everyone.

'I met you downstairs, in the bar.' The man looks at me, strangely – concerned. 'You were with Belle Scarmardo. How did you end up here?'

I shake my head. 'I must have pulled this door open by mistake. I thought it was my cabin. I was already inside when the lock must have caught. Too much wine in the bar, and I've been feeling a bit dizzy – seasick. I panicked.' I don't know why I lie, maybe out of instinct because he's a journalist and I'm trying to protect Belle and the family. I'm still trembling. I rely on their politeness for them not to question me too much.

'The family are at dinner. Shall I let them know you're coming, or would you like to return to your cabin?' Mirka is all smiles. Tears start at the back of my throat. I swallow them – try to give nothing away.

'I'm not sure. I just need a minute. Thank you.'

'I'll get you a glass of water.' Mirka slips away and I see that the journalist is watching me carefully. 'You're Emily Mason, aren't you? You're the other one from that boat. When the man died?'

As ever, I force myself not to react. Of course people will bring this up. I'd known it in advance. Mattia had referred to it earlier. It's not like it's a secret. I still find it odd to talk about it so freely, though, and suddenly it's being thrust into the forefront, seeing Belle again.

He takes my silence as agreement and looks down at something in his hand. I follow his gaze. A silver memory stick.

He hesitates. 'I came up here to find you after they threw me out of the bar. I've been told to stay out of the family's way. I need to keep a low profile. Look, would you like to sit down?'

I shake my head and continue to stare at the memory stick in his hand. What's going on?

He sees me looking and seems unsure, still holding back.

'You're not one of them; they might listen to you. There's something on here I think they need to see. I feel—' He stops as Mirka reappears, smile in place, glass of water in hand. He keeps his voice low, out of Mirka's earshot, as he presses it into my hand. 'Could you have a look at this? I'll find you tomorrow.'

What I *should* do is point-blank refuse, thrust it back at him. But against all the glitz and glamour, he seems like the only real thing I've seen since I boarded.

What I do instead is curl my fist around it and follow Mirka as she leads me to dinner. I look over my shoulder as the journalist turns and disappears round a corner.

What is on the memory stick that is so important? And why give it to me?

The most important question comes to me far too late – did he see who'd locked me in?

11

Belle is just outside the cabin door when I arrive. Mirka slips away and it's just her and me.

I'm still trembling, not able to shake off the fear of being trapped, and I go at her harder than I mean to, hissing, 'What the fuck am I doing here, Belle? I'm the only plus one. Why has Mattia let me come?' I'd bitten my lip at some point earlier and the blood in my mouth tastes metallic. It reminds me of worse times and I force myself again to take a deep breath.

She stares at me, wary. I can tell she's deciding what to say. Her reticence makes me even angrier. After her first burst of warmth, she's pulled back. I've barely seen her since I got on board. And she's playing by her new rules like they're lifelines.

Being trapped has shaken me – a warning far bigger than the notes. More physical. What else is coming?

'Tell me!' I say, louder this time, and she darts a look at the door, more scared that they'll hear than out of concern for me.

'Can you wait?' she asks. 'Tonight. I'll give you more details then.'

I think of her change of direction earlier and I shake my head. 'Someone just hurt me, Belle. I don't know who. But I think someone knows. I think someone knows what we did and is trying to scare me off. Not really bad stuff – not yet. But I can feel it building. What the fuck is going on?'

'Oh my god, Em, what happened?'

'It doesn't matter.' I can't face telling her about the notes, everything. Not now. I just want the truth from her.

'Look, I'll tell you more later? Please? I want to know who hurt you.'

'Belle, this family are treating me like shit.'

'They *are* shits, Em, I told you. I'm scared of them. That's why you're here – to help me. To protect me, from them! I begged Mattia to let you come. Please let that be enough for now, and I'll explain more soon.'

I swallow hard, then nod. 'OK. I'll wait.'

It had been the look in her eyes – the fear. I remember the last time she'd looked like that.

I'm still feeling sick as I sit down to dinner.

On the private balcony, the table is laid out with fairy lights and candles. Belle sits up by Mattia at the head of the table, and I've been seated between Xander and Jimmi.

After we'd gone in, I'd seen Belle have a word with Mattia, who had summoned Xander, his hair wet from the pool.

I turn to accept a drink from a waiter, and suddenly Xander is beside me. The effect of Mattia's words are quick.

'Emily,' he says, 'can I say you look...' He offers up a chef's kiss. 'Let's start again. I will pour you wine, and in return, can you assess the ship's food for me? I can never think of clever things to say about food, and Dad will ask later. I need someone to plan my supportive, intelligent comments.'

He gives me a wide smile – he must have been instructed by Mattia to turn on the charm. Another performance.

I see up close how beautiful he really is. The dark eyes, olive skin and blond hair. Does he dye it? He's striking. I think of all the magazines I've seen him in, the gossip columns, the famous women on his arm. He fills my wine glass, and the question of *why the fuck am I here and not some new, more suitable friend of Belle's* solidifies in my mind. Surely she must have made new friends in this new world?

Plates arrive, and I look at finely arranged vegetables and a puff of foam, tiny pieces of toast. The table is laid with white linen, and the light is soft. Music plays out through the speakers on deck.

I think of Dad and Finn eating the piles of macaroni cheese I left in the fridge and freezer.

'So, what was Dad talking about, when he said he owed you? We all want to know,' Xander says, and leans closer.

'It must be what happened with Belle. You must know about it.' I steel myself and flash the biggest smile I can manage. I even throw in a shrug. I can play this cool and calm.

'The kidnapping?' he practically yawns, like it isn't anything big. 'She was taken for a few days, wasn't she?'

'Yes, pirates. The modern-day ones. We were crewing on a yacht when it happened. It belonged to your dad but he'd loaned it to some friends.' I don't let myself remember too much about it. I drop the words lightly as though they don't still plague me. I play this role for Belle. Even I can carry off one dinner. And although the story hurts every time I tell it, it's not new to me. Or to him. But I need to play this game – I need to find out who knows what.

'It was near Somalia?' he says, the details obviously not burnt on his brain as they are on mine.

'Sri Lanka. They came from nowhere. Belle was taken and held for three days. The police caught them and she was released unharmed. Your dad said in the papers he blames himself, for not providing more security, but it was a small yacht. We were blindsided.' I lift my glass, another shrug, and think that to say Belle had been '*unharmed*' was so far from the truth, it was an outright lie, but they hadn't physically hurt her, at least.

'And the captain on the yacht was killed?'

I can only nod, because my throat has closed and the ocean spins. I can't talk about the captain. It still throws me every time.

I pause and say nothing. I focus on the stars, like tiny crystals. The lap of the sea. And I thank God for Xander's lack of empathy as he moves on without question.

'Had you both met my dad before?'

I shake my head. 'He owned the yacht, but he owns so many boats. We crewed a few back then. He was good friends with the customers and there was a lot of press at the time. They were robbed but were unharmed. I left afterwards. We both did.'

Separately.

I think how fast I'd run once Belle had come back. I'd gone into some kind of paralysis when she'd been taken, but once I knew she was safe, I just couldn't look at her. I'd gone on the most destructive bender of my life: drank until I couldn't see straight. Until the images behind my eyes bled into nothing. My credit card bill was like a red mountain, and I don't know what would have happened if I hadn't collapsed one day. They took me to hospital. Had me checked. Found a fleck of Finn.

Then home. Back to Dad. More debt to pay for the flight back. My tail between my legs. I hadn't been able to work for about a year. Dad had been forced to re-mortgage the house to keep us going. I'd been a mess. I'd spiralled. Then Finn was born.

I look over at Belle now, feeling the guilt afresh, of not being able to face her, to be there for her. My throat is still tight and the tiny puffs of foam on my plate now look like vomit.

The night shades in gently as the main course is taken away; the temperature drops a little but the air still feels like velvet. We must be miles and miles from England now. I've seen no other lights at sea so far. It's like we're alone on this ocean.

I see Mattia lean forward and whisper something to Belle, making her hand close in a fist. She nods and heads inside the cabin.

'I hope you don't mind,' Xander is saying.

I'm drinking too fast, but I drink a little more. I almost miss what he says next. I'm certainly not prepared for it. Not here, not round this table.

'But I did a little digging this afternoon, after I saw you in the lift. Well, I had someone else do it. I figured you must have secrets. Belle's best friend must know some biggies, at least one.'

He looks at me expectantly. He has no idea. *You'd choke on that wine*, I think, *if you knew*.

'Ah, quiet Emily. Cards close to her chest. I see.' He smiles and takes another gulp from his glass.

'I doubt there's anything I know that the great Xander Scarmardo doesn't already know,' I say, and I dole out my biggest smile, drop him a wink.

'Well, I did find out something.' He lowers his voice and raises his eyebrows. 'You're a mama, Emily. No mention of that so far. You have a little boy? And, you know, Belle never mentioned him once. It's like she doesn't know. Almost like you've never told her. Your best friend.'

I take one more swig of wine. Panic stabs quickly. I look again up the table but Belle hasn't returned. I feel Jimmi next to me. Did he hear? Did any of them hear?

Belle needs to know first. I need to be the one to tell her.

And Finn is all mine. If someone threatens me, it's one thing. But not Finn. Being scared about disrupting Finn's happy life is the reason I was most afraid to come.

Xander looks at me. 'Surely you've told Belle though. That's not the kind of thing to keep a secret, from such a good friend?'

Words like tiny knives.

Finn is something I will not share. In the world of secrets, he's mine to keep. I think of Belle and all her pregnancy tests, how she'd feel if I threw my child at her. I think of all the things I haven't told her, and five nights isn't long enough to get through half of it.

'What about Mr Emily? There was no info on that. Is the baby's father still in the picture?'

I open my mouth to reply, but I'm hit by the memory of his

mouth on mine. Soft and hard all at once. The dark of the beach. The taste of the moonshine we'd drunk in buckets. Sand on my skin. How I'd wrapped my legs round him and clung on like he'd save me if I could only hold tight enough.

No one can know. Even Belle. I can't tell any of them.

I realise I'm sat with my mouth open and nothing's coming out, so I play the Xander game. I rally. I put my hand on his arm and drop my head forward, my hair brushing his shoulder.

'Mr Scarmardo, I haven't asked about your past hook-ups. How crass of you to ask after my work flings back home.' I sit back, pick up my glass and drain it. I raise one eyebrow and hold it out towards him. I keep it smooth, aloof.

12

I'm still staring at Xander when there is a clink of a fork against a wine glass. A chime rings out and I see Mattia reaching for Belle. She's back from inside the cabin and she looks braced.

He's always touching her, I think. *Instinctively. Compulsively.*

'Christ, what now,' Xander says, and I glance at him. I have a fairly good idea. From the look of her, Mattia is forcing Belle to announce early.

Around the table, there are shadows of apprehension on all the faces. Does everyone know? Belle said that someone had stolen her pregnancy test so at least one person does. Only Jimmi looks unchanged. His expression has been the same for most of the dinner: controlled. Sober. Relaxed – but contained. Secretive.

'Belle and I have some news.' Mattia is beaming like someone flicked a switch inside of him.

There's a tiny gasp to my left, further down the table, and it's Chloe. Her hands are stiff, pulled into her chest in fists, like she's in pain. Her nails must dig deep into her palms. She's looking desperately at someone. I follow her gaze. Jimmi.

'We're going to have a baby!'

The first thing everyone does is look to Belle, who stares down hard at the plate in front of her. Her face is white. Why on earth has Mattia announced it tonight? Belle had said she wanted to give it a bit longer. It's so early in the pregnancy.

I look again at Mattia. *He's pushed it*, I think. He is a man who has it all. All his family are here – he is forcing the issue. He is confronting it here, where no one can run.

He holds Belle's hand like it's crystal, but he stands like a fort at the end of the table. *If the buck stops anywhere…*his stance says. *If you think you're hard enough.*

'Dad,' Lila says, softly. Her face is pale. The candles flicker and pick out the hollows around her cheekbones, and her voice when she speaks again is fragile. 'Dad? You're going to have another child?'

Jimmi stands; he's the first to move, striding towards the end of the table. He drops a wink at Chloe as he goes. I look back to her and she seems to relax slightly, her hands softening as she watches him.

Jimmi's arms part as though ready to embrace as he says, 'Congratulations, Dad. You and Belle must be over the moon.'

Someone drops a glass, but I can't follow the sound with my eyes. Although I want to know to whom this news is a surprise, I can't move.

No one else speaks, and I look back to Belle, who puts out a hand on the table and steadies herself in her chair, bending slightly, like she's facing the wind.

'What?' Bean mutters. 'Another one to add to the pot?' He's white too, but he looks angry – white-hot rage not just shock. Even his lips have lost their colour, they press together so hard.

'Dad?' Lila says again. 'Dad, is it true?'

Mattia looks round at his family, and he nods. 'Yes,' he says. 'We found out a few days ago, and I didn't want to keep it from you. Belle is pregnant.'

There's a beat, and then Lila lets out a whimper. Jimmi hugs his father, slapping his back. Xander is by Lila's side, his arm around her. The two of them blend into one – a silhouette, insubstantial in the candle light.

Xander looks directly at me and mouths, 'Secret's out.'

13

'Let me take you back to my cabin.' I sit with Belle as she retches over the loo.

'I'm not going anywhere!' She gulps back the water I pass her. 'He said we should just do it – just tell them. Get it over with.'

Outside, I hear raised voices.

When Chloe had started crying, I'd come in with Belle. She'd staggered away from the family, slipping on the deck as though it was wet. I'd taken her arm, and the feel of her skin on mine had sent me back over three years, to when we'd staggered across the yacht after a night out, bambi-legged with booze. Soaked in sweat and sun.

Her arm through mine like a link to the past.

Every now and again we'd wake on the beach, having fallen asleep after drinks, woken by the sun. We'd sleep in a pile of limbs and wake when the first rays hit us, running back for whichever boat we were crewing. Running to get there before the guests woke, before the captain spotted we were missing.

We raced through the private ports, docking areas, moorings – on sand, pebbles. Under an early pink sky.

Our world had still been intact back then.

I wish I had realised it had been enough. I wish I hadn't pushed. Hadn't started all of this.

I look through a crack in the curtains of the huge bathroom, over by the marble-effect tub which looks out over the sea, and see Xander pouring a drink. Lila leans against his arm like her legs have gone to sleep.

Jimmi's voice had been loud to cover the deafening lack of congratulations, but his enthusiasm wasn't enough to mask the fall-out.

'A last-minute golden child,' I'd heard Bean say to Chloe. 'What does that mean for us? Now? Is that why he's delayed retirement? You think it will all go to Belle's kid? We must do something, we must—' I hadn't heard the end.

'How can they be so vile, about a baby? My baby!' Belle wipes her face quickly, pulling away the black marks of mascara below her lower lids. 'Here, can you pass me that?'

I follow her finger and pick up the silk make-up bag. She tips out hundreds of pounds of make-up onto the counter and begins dabbing and smoothing.

'Leeches! The lot of them! He's built his business up from scratch, and they've been given every opportunity. It would do them good to make it on their own! Why do they care so much if he might want to work for a few more years?'

I watch her apply lipstick from a pop-out, shiny gold case, and she opens a jewellery box, running her finger down the earrings. She replaces the ones she'd been wearing, putting in two chunky diamond tear drops.

'Mattia gave me these for our wedding,' she says, seeing me looking. 'Lila looked at them rather than me for the entire reception. I'll give her something to look at tonight.'

I briefly remember times when I'd stared at something Belle had that I couldn't afford. Her mum was always picking a few bits up for her – fancy hair products, make-up. Neither of us were rich back then, but I was always poorer. That gap has only widened. I look at the diamonds in her ears, for a brief moment feeling cheap in the expensive dress she's given me.

But I shake it off. I remind myself I started this. I'm here to make amends. Or at least to try.

'Em, you're all I've got left.' She sinks to the cushioned stool

I sit on and takes my hand. She tips her head to the side to rest it on mine.

We fall silent, and I listen to the furore outside. It seems to be quietening.

Belle tightens her hold on my hand. 'What if he starts listening to them? What if he picks them?' Her voice is quiet, almost a whisper.

The memory of the airless feeling of the cupboard suddenly presses down. I know I can't wait for long. I should tell her about the notes – I need to work out what's going on. What is on the memory stick the journalist gave me? But I don't feel I can leave, not when she has this to deal with.

I feel the heat of her face, her brow still touching mine. I think of Xander burrowing into secrets. I wonder what else he's discovered.

I wonder how much Mattia's decision to delay retirement is because of Belle and the baby. How accurate are the children that this is the reason he's putting it off? Would a man like Mattia ever really retire? Maybe he's doing it just for kicks. Maybe Mattia likes setting the cat in with the pigeons.

'You and Mattia…' I start, but I feel her tense. Can I push the friendship, as flimsy as it is now?

I have to. 'Did he force you to announce the pregnancy? You said you were going to wait. Is he a bit…controlling?' I think of the rumours. The way his staff straighten up when he flicks his hand. How jumpy they are around him.

She's standing before I finish. Her back is to me and she's picked up a lipstick, perfecting her already perfect lips.

'I've told you.' Her voice is cold now. 'He's been amazing. I've already said that, Emily.'

'Well, good. I'm so pleased for you,' I finish. I'm chickenshit. No use to anyone.

She exhales very quietly.

I carry on. 'I think it will be OK. I think they're just as scared as you.' I push a little. 'I suppose you married Mattia so soon after they lost their mum. They're probably not angry with you – they'll be angry with her, for leaving them. You remember grief. We've both been there.'

She nods, and she looks at the floor.

We heard about Belle's parents' car accident while we were dancing in the student union to some nineties throwback night. We'd been wearing Spice Girls t-shirts and clips in the side of our hair, and we'd been high on cheap booze and the taste of real freedom. A call had come through, and it had all crashed so hard I wasn't even sure how we'd got to the hospital. I remember my throat was tight as I'd watched through the glass as a nurse had led her to a bed where machines beeped and blinked, and Belle had sunk into the plastic chair and looked smaller than I'd ever seen her.

For all their wealth, their keys to all the doors they'd ever need, the Scarmardos had lost their mum. Chloe would only have been eighteen.

'Will you come out with me?' Belle says. 'Mattia will need me.' This time her question has the hint of a command.

We rise together, and I hug her, tight. 'You've got this.'

'Girl, no creases, I've just changed my top,' Belle says, but it sounds hollow. Like she's reaching for something out of her grasp.

We head out, and I remind myself I'm here to support Belle, not to hound her, to question her.

It's Belle and me. It always has been. Surely it still is.

14

There's been a quick gear change into a late, drunken evening. There's no shouting when we move back outside, but wine is spilt on the deck of the balcony and faces are tear stained and raw. Mattia had met Belle as we'd come outside, checking on her, and I'd left them to talk quietly.

'You knew something I didn't know,' Xander sing-songs, his voice slurring as he hands me another drink, eyebrows raised.

Chairs have been pulled away from the table. The plates have vanished and, in their place, dessert wine and brandy have been laid. I see Belle head back in, and Mattia moves over to the sofas, where Jimmi and Chloe sit.

Xander takes my hand. 'Come see the view, Emily-with-all-the-secrets. I feel like we should get to know each other.'

Bean smiles at me as we walk away, glares at Xander.

The sea just ahead of us, over the railings, is lit a pale emerald by the ship, but beyond that it is black. No lights anywhere on the ocean. The smell of spray, of sun-warmed water, is familiar.

'I wonder, with all your secrets, if you know the one I know, about your good friend, Belle. About my new mummy.'

I will not let this man scare me. He has a watch on his wrist worth more than my annual salary, and I'm drinking wine which costs over £100 a bottle. I'm light-headed but I will not let him have the upper hand.

I say nothing.

'Clever Emily. Still keeping all her cards to her chest.'

Xander stands very close; his smell reaches me, of expensive and luxurious living. He is so very beautiful. He leans in and whispers, his mouth so close to my ear that I shiver.

'I know something you don't know.' His whisper is sing-song, and he leans even closer. I can feel his lips almost on my cheekbone. 'Do you want me to tell?'

'I'm not sure I could stop you,' I say.

'Your friend Belle, goodie two shoes, pretty, pretty Belle. Innocent, vulnerable, Belle. We all know the story of how she met my father, after Mum died, at some hostage charity evening. But do you know what, clever Emily? That's a lie.

'Belle met my father several times before my mother died. They kept it a secret.' He lingers over the word. Draws it out. 'I don't think they'd ever breathe a word about that.' He's still whispering; my stomach twists at his words. 'But I know. So, when my father said my mother slipped into the sea, that it was a tragic accident, I just wonder how far under darling Belle's skirt my father had already reached. And when my mother *slipped*...' He hangs on the word. 'Well, did the boat capsize due to jutting rocks? Or to roaming cocks.'

I'm back to full alert. There's a cold twist in the summer night air. Why has he told me this? Is he trying to drive a wedge between Belle and me? Is it another ploy to leave her defenceless?

'You think I'm lying, clever Emily, with all your secrets? I could be. But I think you know I'm not.'

He's leaning out now, over the rail. His profile, handsome, striking and so slick, looks quickly sad. Just for a second.

I'm not attracted to Xander Scarmardo, despite how beautiful he is. I haven't been attracted to anyone since the night I spent with Finn's father three years ago. Yet I feel a flash of pity – his mother dying like that.

But Belle being involved with Mattia before Viola's death? No. It can't be true. Of course that can't be right.

'Do you know the truth? Has she told you?'

I think about what I could say. How to gain his trust and find out what is really going on. There's no point wildly defending Belle; I need to be more calculated than that. So instead of speaking, I shrug a little, trying to look enigmatic.

'Come on, Emily,' Xander says, staring ahead, back out over the ocean. 'Now that I've showed you mine, can you show me yours? Why didn't you tell anyone about your son? Do you know anything else about Belle – about Belle and my father – that means she needs to keep you close?'

My hand tightens on the rail. There's laughter behind us and I'm aware of how draining this game-playing is. My mouth is dry. My head aches.

'I reckon that's just a bit of bullshit,' I say lightly.

But what he's said about Belle circles in my head. Could she really have got together with Mattia when Viola Scarmardo was still alive? I feel tired and that the night has gone on long enough.

Xander is clearly drunk and focused now on his own train of thought. He faces out to sea. 'My mother died, and they both were very creative about when they met. Now Dad isn't retiring. Lila—' He looks across at his sister and I follow his gaze. His voice takes on an angry note. 'Lila will be devastated if he doesn't step down. She's given all her time to the company. Even right now, she's holding the whole thing together with paperclips—' He stops, shrugs. 'All of us. We've been brought up one way then suddenly,' he clicks his fingers, 'all change. Bean's income has been cut until he gets a job. I'm on a tighter rein. Chloe has been refused more money for her production company; her new festival plan is in freefall.' He shakes his head. 'This ship – it's eating cash. The company's funds have been diverted. Do you know how much this ship cost? Five hundred million dollars. Christ. You ever had a step-mother who cost you five hundred million dollars?'

I can't move past the idea of Belle lying about when she met Mattia. The implications...But I rally.

'I'm so sorry about Viola,' I probe a little, trying to see the real Xander.

'I remember how she was when I didn't feel very well, when I was small.' His voice softens, locked in full nostalgia. 'With my family background, Grandpa's Italian blood, the work ethic, we put machismo on our toast for breakfast. If we were ill – us *men* – then we took it on the chin. There was only ever Uncle Marcus who was sympathetic, probably because of whatever happened to his cheek to get that scar. He knows pain. I don't think my father's taken a day off in his life.' He pours something in his glass from a hip flask. He must be blind drunk by now.

I look back at the family. They're all scattered on sofas and chairs in smaller, quieter groups. As insightful as Xander's reminiscences are, I suddenly want to go and find Belle and see how she's holding up.

'Not a single day. But if I was ill, mum would bundle me upstairs. She'd bring me toast with chocolate spread on the top. "*Our secret*," she'd say, and she'd turn on the TV in the room, and climb into bed with me. We'd watch old movies – loads of them: black and white ones, seventies, eighties. She loved disaster movies, you know, the planes, buildings.' He laughs, sour, '*The Poseidon Adventure*.' He takes a drink. 'She'd not tell him. She wouldn't tell him I'd had a day off school. It would all be our secret. And he never knew, because he was never there.'

The sound of the sea is gentle. Mattia's voice carries from the end of the deck sofas, calm, steady. He's still holding court, his confidence if not his words, explaining that all will be well, that they have nothing to worry about, but I hear in their replies their worry like mice scratching on skirting boards.

There's silence for a second. What can Xander hope to achieve by sharing all this with me? It can't be anything good.

'I'll go check on Belle,' I say finally, taking a step back. But Xander doesn't seem to hear. He carries on without even looking at me.

'Well, let's see what comes of this week. It will bring something. But it can't resurrect her. Her head smashed onto rocks, her body afloat, face down. And it seems you know secrets that I don't know, Emily-who-holds-all-the-cards. Your son, Belle's baby, and much more, I'm sure.'

He stumbles forward, and kisses me on the cheek, whispering as he does, 'And be careful. There may not be rocks on this boat. But if Dad or Belle find out you know more than they'd like you to, well…' He stands back. 'You have such a pretty head.'

15

Three years earlier, Sicily

Our marriage. What is it like?

I sit with a glass of wine on the beach. Mattia arrives later this evening to celebrate our anniversary. He has never missed one. He is diligent in red letter days, if not the day to day.

'Viola!' Mattia. I look up from gazing at the sea and see our boat, *La Piccola*, out on the water.

'I'll head to the port!' he shouts as he waves from the sleek, white yacht he bought last year. So small it's easy to handle on your own.

He throws a rope towards the rear of the boat, and someone catches it.

I can't make out who it is, but I don't bother looking. Mattia must have brought some crew. He'll dismiss them soon. We only have staff for the first day on boats or in the villa. It's our tradition on our anniversary week.

'More wine, signora?'

I extend my glass as it's filled. I'll give Mattia half an hour to get the boat secured.

Our anniversary week and yet I feel a flicker of unrest.

So many years together. Our marriage has lasted, and this is a good thing, I suppose. Longer than many.

You're so lucky! Friends say. Some smile when they hear this and say nothing. I nod along, because of course I am. More than enough money. Beautiful houses. Beautiful children. Few see the cracks that lie beneath the surface.

What is our marriage like?

What I realised quickly, as the wife of Mattia, is that marriage is often being alone.

Once Mattia's business was set up in Italy, we moved back to England. His parents lived in Newcastle, in the north east of England. It is a beautiful city. It has a port, tall ships and old buildings. It is also near the beach. These are all the plus points to this beautiful city that I must mention, entirely in its defence, before I confide how much I hated it. How utterly miserable I was.

How alone.

I told no one. Least of all Mattia.

For our honeymoon he had taken me away on his yacht, and we had sailed to places I had only ever read about. We had married within a year of meeting. It was before our life together had really gathered pace, and Mattia dedicated himself to the job of honeymooning like he dedicated himself to all undertakings. He was unswerving and thorough. Romantic and attentive.

I was nineteen and just a child. He was twenty-three, but it was like he had circled the world. He had already been at work since he was sixteen, and in those seven years he had achieved more success than many do in a lifetime. I realised later that the honeymoon must have been the only real holiday he had ever taken, if you could call it that for him – I was the full focus of his relentless energy. He switched his attention from business to me. He never just sat around and took in the beauty of the sea, or read a book.

The crew were discreet. There was no part of the boat in which we did not make love. Nothing to which he didn't introduce me. We dove off the boat in the evening and would swim naked under the night sky. He teased off my bikini on the deck in the sun and would rub sun cream into my skin until I screamed for him to carry on. He would inch his chair towards me on the deck at dinner, and kiss me as dessert arrived, tracing my neck with his finger while he fed me from the spoon. He would pause only briefly to ask the crew to leave us – I lay on the table from which we ate as he buried his head deep under my dress, and I would lie afterwards in his arms, undressed and undone.

It is what I remember; I remember craving him, him always being ready. There was nothing he would not do for me. And there were gifts too: jewels, trips to private beaches. There were picnics he arranged, but overwhelmingly I remember the feel of him.

When we got back to our house in Bologna, after we had greeted my parents, I remember him looking at me from across the room, and I blushed.

'Will there be grandchildren soon?' Mama asked, and it was the first time that it had occurred to me.

Sex leads to children. In all our honeymooning, we hadn't used protection once.

I looked back to Mattia, his head nodding seriously at something Papa said, and that was the first time I suspected him of having a motive other than pleasure. The first time I began to understand him. The first time I questioned him.

All the sex would lead to a child. Mattia was bent on pleasing me, not just because I was his wife. It would also make me the mother of his children.

'Maybe,' I replied, and my fingernails dug into my palm. I wasn't sure I was ready – that we were ready. We had only just married. Children could wait.

But I had done nothing to prevent it. I hadn't even thought of it. And it wasn't as though I didn't know. Of course we'd have children. But did I want them now?

We hadn't discussed it at all.

We moved to Newcastle after about a year of marriage. There were still no children, for which I was grateful at the time, and in Bologna I had been enjoying my status as the wife of a successful man. Invitations arrived for art galleries, for the theatre. Mattia was happy for me to indulge my passions for the arts, as the Scarmardo name appeared alongside other names on the walls for funding, for sponsorship.

When we moved, I think I'd expected it all to be the same, only somewhere different. But the change. Oh, the change.

First, a language. Mattia was fluent in Italian, the language of his father. But in England he spoke English, and I needed to learn it like I spoke my own tongue. I stumbled over the vocabulary, all the rules. The accents.

And the weather! We moved in September, when people in Italy still eat gelato in the piazza in the evening.

Here, it rained, it was damp. We moved into a large, old house where the heating rattled as it warmed, and my hair curled quickly when we went outside – a thin layer of moisture laced through the day.

People looked at me before talking to me – they would take in my clothes, my accent. They rushed to make friends – Mattia was already a force, an employer of many and a man to please, and his Italian wife was something of a dinner-party invite. But I was unused to being the subject of such fascination, of being quizzed on where I grew up, what foods I ate. In Bologna, I was admired; here, I was assessed.

Mattia worked long hours, went on long business trips.

In the end, it was his brother, Marcus, who came to my rescue. He was a piano teacher – utterly unlike Mattia, quiet, unassuming, and he worked at the local school at weekends, teaching classes. He visited houses when school finished, teaching children in their lounges. It meant that he was free during the day. The time I was most alone.

Mattia is walking up the beach now, and I see someone on the boat climb down to secure it.

There's a flash of a brown limb and I catch sight of a dark-haired ponytail swinging against the sea.

We usually only have minimal staff for our anniversary weekend. I hope whoever Mattia has brought to crew isn't hanging around. I don't recognise who it is, but then I don't keep track of all the staff. Mattia is constantly firing and hiring people.

I stretch out long and relax under the Sicilian sun, ignoring the uncomfortable whisper of doubt. I am on our beach, where I have holidayed since I was a baby, to celebrate our thirty-eighth wedding anniversary. What can go wrong?

DAY TWO

16

At first, I'm not sure what wakes me. Light streams through a shaft in the curtains and then I hear a gentle knock at the door.

I'm still full-bodied in a dream, and it's the one I've often had. The panic I'd first felt. That feeling – when you're asleep and you open your mouth to scream but nothing comes out; you try to run, but your legs don't move.

It's the panic from the attack on the boat three years ago. The utterly paralysing panic that had made me freeze, and I block it out whenever it raises its head. I tell myself I've moved on, even as I watch myself unable to move from the house I was born in, not daring to try anything new. Belle has managed it. Why can't I?

In the dream, the footsteps coming for me are as real as the blood in my veins, and I know I'm about to be taken. I can't run. I can't scream.

And then the second before I open my eyes, there's a hand on my arm, a voice in my ear. As I feel water swirling around my waist and I'm seconds from the worst thing that could happen, I'm back from the brink. I'm back because someone has reached out for me. Him. Always him.

I see him in Finn. He's alive to me every day.

I open my eyes, the shaft of light lies across my chest, bright and warm. The gentle knock on the door has stopped. Belle?

Instead, when I open the door, I see the retreating back of

Mirka. There's a coffee outside the door and I call out, 'Thank you.'

She turns, lifts her hand, her smile bright like the sun shaft and instead of walking away, she heads towards me.

'Morning, Emily, can I get you anything else? Some pastries, yoghurt or fruit?'

I nod. 'Yes, please. Mirka, have any letters been left for me?'

The smile doesn't falter, but she gives a brisk shake of her head. I wonder if she has any sense – or even any interest – in what yesterday's note was about. And she hasn't mentioned the cupboard at all. I wonder what else Mirka notices that remains unsaid beneath the professional front.

'Lila Scarmardo asked to be alerted when you woke,' Mirka says. 'Shall I let her know? She said she'll visit you in your cabin.'

Lila wants to talk to me?

'Yes, and thank you.' I pick up the coffee and watch Mirka walk away, wondering how long she held the smile for after she'd turned around.

The memory stick. Why had he given it to me? I must see what's on there.

As I let the door swing closed, once again, I'm sure I see Bean in the corridor. When I notice him, he disappears round the corner of the ship.

'Bean!' I shout and I run out after him, but by the time I turn and look down the long stretch of corridor, he's disappeared. There's no one else to be seen, and I put my hand to the wall to steady myself. I'm breathing hard, and I'm light-headed after last night's wine.

Why is he hanging round my cabin again? Xander implied he was flirting with me. But I don't think so. Is he waiting for me to leave, to try to get in? Could it be him who pushed me into the dark? I remember the feeling of the walls closing in and pause to take a slow breath. I need to keep my wits about me today.

With one last look, I head back and dress, pulling on work-out leggings and a vest top. I tie my hair up into a ponytail.

Apparently, there's a yoga class broadcast across the sports channel on the ship for those who wish to take part in their cabin. I'm going to do it in the sun. I may as well take full advantage of the luxuries. I feel some panic kicking in at the thought of Lila coming to see me. So far, Bean has questioned me, Xander has landed some fairly heavy news about Belle and Mattia, which he appears to believe. Are they all trying to turn me against Belle?

I mull it over as I head out into the sun. I look forward to some exercise. I work out hard at home. It's what I've clung to ever since having Finn. I need to stay healthy to look after us. I don't just mean low salt and exercise; I mean I need to be *strong*. I need to be able to respond next time, not flail. Not fail.

Sliding the doors back to the balcony, I raise my arms up to the sun for a salutation. The iPad is propped up on the deck by my yoga mat, which faces the flat of the ocean – it can eat you up, but today it's so still, you'd never know how ravenous it can be.

I take a deep breath through my nose, and hold it. Jimmi Scarmardo appears in my brain. Why am I thinking about him? Was it his unsettling ability to fake enthusiasm for Belle's baby? I can't decide if he was trying to be kind or trying to suck up to his dad. Xander had made some reference to Jimmi being the new favourite after Mattia's speech.

Jimmi didn't talk to me at all last night, but then why would he? I was locked in conversation with Xander for most of the evening. A conversation that now, on a calm, sunlit morning, seems wildly far-fetched – the conspiracy theory of a son grieving his mother. Jimmi must have grieved, too. I knew from the Sunday papers and from Belle that his fashion label had been growing in strength, that he had dropped out of the gossip pages of magazines; no longer snapped with women leaving clubs, drunk in cars late at night, on beaches, surrounded by an entourage or with another girlfriend. No more photos of him riding a jet ski, a fast car, getting off a private jet. He's so controlled now, there's something almost sinister about his ability not to react when the rest of them spit and stew.

I hadn't known that grief could make a man like him change so much. Is there more to it? What had Xander said? He had turned on him, asking if Mattia had promised Jimmi that he was in line for succession; suggesting Mattia was favouring him over the rest of them: *splitting the wolf pack.*

I bend into a downward dog and exhale. Maybe it's not just about uniting against Belle. There might be something else causing all this tension and infighting.

The sun is warm, and the ship feels so still it could be anchored.

There's a knock on the door. I jump.

'Emily,' Lila says, wearing workout gear as well, tall and the picture of health as I let her in.

'You're doing yoga,' she says, looking out to the balcony where the iPad is still playing. 'I'll join you.'

17

I lower down and watch Lila bend like she's made of rubber, wondering what she wants. 'Last night was crazy,' she says. She lifts up now and stands in warrior pose.

I follow, stepping forward and lifting my arms. The likelihood of Lila Scarmardo and I becoming BFFs is so absurd it would make me laugh, if I wasn't so convinced this family means me harm.

I play along. 'Are you OK?' I remember her face last night after Mattia announced delaying retirement. Then later when he announced the baby.

She shifts her weight to lean back. 'Of course.'

She's so relaxed when she speaks, but it's all a front. I know how cut up they all are. I saw it last night, particularly Lila. She's clearly not here to share confidences with me. I wonder what she wants, and it makes me uneasy. But she wastes little time getting to the heart of it.

'I know what Xander told you last night.' She sinks down to the deck, crossing her legs, then she raises her arms above her head, and lowers them again, her hands together in a prayer motion at her chest. Her eyes are closed, and I mirror her actions, wondering if I'm supposed to volunteer his stories about the affair that Belle and Mattia supposedly had.

Instead, I opt for saying nothing. The yoga instructor signs off and I can feel the sun getting hotter, my arms taking the heat. We're further out to sea, under a foreign sun.

Dad still talks about the dangers of a foreign sun. *So much hotter than our back garden*, he used to say, suspicious of travel. He and Mum had only been out of the UK a few times. Once to Spain and several visits to France. After Mum died when I was ten, holidays had been camping and caravan parks. When he'd picked me up at the airport three years ago, the state of me had only solidified his impression about the perils of travel.

What have they done to you? he'd said, referring to everything so far away it was out of his reach.

Lila opens her eyes and looks at me. 'You're not saying anything.'

'You didn't ask me a question.'

'Ha!' She laughs and for the first time I see her smile. 'Come on. Dad wants us to show our faces today on board. Let's go and get some coffee. And ice cream. You know there's a twenty-four-hour ice-cream station? The caramel crunch is the best there is.'

Passengers point and stare at Lila. Some stop to say hello. Lots of smiles. She poses for a few selfies and people hold phones up as we pass. I bask a little in the stares, smile at some families. Someone even asks me for a photo.

'Sure,' I say. I stand and smile, enjoying the brief moment of celebrity by association. It's a bit addictive.

Lila is a pro. She smiles, keeps moving. Waves, keeps moving. At the ice-cream station there's no queue, and the crew members beam at her.

I choose mint choc chip – it always reminds me of caravan holidays in Scotland when I was a kid – and we walk out onto the deck and find the play area. There are no children allowed on the ship so this area is for adults only. Huge basket swings are set up, and they swing out as though over the ocean. Not quite, but the illusion makes it feel real.

'Here,' Lila says, and she flops into a basket swing and gestures for me to climb in. It rocks gently, and I slip my sunglasses down as I look out over the sea. It must be thirty-eight degrees today and the air is still.

'Dad wants to try one of these swings but he can't face having to chat to the little people. I think he's going to reserve one for tomorrow night – once everyone is a bit more used to the ship and hopefully also already in bed. He can't move around without selfie requests. We're meant to put up with it, though.'

I get the sense that Lila is building up to something. She's doling out small talk like a prelude. Holding back seems to work well with Xander, so I say, 'Your dad knows how to build a ship!'

I hold the ice cream on my tongue, feeling all the miles and then some from my real life.

Finn would love this basket swing. He'll be at nursery now. He runs in every morning with his best friend, Eddie, coming out beaming, paint splashes on his t-shirt and sand in his shoes. Dad collects him, and I get home from the factory at four p.m. for tea. I read him stories, put him into bed, then work until nine. The mortgage is paid slowly, the bills are met. There's not much left over, but that's OK.

It was only yesterday that I said bye to Dad and Finn. It feels like it's been months. The sun has ironed out some of the fear from last night. I'm wary around Lila – she must want something from me – but the panic I'd felt when I'd been trapped seems unreal somehow.

'I know that Xander told you about Belle,' Lila says, 'that they got together before Mum died.' The quick, intense look she shoots me belies the casual tone she attempts.

I nod. I still don't believe it's true, and I remember Belle telling me about the lawyer offering her five million dollars to walk away from the family, and despite the hot sun, I feel a chill. Was Lila behind that?

'He's just guessing though, isn't he,' I say. 'I heard what he said about her in the lift, the *Bloody Belle*, he said, angry her name was on the side of the ship. Angry I've been invited.' I shrug. 'I mean, he's trying to stir the pot.' I glance at Lila, testing the waters.

'I guess if anyone might know the truth, then you might,' she says, slowly.

'Why me?'

'Because you're invited when we've all been asked to leave our other halves at home.' She stretches out, her legs longer than mine, tanned and toned.

I wait while a couple walk past, gazing out at the ocean in shorts and bright t-shirts. It's the couple from the queue. I recognise the new blue hat, with the wide, floppy brim. The husband is carrying a bottle of Coke again and they disappear out of view.

'I don't know why Mattia agreed to me coming.' I look at her again. I know why Belle wanted me, but I'm not sharing that. 'Belle and I have known each other since we were tiny. We lived next door to each other. We did everything together, but I haven't seen her since…' I trail off.

'She was kidnapped and you weren't?' Lila finishes. 'Why is that a problem? She can't blame you for not being taken.'

The prickle up and down my spine is familiar; I've never been able to think of it without having some sort of physical reaction.

'It wasn't just that she was kidnapped and I wasn't,' I start, knowing I won't tell the whole thing, not aloud. There are two versions. The public and the private. The glossy, and the shameful. It's shame that's left me shrivelled for everything except Finn and Dad.

'We were on the boat, it was morning. We were washing the decks down. The four clients were asleep and other than them, there was only the two of us and the captain on board. Have you ever been on it? It's quite small for a super yacht. Luxurious, but only two client bedrooms, our bunk bed right at the bottom of the boat and the captain's room. The rest are communal areas – small kitchen but a huge lounge and inside dining area. Big deck space. There's even a small lift.'

Lila shrugs a little, almost bored. Her sunglasses obscure her face and the sun is so bright I don't really see her. She hasn't asked to hear the rest, but I can't stop. It was the same with childbirth stories. People didn't have to ask for me to recount it. I needed to say it, over and over.

'We were plumping cushions; we'd hosed the deck. A bucket with the mop was still out. There was breakfast to prepare.' I remember the smell of the rising heat, the feel of the sun on my skin. I'd been in shorts and a bikini top. Nothing had mattered. I was in charge of breakfast that morning and my biggest worry was not over-cooking poached eggs.

'There was a bump on the side of the boat. We'd been going gently, no wind, so I wondered if we'd hit something. I looked over the side and saw them.'

This is where the narrative splits. I'd started freezing even then. I never spell out the tiny details – the masks, the guns, knives strapped to their waists. The way my breath had shortened, my chest had become tight. The way tiny black dots flashed in my vision, my mouth tasting sharp and sour.

'There were five of them, all armed, and they wanted money, jewellery. The women on board had stuff worth hundreds of thousands. It all went in the safe most days. They talked about it freely. One of the men had a watch that was worth over forty k – I recognised the make. They asked us to show them where it was.' I fall silent and the scene plays itself out in my head.

I'd opened my mouth to scream when I'd seen them, but like a dream – like my reoccurring dream – nothing had come out. I'd tried to run, but my legs hadn't moved. And I'd known if I didn't move soon, then it would all be worse. It was already very bad. I'd gripped the mop handle I'd still been holding but it was redundant in my hands.

Belle had shouted, *'What is it?'* And I'd barely managed to turn. I'd gone limp. I'd opened and closed my mouth, which is why she'd gone up ahead of me to look over the side. It was why as they were mounting the deck, they grabbed her first, and not me. And the one who grabbed her, pulled the knife from their belt, and held it up against her throat, cutting her the tiniest amount, so that blood was already beginning to trickle down her neck as I'd stood there.

'They took Belle,' I say. 'They took her hostage and kept her for three days. Until a payment was made.'

The moment is still crystal clear in my head. Like a photograph, but real with the sweat I can feel and terror I still taste.

I'd had a split second to do something. Sometimes I justify my actions out loud, I say things like I say to Lila now. 'There was no time. No time to think even. There were five people inside and we had to lock the doors. One of the women was pregnant. It was all I thought about.'

But I didn't think about her. I was congratulated later for putting her first, of thinking of the baby. But I didn't. I'm not sure what I thought of. Time both sped up and slowed down. I looked at the knife, I looked at the blood on Belle's neck. It had reached her chest by then, her white bikini top tinged red, and drops were almost at her navel. We were both skinny, brown, and I remember looking at her belly button, stretched long as she was pulled backwards, pulled up against the masked man. I watched the blood reach it, and Belle…She was terrified – crying, eyes wide.

And they were all shouting, all of them, screaming, shouting – '*Money! Money!*'

Something in my mouth tasted bitter; I was numb, and then it goes misty – unclear. I remember running – and nothing would have slowed me down. I ran – all I can really remember are tiny details: the door to the inside deck was ahead of me; the sound of a clatter as I must have knocked over the bucket; shouts; blinding sun. I ran and ran.

Then I was inside. I don't know how I managed it, but I locked the door behind me. There was sweat in my eyes, and despite the heat of the morning, I was freezing.

Three of the men were already at the door as I was turning the key, and one swung a gun round so the butt was facing the glass and started pounding hard. I ran to the next door, leading to the lounge, which I locked again, and I hit the alarm.

That was when the captain appeared.

I pick it up here for the sake of Lila.

'I sounded the alarm, but they had Belle. She was caught outside. I was helpless. The captain ran out and took over. We had weapons on board and he grabbed one; the mayday had gone out. We thought we were lucky; there was another boat nearby, and they came quickly. The pirates shot at the glass, and were just getting in when the other boat appeared.'

They got away – they took Belle with them. And Juan…I've never been able to forgive myself. My throat closes at this point and I can smell it. The sweat, the heat – the breath of the captain.

I open my mouth to speak but I realise I've gone too far. I can't continue. My vision blurs.

'Emily.' At first it sounds as though it comes from far away, but I hear it again. 'Emily.'

Lila's face is close to mine. She has lifted her sunglasses and I realise her hand is on mine. 'Emily, it's OK. I'm sorry, I shouldn't have asked you. I forgot about the captain. I didn't really think.'

I blink a few times and force a smile. 'Oh, it's OK, it's good to talk about it.'

But it's not. I feel weak afterwards. Even that protestation has cost me. I sit and pray she takes the lead.

Lila gives me a few minutes. The sun is hot and I breathe slowly until the air comes naturally again, and my heart rate slows to something that feels almost normal.

'And Belle? Afterwards? I mean, did you both meet Dad after the attack?'

I remember what Lila had been talking about originally.

I stare straight ahead. 'She met your dad a bit later, after your mum died, and she never came home. I suppose her life and mine split.'

The last bit is true.

There had been a moment, when she'd got free from the arms of the man holding her. She'd run to the other side of the deck and they'd not seen her as they'd tried to get through the door I'd locked. She'd banged on the sunroof on the other side of the boat – it opens from the inside. It's glass and looks down towards the lift shaft and the lounge area. I'd seen her. Entirely alone.

I'd seen her bang on the glass, and I'd had a chance to open it. I'd had a chance to save her.

A split second when I'd seen her look down, but I hadn't been able to move. I'd frozen again – limp like I'd been when they'd first arrived. I'd just watched as she banged on the glass. I did nothing.

I was petrified – and I wouldn't open it.

Belle looked terrified, watching me do nothing. She banged harder on the glass. She looked utterly abandoned.

Instead, I took a step backwards. I left her there. And I ran deeper into the boat. I hid by the door, just watching her. All alone.

Seconds later, a man came and grabbed her from behind, pulled her backwards as the alarm was ringing, and pulled the knife back up to her neck. The last memory I have of that day is the knife pressing against her neck, as the blood smeared its path across her skin.

And the captain. Well, when the glass broke and the end of the gun appeared through the hole, I froze solid. Like ice, so cold.

And he...

He...

The sound of blood, choking on his blood.

Belle disappeared from view, and we didn't speak for three years.

That's why I came. Not just because of Belle's invite; her pleading. But because of the note. *I KNOW WHAT YOU DID.*

I came to save her this time, so I can wash away the guilt of the time I left her to die.

18

The champagne bar smells expensive, polished brass, plates of croissants. Huge ice buckets stand ready next to Jeroboams of the most expensive kinds of champagne. A brass coffee machine sparkles from behind the bar and we pass through tables surrounded by low chairs or sofas, and booths tucked around portholes.

Lila had grabbed my hand and declared I needed a drink, after looking at my face when I'd finished recounting the attack. She'd led me to the outside deck, sitting up at the tall round tables.

Lila pushes one of the two drinks that arrive towards me. 'Here.'

'Thanks,' I say, sipping at the champagne cocktail she'd asked the waiter for, pale red and sweet. It had been good to walk for a minute. I feel like the reset button has been pressed. I can breathe again.

'*Do* you know how long Dad and Belle were together, when it all started?' she asks, pushing again.

'As I said earlier, it was at the charity event. I have no reason to think otherwise.' That's when Belle had said she'd met him.

Lila takes a drink and her expression becomes hard. Her eyes narrow slightly and she swallows.

'Belle spent some time in Bali after the kidnapping, didn't she?' Lila asks it as a question but she knows the answer.

'She could have done.' I have no idea. I'd been drunk for most of that time. But I want to hear what she has to say. It feels like Lila has been desperate to tell me something, and I'm interested.

'Well, Dad and I flew out to the East for a meeting quite soon after the attack you experienced. Afterwards, I flew home. He stayed on for a day or so, but then he called me from the Bali house. He must have gone there rather than come straight back.'

The sweetness of the drink counteracts the acid of her tone.

'I didn't think anything about it at the time. But I had a call from our housekeeper there a few months later.' Lila lifts the drink and sips, signals for another. 'She said there was a pile of clothes she'd washed and had ready to post to the lady who had been staying in the house – the lady who had been staying there when Dad had so kindly given her the month off, paid. She was *so grateful* for the break, she said, and if I could get her the address she'd have the clothes posted off right away. She apologised for coming to me rather than have my secretary deal with it, but she said Dad had asked her to keep the house guest quiet as she'd needed some privacy. But she had assumed Dad meant keep it quiet from most people. At the time, I was Dad's second in everything.'

As the sun climbs higher, the shade creeps over us from the umbrella above. There are still no boats anywhere as I look out over the flat ocean, thinking of Belle and all the secrets that could have built up over the three years.

'Dad likes his secrecy. If he'd wanted me to know about it, he would have told me. I had everything sent to me, then I checked the CCTV on the driveway. Guess who I saw?'

She falls silent as more drinks arrive. The bubbles are a mix of dry and sweet; dark-red liquor swirls at the bottom.

The waiter smiles.

'Thank you,' Lila says as he walks away.

I sip, but struggle to swallow. I think of Belle, living with Mattia in the family villa while Viola was still alive. I wonder if it's possible that at that stage it was innocent. The wealthy yacht owner looking after a traumatised employee. I desperately hope so. I can't bear to think about the implications otherwise.

'Why are you telling me this?' This is the part I don't understand. 'Why confide in me?'

'Now that you ask.' Lila turns her brown eyes my way. They could be Xander's. They must both take after their mother – unlike Jimmi and Chloe, they don't look like Mattia. 'We were hoping you could help us. It's just Xander and me asking right now – we haven't spoken to the others. I didn't want anyone letting it slip to Dad that we've been snooping. We checked you out. You need money. We're happy to compensate. We're not asking for anything underhand. We just want the truth. You see—'

'You're offering me money to betray Belle?' I laugh out of shock. 'What, you buy me a drink, call me poor and think I'll throw my mate under a bus?' It's crazy. They must be crazy. It's not only a reach but wildly insulting. I look at her, mock seriously. 'Twenty million and I'll do it.' Then I laugh again, pick up my drink and roll my eyes.

'Emily, please.'

'Really?' I want to take the piss out of this utterly entitled bullshit, but there's something in her tone. She sounds like Xander. She rubs her hand roughly across her face.

'Please,' she says again, and her voice is tight, quiet.

'Christ, you lot think you can buy anything, don't you?' I say, but quietly, and I keep my tone steady.

The customers at the other table are pointing, having noticed who I'm sitting with, and Lila forces a smile onto her face. She waves.

'Emily. Just hear me out?'

I may as well listen.

'After Bali, once I'd seen the CCTV, I kept tabs on her. I knew who she was from the press, and I thought Dad must be having an affair.' She shakes her head. 'It wouldn't be the first time.'

Oh Belle, I think, *who have you married?*

'His occasional infidelity is no secret – it's not like it's never featured in the press.' She shrugs. 'But I had a feeling. He talked about that documentary she took part in, where she was interviewed about being a hostage. He couldn't stop bringing it up.'

I remember it. I'd watched it on TV. Dad had suggested we both watch it but I told him I couldn't face it; then I stayed up into the early hours of the morning and watched it alone, in the dark. She had only been on for five minutes. I'd played it on a loop for hours. I'd sunk a bottle of wine and turned the volume right down. I'd gone over the outline of her face like she was a ghost.

'Anyway, it gets worse.' She looks at me. 'Are you ready?'

Dread twists in my stomach but I nod. Part of me worries I'm betraying Belle by even listening, but I'm in the middle of a puzzle and only have a few pieces. I need the rest.

'Dad said he was meeting Mum for their anniversary in Sicily and taking the boat from France, not the jet. He can sail that one without crew. They keep crew to a limit on their private weekends. I was over in Sicily, after Mum…'

She takes another drink, steadies herself.

'I spoke to the housekeepers. They gave me something they'd found on the grounds. A charm, the letter B. From a bracelet, or a necklace. They thought Mum must have lost it – she did have a bracelet with the first letter of all our names on there. Except she never wore silver. She only wore gold. It was nothing to do with Bean. It must have been everything to do with Belle.'

I can't breathe.

'It was picked up the day after Mum's body was found.' Lila lifts her drink and swallows hard. 'She was there, Emily. Mum died and I'm sure Belle must have been there too.'

My mind races, crowded with thoughts – with doubts.

'What are you saying?' Although I know, I need to hear it spelled out.

'Oh, Emily.' Lila picks up her drink, swilling the heavy crystal the way she had swilled the pink cocktail the night before. 'Belle was there when Mum died. She's the one who stood to win everything with Mum out of the way. What do you think might have happened?'

19

I stand in the shower, the water turned up as hot as I can take it. Lila thinks that Belle was at the villa in Sicily when Viola died.

What does that mean? Is Xander right? Was Viola's death not really an accident – was she murdered?

My head spins.

This is the second day of the cruise and so far two of Mattia's children have accused him of having an affair with Belle, and have implied that their mother was murdered.

I think about how Mattia forced Belle to announce her pregnancy early to a family he knew would be upset. He told the press and the world he was delaying his retirement and his children's inheritance, before he'd told his children. I think of the woman with the green earpiece, how she'd instinctively flinched when he'd flicked a hand.

If something else had happened to Viola, it won't be Belle's fault. Belle's asked me to come here to help her – to protect her. But who does she need protection from?

Has Belle asked me to come here because of Mattia? Is that what she's not telling me? He seems to inspire fear in those around him.

I reach out and turn off the shower, feeling cold with shock despite the heat of the water.

I climb out and wrap myself in the fluffiest towel I've ever seen. I look round at the staggering luxury of the cabin – lights round the mirror, expensive toiletries, a marble bath.

As for Belle lying about when she got together with Mattia, well I suppose that wouldn't be the biggest shock. She would hardly announce to the world they got together when Mattia was married. I can only imagine how tempting all of this must be. After what she'd been through…I close my eyes. I still haven't really asked her about the aftermath of the kidnapping. And I know I must. All I know is what she talked about in the documentary, but I can imagine that isn't the whole story. Not even the tip of it all. And I need to apologise. For abandoning her. For not being around to face her afterwards. For letting her go through it all on her own.

Belle must have looked her life in the eye. Her value defined by a ransom for her freedom. I wouldn't be surprised if Mattia was something she decided she was owed.

But nothing more. Certainly she wouldn't murder anyone. There's just no way. Maybe Belle had been to the villa, but she wouldn't have been there that weekend. If she'd dropped the charm from a necklace on the grounds, then it could have been there from months before.

I know Belle. She's not capable of killing someone. More than that – I'm here to protect *her*. She needs my help.

I would turn myself inside out to save her.

But I didn't. The voice of self-doubt niggles at the back of my brain. I'm not the lit match. Not anymore.

I hadn't saved her. I had stared up through the glass.

Belle was taken and the captain had been killed. The glass to the inner reception room had smashed under the weight of the butt of a gun, when the captain had screamed at me to get behind him. I remember the whole thing in a blur. I'd been crying.

Then there was the shot.

Blood everywhere. Belle gone.

All I could do was run away.

I hadn't just come to save her. I'd come to save me. Kill the demons. Find myself. And find out who sent the note. Who claims to know the full story. What we did.

I need a clear head. To work out what's going on, I need to watch Mattia. Watch the children. If Belle is really in danger again, I won't fail her this time.

Out of nowhere, I have an image of the man in the Blur t-shirt and the shiny chrome memory stick. His hesitant voice – cheap clothes, the kind I understood.

What had I done with it? I'd been so distracted by the family, the disastrous evening, it had slipped my mind.

Wrapped in the towel, I head into the main reception room in the cabin. I find it in my evening bag.

I pull it out and look around for something to use. There's a memory stick attachment in the TV in the second reception room. A PlayStation and various controls are all lined up ready to use. I find a slot that works for the stick and turn on the TV. The sun is bright in here. The horizon is hazy in the heat.

It takes a while, but finally a link appears, which I click on and find a file with a screen full of photos.

I expand the first. It's a photo of the family on holiday – the siblings look a lot younger. It must have been taken at least ten years ago. They're all at a beach, and looking closely, I recognise it as the beach of their villa in Sicily, the one that was all over the news when Viola died.

I click on the next picture, and it's the same beach, only this time there's just a woman – Viola. The next few photos are of a woman and also a young boy. Maybe a young Bean. The next couple have Viola and Bean in them, but also the twins – their blond hair flashing up, and there's also one of all five children, digging sandcastles with Viola.

In the next few, the children are on the beach, and with Mattia. I manage to zoom in very closely on the image. It's not Mattia – it's the image of him, but there's a scar down one cheek. He must be a close relation.

I think back to last night. Xander had mentioned an uncle

with a scar. He had spoken kindly about him, said that he was different to Mattia. Uncle Marcus.

This doesn't make any sense. Why all the secrecy around a bunch of old holiday snaps that wouldn't even pass muster at a gossip magazine? And why would the journalist want to give them to me of all people?

There's a knock at the door and I jump.

'Emily, it's Belle. Want to come and get changed? I've got a few things for you – picked out some great outfits!'

'Just on the loo,' I shout, and I close everything down, pulling out the memory stick and dropping it into the drawer with the PlayStation games.

The photos will have to wait. It's time to confront Belle.

20

Belle hands me a scarf as I enter her cabin.

'Wear this if you like. It will go perfectly with the outfit I've picked out.'

I throw it back at her. 'You keep saying you're going to tell me what's going on. This is as good a time as any, I reckon.'

'A different scarf?' Belle pulls a questioning face, looking hopeful I'll let it slide. 'I don't think we've got time, the—'

'Belle. I've had the Scarmardos plying me with booze and sneaking rumours into my ears. It's about time I heard what really happened, about when you and Mattia met.' I sit on the bed, and pull my knees up to my chest. 'We haven't really talked.' I look at her carefully. 'About any of it.'

'OK.' She flops on the bed next to me, the scarf twisted in her hands. 'Full disclosure. Where do I start?'

'Start with Mattia. Remind me, *when* did you meet him?' I might be here to protect her, but she needs to be straight with me.

'We don't have that long.' She glances at her watch.

'I think you'll find we do.'

'Well I've already told you – I met him not long after Viola died. We were at a charity event. I was speaking as a hostage and—'

'Start again.' I close my eyes briefly, frustrated. Also, the mention of Viola's name is unsettling. Why does she need to mention her? 'No bullshit. I'm not joking, Belle. I know I can't get off this ship, but I'll find a way if you feed me any more crap. You say you brought me here to help you, but you haven't told me much of it at all. Plus someone is trying to scare the shit out of me and it's working.'

'What's happened?' Belle reaches for my hand. 'You never did tell me what happened last night.'

'No, not me first. You. When did you meet him?'

She waves her hand. 'It *was* at the charity…'

Tailing off, she stares long and hard at me, and slowly the eager expression slides away to nothing. It wasn't real at all. She looks blank. 'What do you know?'

'The same as them. You met him *before* her death.' She clearly won't tell me unless I push hard. I think of being locked in the cupboard, of the notes, and I hear the volume of my voice rise. 'You stayed with him in Bali, after the kidnapping.' I pause, then decide to say it anyway, because I want to wound her – for not being honest with me, for leaving me in the dark. 'And I know you've been to their villa in Sicily, where Viola died.'

She reels like she's been slapped. Starts shaking her head, but I lean in and reproduce her new wave, exaggerated. I can't help it. I need her to be honest now. I say, 'Tell. Me. The. Truth.'

'They know?' she whispers. The scarf twists tight in her hands and her eyes close.

I stare at her. So, it's true.

Christ.

'OK.' She exhales as she looks at me. 'Yes. I met him at the hotel, after I'd been rescued. They snuck him in the back – no press. He didn't want to be associated with the incident so soon after it happened. But he was rocked – he felt awful. That apology he gave you at the drinks yesterday – it was real. His boat, his crew. He visited the family of the captain first.' At this she stares at her hands, still twisting the silk, and I close my eyes, willing her to push past this part.

'He invited me to a private room. Apologised. Offered me some compensation.' She looks at me, her dark eyes as blank as they had been a second ago. 'I haven't seen you since. You didn't take my calls. It was fucked up, Emily. I was fucked up. I spent three days in their boat hole; it was so hot. Not enough water. Terrified. I had a bucket – barely any food.' Her voice rises as she speaks, and I see her careful control start to slip. Her hands are shaking. The scarf falls to the floor. 'Once the press got hold of the story, it was all over the radio. They were more terrified than me. They argued constantly – fought physically. I thought about what I'd do if they killed each other and I was left in the hole, how long I'd last and whether anyone would find me before…'

I bite my lip. At the time, I had also wondered if she was coming back.

'Where were you? I needed you, Emily.'

I feel a kick in my stomach and I reach out for her as I say, 'Belle, I—'

But she pulls away, bending forward, pushing the heels of her hands to her forehead. 'Even now. I don't go out on my own after dark. I sleep with all the curtains open. In restaurants, I need to face the room. If there is a big crowd, I can't breathe properly. I…' She slides to a stop, shakes her head. 'Well, Mattia was kind. I was a mess. I shook the whole time. I couldn't even look at him when he suggested money. I barely heard it. That's when he offered me the Bali house. For as long as I wanted. I had nothing to go back to. Mum and Dad gone. I couldn't get hold of you.' At this she looks at me, angry. The bitterness comes off her in waves.

It must have been the time when I was so drunk I wasn't sure if it was day or night. When I hated myself. I just wanted to swim down, into the darkness.

Shit, I should have been there for her. I should have made her talk about this the minute I saw her. 'I'm sorry, Belle. Really.'

'So, I went. I went to Bali, and he was just there – if I wanted to talk. And who else could I call? So I called him. And I called him again. He came to see me. Then one time he held me, and I thought, fuck it – he might sixty but why not? He was clean.' At this point she laughs – it was something we used to say if we rated men in bars. Belle once went home with someone because he spent fifteen minutes outlining the importance of vacuuming inside the kitchen cupboards.

Her laugh dries up.

'He was good. Much better than I thought. I thought it might be...' She screws up her face and even I laugh at this point. It splutters out and dies.

'Spare me details,' I say. 'Keep going.'

'Well, you know what? I figured why the fuck not? I felt like shit. I had nothing. I was alone. So it started properly, and it was so...liberating.' She stares down at the scarf. 'I could go anywhere. Have anything. Do anything. I had so much money, and he was always there. Whenever I called. We talked for hours. I think there was such a hole in me – something so huge, that I gave him a purpose.' She sees my face and shakes her head. 'Oh, I don't know. But I became his project. All he wanted to do was make me happy. In bed, out of bed. His listened to me for hours. Took time off work. I know Lila was getting frustrated he was taking so much time away from work. He told me about it. But things weren't easy for him. He was ready to retire – and he was dreading it. He needed something new. I was it.'

'And Viola?'

'I sailed to Sicily with him before she arrived. We had a few days there. He didn't tell me she was coming, or that it was their anniversary. He only told me after we'd arrived, so I made sure I was gone before she got there – I didn't want to hurt her. I promise! I know I was in the wrong. What we were doing was wrong. She didn't deserve his betrayal. He said their marriage was over. That they'd stayed together for the children, and they lived separate lives. I didn't know what to believe.'

She stops at this moment. Looks down. 'But we were in love.'

Silence ticks over in the cabin as the heat from the sun comes in through an open door. It's flattening. I remember just how far away from home we are. How far away from land.

I check her face for clues, decide to go in soft. 'Belle, do you believe him? Do you believe his version of what happened? He seems obsessed with you. He can't stop looking at you – even now. And apparently the whole company is mortgaged or whatever the word is to pay for this new cruise line. Is that all for you?'

'Of course not! We fell in love and that was it. Some things are simple.' She waves her hand again, dismissing the implication. 'I told you.' She stands and pours a glass of water, downing it. 'He wanted to do something new. He likes a project. He wanted to turn what happened to me into something better – a shiny boat. A new twist in his legacy. It's not really a risk – it can't fail.'

I wonder if this is really Belle. If she's really bought into this story, of the fortuitous timing of the accidental death of the first wife. Of the cruise line sailing to certain success.

'And why has he allowed me to come?'

She sits back down, and I see her fingers are white, she's gripping her knees so tight.

'Because I begged. I said if the baby news got out they'd be angry, and I would need a friend. But you know the real reason, I already told you – I asked you to come, because one of them is out to get me. Maybe all of them. First, they offer me money to get rid of me. That didn't work. Now they're planting stories about me in the press. There are loads more than the one I mentioned. Lila accused me of stealing her mum's jewellery; I read about that the other day. I think it's those earring she keeps staring at. The car wheel was loose – I mean, I could have died! A brick came through the kitchen window when I was in on my own. I told Mattia and he said it was just local kids. I don't know what they'll do next, but I'm worried it's going to get much worse. The way his family look at me – they don't just want me out of the picture, they want me gone for good. I know it. It's part of the reason I told Mattia we should announce the pregnancy last night. I wanted the upper hand. If they've been rooting around in my things, stealing my pregnancy test, then I needed to come out with it – to stop any scheming they're doing.'

My brain is like a fog. I run over last night. What had been said? Her hands had tightened into fists before the announcement. 'But you told me Mattia had *forced* you to announce early, to use the news as a way of bringing everyone together?'

She looks blank. 'I didn't say that.'

Had she? I was sure of it, but maybe the alcohol had got the best of me.

'They're after me.' She looks at me, and she's not blank this time, she's pleading. 'Having a baby was the only way…' She stops, then starts again. 'I asked you to come to help me. To either save my life, or to be my witness. Something terrible is going to happen. I know it.'

21

'Here we are!' The captain beams, indicating huge screens sitting in front of an elaborate grey desk covered with large knobs, green, red and white buttons. Dials are surrounded by a clock of degrees, like real-life protractors. There are clocks on a display above which hang from the roof, along with more screens. The wider room looks like a fancy tech shop. I've never seen anything close to this. Even compared to the most luxurious of yachts I worked on, this ship is something else. More than that, I haven't been on a bridge in three years. The last time I was, I had been radioing for help as Juan bled out. I remember shouting like it was five minutes ago: *The captain has been shot! One of the crew has been taken!*

I look out of the glass at the sea and the flat, heavy calm of the heatwave. It had been hot that morning too. Bile rises in my mouth. I close my eyes quickly and swallow hard.

We're days from land, and I'd give anything to avoid another traumatic incident. But from what Belle has just told me, it sounds like we're on course for one.

This bridge is impressive, but I could really use the time to look through the memory stick, process everything. I wonder if the journalist is just after some easy money. Maybe he thinks I have direct access to Scarmardo cash.

'There's always someone here,' the captain is saying. 'An alarm goes off if nothing's been touched for a while. Just to make sure we haven't fallen asleep.' He grins, then looks at Chloe. 'Would you like to blow the horn?'

Chloe wears a short, white, floaty sundress with an array of necklaces, making her look about sixteen. 'Ooh, can I?'

I force myself to smile along with everyone else. The morning has stretched long, but suddenly I've blinked and it's almost four p.m.; Belle and I had been called to the bridge by Mattia's assistant with the green earpiece. I felt our conversation had been cut short. She'd thrust a summer dress at me – pale yellow with white daisies. It's short, silky and it swings when I walk.

I glance over at Belle who holds Mattia's hand. I wasn't sure what to make of everything she told me.

The mood is light. Chloe is posing for photos in an elevated chair, holding a pair of binoculars. She shrieks as Bean drops her phone as he angles for the right shot. Mattia laughs at this, even Jimmi smiles. The captain indicates to a button in the centre of some controls and she jumps down. 'Just press here. You know the Disney cruise ship plays "When You Wish Upon a Star" when you press its horn?'

Mattia laughs again as the sun comes in like the world is full of promise, and none of us have anything to worry about.

'What happens if all the electricity stops?' Belle asks, as Chloe sounds the horn.

'We've got another bridge on board, from where we can run everything. If one goes down, there's a back-up.'

'What happens if someone falls overboard?' I ask, thinking of the very worst of things that could go wrong.

'Safety is our top priority,' the captain says, very seriously. 'If an alarm sounds, we have a response from at least an eighty-strong team.'

'And if a crime is committed?' This time it's Lila. She'd smiled for the press photos before the bridge tour, but she isn't smiling now.

'A serious crime is reported to two destinations. Where the

ship is registered – in The Bahamas – and our destination. But The Bahamas first.'

'So, if someone is killed and you're sailing in Bali, then you tell The Bahamas?' Bean says. 'What can they do?'

'In all honestly, very little. People do die on cruise ships – people die everywhere. But I think killed is a strong word!' He laughs. 'There is a morgue on board, but we don't put that in the brochure. There is on every cruise ship of this size. We also inform our destination port, and we have procedures in place to lock down the ship if there's anything suspicious. If necessary we can sit tight until either help reaches us or we reach our destination. We have a doctor on board and a security team.'

'But plain sailing for us!' Mattia says, smiling round the group.

'How's the weather?' Bean asks.

'Good, we think.' The captain hesitates. 'As you know, it's been very hot recently – unusually so. There's a storm heading towards the US East Coast some time tomorrow, but hopefully it will have dissipated by the time we reach the port. If it crosses us, I'm hoping it will be fleeting.'

Looking at the screen, we're a dot in the middle of the ocean.

'How close is help, if we need it?' I ask.

'Help?' The captain smiles. 'We won't hit any icebergs, if that's what you're worried about. But look at the screen.'

We all look.

'These are the nearest vessels. And when I say nearest, sometimes they're days away. But don't worry. We'll be fine.'

Days from help. Here, on this bridge, it suddenly feels like this heat can only end one way. I think of all the rage on board, all the secrets. I worry about an explosive finish. 'When you say *if* the storm crosses us. How likely is it?' I ask.

The captain looks out of the window over the sea, blue and calm and promising to remain so.

'Well,' he says, 'weather will be weather.'

22

My cabin is being cleaned when I get to it, so I need somewhere else to get my thoughts in order. The ship has a twenty-four-hour pizza restaurant and the idea of dough and cheese and some time on my own, with no one observing me, is exactly what I need.

As I walk, I'm focused on what I've learned about the family so far. Bean for one. I can't read him. One minute he's blushing when he speaks to me, the next he's sharp and asking why I'm here. And he was lurking outside my cabin. Then Xander admits burrowing away into everyone's affairs – he had someone dig into my life.

And the revelations from Belle – the fact she lied to me to begin with was a shock. And the only reason she told me the truth was because of Xander and Lila. What does it mean?

None of it is making me feel any easier about being on the ship. For all my attempts to stay in control, I've started to feel my anxiety levels rise. I've thought about the attack on the yacht more in the last few days than I have for years.

Watching Belle be taken, watching the captain die. Finn is ninety per cent of the reason I was able to find my feet. Yet here I am, back there again, mouth dry, that bitter taste on my tongue, heart rate sky rocketing.

I lose myself on the decks and browse in the shops on my way to the restaurant, jewellery way out of my price range; I touch the silk kaftans in the clothes shops, the memorabilia. The late afternoon sun dims its burn and people drift outside to the decks for drinks. There is music coming from different bars as I walk through, and I think of Finn again.

He'd love this. His tiny, fat fists flash up, his dark eyes staring at me – waiting. For snacks, for stories. For me to be a dinosaur. He knows the names of all of them, and we read books about them at bedtime; they stick out of the pages, all furry, and he knows when I'll hold them out for him to stroke. He sleeps with his squishy red t-rex tight in his arms, and there are moments when I look at him, asleep, and my heart is so full I can't breathe.

'Look, you need to be quick. I can't talk for long.'

I know that voice. I eat cheese, truffle and mushroom pizza as I hear Jimmi Scarmardo talk. There are a few tables taken up outside, but most people are out on the decks. It's the wrong time for pizza – dinner will be soon. But I missed lunch, and I can't wait anymore.

Neither, it seems, can Jimmi. He sits on a table by himself, a baseball cap pulled down tight, and sunglasses shield his face from anyone on the lookout for the family. In t-shirt and shorts, he could be anyone.

I can only just make out his conversation. There's a tight finish: '*Look, I need this kept under wraps. If this gets out…*'

I don't hear any more because a waiter comes round with water and tops me up.

Unlike Jimmi, I'm not in any form of disguise, and as the waiter walks towards him, I sneak a look. He's sat in the far corner of the deck area. He sees me, and lowers his phone.

I need to be brave. I lift my hand in a wave and he switches to Italian, not knowing I can understand, and says, 'Keep it quiet. Call me back. I have to go. I'm serious though – I don't want this getting out.' There are echoes of Mattia's authority there, which make me shiver.

He pockets the phone, picks up his plate, the water glass, and heads over.

'I thought you'd be busy with investment meetings and the business. Or with the news of a new sibling.' I shift my chair around to let him sit, and flash a smile. Public smiling face out on display.

'The ship is under control. Lila is holding us all together. It seems to be going well.' He grins, but still no part of his smile reaches his eyes. 'And the Scarmardos are officially delighted with the news of a sibling on the horizon.'

I can't think of anything to say, so I swallow pizza, but it goes down too hard, too fast. I start choking.

Grabbing a napkin, I lean forward, as Jimmi lifts a hand and pats me on the back, an action that is so light it would make no difference if I were seriously choking. My eyes are now running.

'OK?' Jimmi asks, hesitantly.

I must be red with coughing, eyes streaming, and I take a gulp of water, nodding. I manage a raspy, 'Yes.'

Questions I want to ask are lodged in my throat, taking up much more space than the pizza dough.

I drink more water, waiting for him to speak.

'A late lunch for one?' Jimmi asks, after a few moments.

I nod, looking out at the sea. 'Thought I'd give you all some room. Since Mattia's announcement, you've all seemed a bit… tense,' I say, carefully. I decide to push a little. 'I figured you wouldn't want little old me witnessing unrest amongst the Scarmardo children.'

This time Jimmi smiles for real. 'Don't tell me you've been hiding from us. I'm disappointed.'

'Nah – not me. I was opting for the finer life. Pizza and a glass of water. My idea of heaven.'

I lift my glass to his, and he meets mine. There's a brief clink.

He looks at me strangely for a second.

I think of his call. In for a penny.

'I heard you on the phone just now. What are you hiding? What's the big secret?'

He chews his pizza, takes a drink of water. 'You were listening in to my conversation? That's not polite.'

'Well, I wouldn't call it listening in. You were having it at the next table. It's not like I came here for anything but the cheese and bread.'

He looks out at the sea. 'A few more days left, until we hit land,' he says, expertly changing topic. 'They can be claustrophobic, can't they, boats?' He lifts his glass. 'You know sailors used to be seven times more likely to go mad than anyone else? Lack of fruit and veg, weeks on only salted meat and fish. The original cabin fever. And don't forget about the dangers of the sea – the Fata Morgana mirage will get you every time.'

The sea has never felt claustrophobic to me. It's the biggest thing on the planet. But he's right, this ship – with all its luxury, it's a dream come true, but with the Scarmardos right now, it feels like a jail. Jimmi has avoided answering my question but I decide to let it pass.

'Are Bean and Xander OK? They seem to fight constantly. Not just what I saw in the lift.'

Jimmi's fingers drum on the table. His nails are short and his hands are tanned, his forearms toned – no booze, water only, exercise. He should be the picture of health, but there are faint rings of dark around his eyes – there's something which seems to be stressing him out. He's not giving anything away, though. He doesn't answer and glances at his phone. I have no idea what's going on with him but it only adds to my unease.

I mask my irritation with a smile and say, 'Are you going to avoid answering every question I ask?'

He lowers his sunglasses and leans back in his chair. 'What are you asking, Emily? How we are feeling about a new brother or sister? A new step-mum? A new cruise line that is hanging by its nails? Bean and Xander at each others' throats? Who's leaking all the stories to the press? No fucking clue, to be honest.' From nowhere he laughs, but with real humour this time. He throws his hand up in the Scarmardo wave. 'But I'm pleased to see you've been paying attention. And here was me thinking you were just the little mouse.'

My irritation vanishes; it's been ebbing and flowing all day. I watch him laugh like a release, and it's my first flash of the real Jimmi Scarmardo. He looks at me again, smiling, his eyes thoughtful.

He pushes his chair back and stands. 'Let's go. No point hiding. I do not, Emily, have a fucking clue if something else is going to come out. Shall we go back and find out?' He raises one eyebrow, and I stand with him.

'I'm scared of what may happen,' I say. And I realise how true it is. But I also panic that it has slipped out in front of Jimmi Scarmardo. I've been so focused on everything I've learnt, I've let my defences slide. He has secrets he hides, too, and the ability to control his emotions. He's the one who scares me the most.

We both stand there for a second, and the waiter comes over as Jimmi lays a tip on the table and thanks him.

'Come on,' he says. He pauses. 'I get it – there's something in the air, no? But we have a fun afternoon planned. Dad has arranged karaoke now, and some photos.'

I need to get back to the memory stick. It's part of the puzzle I still don't understand, but the journalist seems far less interesting than the family. And I love karaoke. 'I'll come. I'd like to check on Belle.'

But I do not say what I'm really thinking – that, if nothing else, I do not want to leave Belle alone.

23

'Karaoke this way,' Mattia strides through the ship, beaming like a lighthouse. I notice again how quickly everyone falls in line. He is all smiles for the passengers, who pause and wave as we pass, but any oncoming crew flatten themselves against the wall to give him space, and I catch the edge of a frown as one doesn't manage to move a trolley out of his way fast enough.

Then Mattia is back to all smiles, his arm through Belle's and we follow in his wake.

Lila walks alongside me and I keep my eyes on Belle. I realise, now that she's lied to me, I don't know quite who she is anymore. But that's partly my fault. I'd been drunk in a beach bar when she'd needed me most. The fear of the pirates – the dreams. I couldn't shake any of it. I was so frightened afterwards. Even now, when I think of it, my mouth goes dry. The feeling of the gun, pushing up against my back and I—

Something touches me from behind and I startle, shouting in surprise. Eyes spin as my heart beats quickly. Mattia raises his eyebrows, and I receive my first reprimanding glance, which is chilling; it makes me even more scared for Belle. His eyes are cold, and they narrow, taking in the reactions of a few passengers who have looked over.

I shrink back.

'Sorry,' Bean says, 'didn't mean to make you jump. I was going to ask if I can order you a drink? They're having them sent to the karaoke booth ready for us.' I see the woman with the green earpiece standing nearby with a list.

My tongue is still stuck to the roof of my mouth. It's Jimmi who comes to my rescue, saying easily, 'Emily likes mojitos, am I right?'

I nod. My hands tremble; it's still so real. The sweat on their skin, Belle bleeding, and the captain, when I'd seen…

Will it stop? Will it ever stop?

'Mojito it is,' Bean looks at me. 'You OK?'

I haven't spoken to Bean since before the dinner last night. But he's been outside my cabin and I don't know why. Right now, I don't know who to trust. Bean has been the kindest to me, but is he an ally? Xander and Lila have shared secrets, but only to get what they want. Chloe is sweet, but I know little about her. Jimmi is a closed book. Mattia is all charm, but he can be cold. Then, of course, there's Belle. There was a time when I trusted her word more than my own. If she's telling the truth, one of the Scarmardos is out to get her. They must be out to get me too.

We climb some stairs and Bean falls in step with me. I take a breath and decide to show my hand as I whisper, 'Bean, you were outside my cabin earlier today.'

He raises his eyebrows and looks ahead to where Chloe is taking selfies with passengers.

'What were you doing there? Did you need to see me?'

He tilts his head, and gives me a tight smile. But then he colours quickly like he had during the drinks last night. It's not the blush of attraction, I realise. It looks more like guilt.

As if to confirm the thought, he shoots the shortest of glances in Mattia's direction before he answers.

'I was just going to check you were settled,' he says.

He's been there twice, though, I'm sure. I'm about to press him when he steps away slightly, and turns to Lila, as though to ask her a question.

'Bean?' I say again. But this time he doesn't hear, or pretends not to.

24

The heat in the room comes off bodies dressed for the sun. Chloe's tan shines under the karaoke booth as though she has flecks of gold in her skin. Lila flops next to me after singing 'Valerie', perfume subtle but sure. I have a flash of her as a teenager singing along in her bedroom. Belle and I used to do the same.

Away from the eyes of the passengers, with the door closed on this booth, the atmosphere has loosened. The Scarmardos clearly love karaoke.

I love karaoke.

In other circumstances, this would be the fun.

'You look like your puppy just died.' Bean slides onto the seat next to me, digging his elbow in and grinning at me.

Chloe is singing again, this time 'All About That Bass' by Meghan Trainor, moving like she's born to perform, and the rest of them are joining in. Belle is enjoying herself, and I think, fuck it, and throw a smile at Bean, starting to sing along too.

He leans closer, his breath on my cheek as he says, 'What are you going to sing?' He shuffles even closer, hands me my mojito.

Bean is on gin and tonics from the laden tray in the corner of the room. Belle had made an effort when we'd entered, serving all the drinks.

Lila had barely glanced at her – but Mattia had held his daughter's gaze until she'd mumbled a thanks, like she was eight.

Lila is on her phone again now between songs. She'd mentioned something to Mattia as they'd entered but he'd brushed it away. I'd seen her roll her eyes at Jimmi and mouth, 'Investors call later?'

I swallow my drink and let the alcohol soften my limbs, tease out the worry from the past couple of days – Belle's mention of the brick through the window, the notes I'd received. What if all this is just noise? Maybe Mattia is everything Belle says he is. Maybe his children are just grieving their mother, and angry about having a new step-mother, one who is around their age. Let's face it, fairy tales don't give step-mothers the best look. It's got to be more about who they're not, rather than who they are. They were probably bound to resent the next wife of Mattia – no matter the circumstances. Maybe everything that's happened is just silly protestations, no more than tantrums.

The music is loud and the lights bright. I've drunk more today than I would in a week; I suppose I should at least try to enjoy the holiday.

Jimmi takes the microphone and starts belting out a Killers track with a surprisingly good voice. Chloe joins him in the chorus – they're arm in arm, and I catch Belle's eye. She smiles. This was one of our things. The local pub on the edge of our estate ran karaoke nights once a month. Belle and I used to stand up and blast out our favourite songs. We delivered a perfect 'Poker Face', we had 'Love Story' down pat. Half pissed on cheap drinks and the lights shining our way, we sang and danced. Belle would improvise with raps and I could drop into the splits once I'd drunk enough; we ruled the corner of that pub. We made our way out, peeling our shoes from sticky carpets and clutching each other to stop ourselves falling down with laughter.

I can feel the mood lifting. Belle hands out more drinks. Chloe is dancing with Lila. They're swinging into some kind of routine with their arms, dancing like it's something they've been doing for years.

It's Xander's turn. He is the only one who looks mutinous.

Mattia sends him a look as Rage Against the Machine blasts into the booth. Under Mattia's stare, Xander heads to the screen, and the music goes quiet for a second as he cancels the song. Instead, he scrolls and hits Blink 182, 'I Miss You'.

I watch him sing – gruffly and with an edge – and think of him last night, of Viola. I can't help but look back to Mattia. He's staring at Belle, and he glows.

'Come on, Emily, our turn,' Belle says, grabbing my hand.

We stand up in the centre of the booth as the first lines of 'Islands in the Stream' play out.

Sliding her arm around my waist, I'm overcome with nostalgia for who we were. Our history, our friendship.

Relaxing, I sway to the music as we sing. We've been performing this song for years. Our mums used to sing it in the kitchen when they were doing the washing up after shared Sunday lunches. We'd copy them, holding up a rolling pin or a dish brush and sing along, when all we wanted was to be grown up and cool.

We're so well practised, I know we are pulling it off. She grins with the face I know so well, her breath familiar as we lean together for the chorus. We could be ten years old again.

There is applause when we finish, and Belle takes a mock bow, flushed with success, and she looks beautiful – I laugh. I'm surprised to realise I'm enjoying myself.

Mattia stands and takes Belle's hand. 'Our turn.'

I fall back on the booth seat without thinking, and this time I land between Jimmi and Bean. Our bodies are way too close for comfort, and I squirm.

'Dolly would be proud,' Jimmi says.

The surprise of it makes me laugh, and I go to reply but stop when a shadow crashes down quickly on his face, wiping off any hint of humour. He stares forward and I follow his gaze.

The first bars of 'Sometimes When We Touch' have begun, and Mattia has taken Belle's hand, his fingers interlaced with hers. He stands close, staring at her: adoration, infatuation.

There's an intimacy there that makes me want to turn away but I'm compelled to watch – they're magnetic.

'Find someone who looks at you like my dad looks at his *second* wife,' Beans says, swallowing half the contents of his glass.

I look around at the booth. No one speaks, no one joins in. The atmosphere has soured.

Chloe stares and Bean passes his gin and tonic to her. She takes a large gulp, wiping her mouth with the back of her hand. Lipstick smears the outline of her lip like a bruise.

Lila stares at them blankly and Bean pours another gin from the bottle.

I haven't really thought about whether Mattia ever loved his first wife. What had their relationship been like? He'd told Belle they were staying together for the kids. I suppose if he didn't really love her, killing her would be easier. God – the mess on this ship. I don't know what to think.

His love for Belle falls before him like sparks of something so big he can't carry it whole. Shards of it spike the new path he's forcing between him and his family.

Maybe they feel that by accepting Belle, they're abandoning Viola's memory.

Maybe I can help them see the good in her, to accept her.

Turning to the room on the closing chords, Mattia says, 'Who's next?', pouring champagne as he does, and I see Belle's stricken expression as she looks at the wall of faces.

She shoots a panicked look at me, then ducks her head, busying herself with more drinks. Mattia may be tone deaf to the room, but Belle isn't, and I feel a protective surge.

Standing, I pick up another mojito from the tray, and say, 'I'll do it.' Lila looks at me, almost scathing. My defence of Belle is transparent and flimsy.

I grab the microphone and the next song flashes up on the screen – Taylor Swift and Ed Sheeran, 'Everything's Changed'.

'Who's with me?' I say to the family, hoping for Lila, but it's Bean who rises.

He winks, and picks up the other microphone.

If I'm going to sing a duet with Bean, knowing that he's been creeping around me, it will require my best acting skills. His gin and tonic swills in his hand, splashing on the floor. He abandons it and reaches for my drink, taking a gulp and hanging on to it.

I pray this isn't a car crash. Belle still looks like she might cry.

I raise the microphone to my lips, and do an exaggerated twirl for the booth, trying to catch Lila's eye in a plea.

And it works.

As I sing, Lila joins me. And now she's smiling. The mood changes. Jimmi starts singing along from the booth seats, and Chloe blasts out a line of harmony.

Lila joining has lessened having too much intense eye contact with drunk Bean and he hams up a love-sick expression in comic style; his shimmy of earlier, which had felt awkward, he now exaggerates, and I find myself laughing. As does the room. He dad-dances as he sings, swinging his hips, and Lila matches him, playing for laughs and for the first time I think it will be OK. I don't think Xander or Lila truly believe that their mother's death was anything other than a tragic accident. It's just too far-fetched to imagine Belle had anything to do with it. Yes, Belle and their dad had an affair while Viola was alive. But these things happen – especially when the rich and powerful are involved. Surely everyone can see that.

Belle mouths, 'Thank you.'

Bean's dancing has stepped up a pace. Working to the laughter of his audience, drunk Bean is enjoying his moment. It is genuinely funny, watching him flail around.

I'm singing when I notice he has stopped.

His face has taken on a pained expression, and he clutches his throat, as though he's choking himself. *Stay funny*, I think, *don't push it.*

It's moving from funny to clown-like. I force a laugh as he swings his arms up again, but then he grabs his stomach and falls against the wall.

'Bean?' Chloe jumps up. 'Are you OK?'

It's Jimmi who gets to him first, shouting, 'Stop the music!'

But no one can take their eyes from Bean, and the music plays loudly as we watch him, writhing on the floor, in horror.

It feels an age that we stand, helpless, until someone hits a button and the suddenness of the silence, the loudness of Jimmi's shouting echoes in the booth, the sight and sound of Bean, gasping for air and clawing at his throat – it's too much. I grab the wall for support.

'Oh my God!' Belle screams.

'Bean!' Lila falls on her knees to the floor next to him, grabbing his hand.

But it is Jimmi who leans over his mouth, listening for breath, and as Bean's movements slow, then stop altogether, Jimmi roles him into the recovery position and looks at his dad.

'Get a doctor!'

25

VIOLA
Thirty years ago, Newcastle

He's never here. In Newcastle, it seems I live alone.

We've moved to an even bigger house. We have a housekeeper, a gardener. I read books, I meet women for coffee.

As for my marriage, there are still no babies and it's making him pull away. He pays for me to make a quick trip back to see Mama. I'm covered in expensive clothes and a watch he gave me for my birthday. But under the sparkles and the silk, I'm so scored by loneliness that if it was visible, my wounds would be open and weeping. But it's not visible. You'd never know to look at me. You'd never know I've lost my way and my heart is breaking.

La mia vita. My life is not how I planned. The romance has gone. I have become nothing. I still read the stories of the gods, novels of passion, but they leave me empty. They highlight only the lack of love in my life. I live for the flashes of him. Then most of the time, I live alone.

'You give him a child,' Mama says. 'You become a mama, like me. This will change it all.'

She says this as I lie with my head on her knee, and I cry my broken heart into the pleats of her skirt and I can't tell her that I don't think I work like that. Nothing has happened.

Mattia has stepped up the love-making, even for him. It is the only area of our marriage where he is still attentive. He's religious in his devotion to it. I'm left sweat soaked with a fading throb that becomes the highlight of my day.

When he is here.

Sometimes he's away for weeks. Opening new factories, attending meetings, investor conferences. The business grows faster than either of us can believe, and we're in it together. He tells me this all the time. He does it for us. For our family. And his hand will move to my stomach without thinking about it and I feel empty.

All the intimacy that is promised during sex, vanishes when the sun is up. Mattia goes off to work, and I am bereft. Rich and alone.

I look in the mirror and I don't even know what I see.

I never did earn money of my own, and when I suggest it, he shakes his head. For all Mattia's drive, he is old fashioned when it comes to the role of man and wife. I am the jewel that will not lift a finger, and I married so young, I never did have time to learn who I am and what I want. What I could even do to make money.

I am crying one afternoon when the housekeeper has her day off, smoking a cigarette. I've taken it up to stop me eating, because something has to fill me up.

The doorbell.

I ignore it. I light another cigarette. There's half a glass of wine on the coffee table and the rain falls from the grey sky. I may as well drink.

The doorbell rings again.

I wipe my eyes and haul myself off the sofa. It is likely to be a delivery.

Opening the door a crack, I look around.

The face that appears is so like Mattia, for a second, I recoil. I don't want my husband to see me like this. But it is only Marcus, my brother-in-law.

'Viola!' His voice is filled with shock. 'What's happened?'

I step back to let him in, and I don't have the energy to protest that all is well. I remember that the glass of wine is the last in the bottle and it's only eleven a.m.; even Marcus will be disgusted with me now.

I open my mouth to say something – anything – but instead, I howl. I drop the cigarette I hold, and it falls to the expensive rug, and I watch as a tiny hole burns and I howl again.

'Viola!'

His arms are round me quickly, he picks me up, and I'm sobbing like I sobbed on Mama. He carries me into the lounge, and lies me on the sofa.

His eyes flick to the wine, and he strokes my brow. 'I'll make coffee.'

I turn my head. If Marcus tells Mattia who I really am, who I have become, then what will I do? But there is no point thinking of that now. All I think of is how soft his hand was as it touched my forehead, and how good it felt to be carried away by someone as I was crying.

'Here, drink this,' he says, and he sits in the armchair, drawing it close to where I lie. He pulls the throw draped over the back of the chair and passes it to me. 'You look cold.'

I sit up and sip at the coffee. It's strong. It reminds me of home.

'Now begin,' he says, 'at the beginning.'

And I do.

DAY THREE

26

I wake, sit bolt upright, and remember yesterday: as Bean had clutched his throat, the noise spilling around the karaoke booth like a wave. Lila had run out of the door, already on the phone; Chloe in loud, hiccupping sobs, holding Bean's hand.

There's a soft light in the cabin, and I see how late I have slept. What happened last night?

Jimmi had sat with Bean as he struggled to breathe, talking Mattia through the symptoms as Mattia had spoken to someone on the phone: *'still breathing'*, *'burning throat'*, *'pulse fast'*.

I'd seen Belle, leant against the wall of the booth, ashen. *'What's happening, Em? What's happening to us?'*

I wonder if this is what Belle meant when she said she was expecting something.

I think of Bean, eyes closed, of his wild movements, clawing at his throat.

And Mattia shouting when the crew had arrived and the medical team had appeared, *'No press! No press!'*

I shower quickly. The doctor had said last night that Bean was stable. Whatever had caused him to collapse seemed to have abated: *temperature normal – a little dizzy and weak. Making a full recovery.*

It had been a late night. The doctor had spoken quietly as we sat in Mattia and Belle's cabin. We'd looked in on Bean once he was calm, trailing in – a drained crowd of well-wishers.

White faces. Sober. Shell-shocked. The speed of it had been the hardest thing to process.

'What is it?' Chloe had asked, her face pink and blotchy with tears. 'What happened to him?'

The doctor had shaken his head. 'I don't know. He could well have eaten something. It seemed like an allergic reaction. They can be very violent, but then it's possible to recover quickly. He's complaining of feeling sick. He said he had a burning sensation in his throat – stomach cramps. I think he panicked, too – his airways were open, but there was certainly swelling around his throat. He said afterwards he struggled to breathe. It's common to panic when you have such a reaction to some kind of substance. He's not allergic to anything?' At this point the doctor had asked Mattia, but Mattia's face had been blank and he'd looked to Lila.

'No – oh, some kinds of peppers. That's the only thing,' Lila says. 'He's lactose intolerant, avoids gluten.'

'Well, bed rest then. Lots of fluids. I've treated him with drugs that should help if so. It wasn't as serious as it may have seemed. His airways were clear. It clearly felt unpleasant, but I'm hoping the worst has passed.'

'He's fine,' Mattia had said, his voice once again filling the room. 'It was an accident. Let's not forget whatever it was simply upset his stomach. He's sleeping in the other room, and he's absolutely fine.'

'Dad,' Lila had muttered, but she hadn't finished whatever she had been about to say.

I had tried to catch her eye, but instead she'd stared at her dad long and hard, then briefly at Belle, before her eyes had found the ground.

For a brief second, I remember that Bean had grabbed my glass as he'd started to dance. It was fresh – I hadn't touched it.

I feel cold. Whatever was in there – had it been intended for me?

27

I run hard on the track around the top deck of the ship. Running makes me feel more like myself. The track skirts all the way around the edge. There are four lanes with metres and kilometres marked out like a race track, but rather than look down, I look out. The sea is everywhere – nothing else in sight. There are a few others up here, but because we all run in one direction, I don't need to look anyone in the eye. I feel alone, which is a relief. But it reminds me of how very far we are from anywhere.

The heat is heavy. The sky blends with the sea as I look out, and I think of the storm the captain warned us about. It's hotter than ever today, oppressive; something has to break. I push myself further, taking in the hot oxygen in gulps, dreaming of rain.

I run until my insides are empty and then before heading back to the cabin, I pick up iced coffee and cakes. So many food outlets, even a pick-and-mix stall. The passengers are moving around in summer wear, and there's a sophisticated holiday vibe that is not what I was expecting. I suppose I'd thought it might feel like some all-inclusive holiday camp, with group activities designed to torture the soul. It's more like an upmarket hotel resort. Roomy, sophisticated, decadent. It's the opposite to how I feel right now – I might not be trapped in the cupboard, but I feel a noose tightening its hold.

Letting my sweat dry off in the sun, I slip on sunglasses. The sun feels good. I hang out on the deck with the swings, and kick back with coffee, telling myself this is not a claustrophobic nightmare. I force myself to let the cruise feel like the relaxing holiday people pay top dollar for. It works briefly – for a second, there's nowhere I'd rather be.

Once the sun becomes too much, I linger in the cosmetics shop and choose a new lipstick, picking up one for Belle too; I grab magazines and head back to the cabin, laying them all out on my balcony.

I want to look at the memory stick before I see Belle. I'd called her first thing, and suggested she come round to talk. We need to go over what's happened.

I head in for a shower and pull up short.

Across the mirror, in what looks like red lipstick, I read: 'YOU BETRAYED THEM! MAKE IT RIGHT BITCH!'

First, I check the cabin, racing round to make sure no one else is there. I pull back all the curtains, letting the sun burn the corners of the room; I check behind the sofas, under the bed.

The urge to run out and not come back is overwhelming, but I force myself to breathe, to be thorough. Someone is trying to scare me. I need to not let them. That's how I win.

Once I'm sure I'm on my own, I return to the bathroom. It's still there. Red and taunting.

I grab the hand towel and rub at the glass. It smears, so I turn on the tap; hot water and soap fill the basin. A little too late, I take a photo, in case I need it. There's enough there to get the gist.

As steam rises, I stare at myself in the smeared mirror.

I'm not safe anywhere on this ship.

After a shower where I keep my eyes firmly on the door and don't turn my back once, I force myself to focus. Belle is coming. She's scared and needs reassurance. It makes sense that whoever is scaring her is trying to scare me away too. To force me to step back from helping her. Is it just about Belle? Do they want something from me? Is it really to do with what happened three years ago?

I check my watch; she'll be here any second. I lie on my cabin deck, letting the sight of the sea work its magic, trying to calm down.

The ocean is my happy place. The town where Belle and I grew up is near the coast looking out at the North Sea, but the beach is not like the white shores of luxury cruises – it's wilder, rugged. The wind blows through you, and there's no hiding place. It's raw. You can't lie to yourself on a beach like that – it opens up to the sea, where the horizon is empty and taunting. Kicking pebbles, running to the edge of the waves and then back up the beach as they came in. Weekends on the shore with raincoats and a thermos of hot tea, the odd drug deal near the skater park, and the cheap fairground with the old rollercoasters that threatened to lose their nuts and bolts with every turn. Cheap thrills. Ten doughnuts for less than a fiver. Fathers rolling fags as their kids rode the ghost train. It was raw. It was real.

This life isn't real. On holiday, people get to reinvent themselves, to be creative with their actual lives. Maybe it's because the heat soothes edges, melts the corners of truth. And it's easier to walk in a bikini, almost naked, and lie about where you are from. Wrapped up in boots, clothes, cars, the tell-tale giveaways of money and origin speak before you open your mouth. Not so in the sun.

There was truth on all the streets where Belle and I grew up. Litter, concrete new-town buildings, industrial estates laid out in portions of land filled with car parks and huge buildings that housed twelve-hour shifts: four days on, three days off.

I almost text Dad, needing the comfort from home, but I can't tell him about this. I'd said I wouldn't contact them, because the one time I'd tried to FaceTime Finn, he'd been upset, running round to the back of the iPad to look for me. I'm either there or not there.

Instead, I wonder what I will say to Belle. I won't tell her. Not that someone has been in my cabin. Though I can't keep this to myself for much longer. I will go mad. But now isn't the time – I remind myself that I need to be there for her. This will just make her panic.

The sun has turned its dial up a notch and I stretch out long, needing the sensation of burning on my skin, when there's a knock on the door.

'What the absolute fuck is going on?' Belle stomps in carrying bags. 'I've brought crisps, loads of crisps. And chocolate. You look great, by the way.' She looks at me. 'White like milk, but otherwise fabulous.'

We collapse on the sofas outside and she tips snacks into bowls.

'What the absolute fuck,' she says again, then she bursts into tears. 'No!' she says quickly as I reach for her. 'I'm angry – I don't need comfort. I'm so angry I could burst!'

She says angry, but her hands are shaking again, and she has that worried look back in her eye – haunted.

I stuff a handful of crisps in my mouth and lie back. The salt tastes good. I almost change my mind and tell her about the mirror, but no. Not yet. I feel more relaxed now she's here – now I'm not alone. It can wait.

I know Belle, and she's mid-vent. I've got at least five minutes before I need to say anything. I take another handful of crisps. She's still going.

'…and the looks Lila keeps giving me! And barely anyone's mentioned the baby…'

Taking yet another handful of crisps, I think of Bean lying in bed, of him clutching his throat in the karaoke booth.

'What do you think is going on?' I ask.

At this she falls silent. She lifts a bowl of chocolates, already softening in the heat, and sits back against the sofa, reaching her legs out long before her. She lifts her sun hat and pulls it on her head. Her eyes are covered with sunglasses and I have a quick pang of sadness that this is how her first pregnancy has begun. It shouldn't be like this. I remember crying about everything – adverts on TV, a puppy. You feel so raw. It's the beginning of your heart ripping open, being exposed to the world; to give birth to something takes a chunk of your beating centre and let's someone else walk around with it, vulnerable, throbbing. This was supposed to be a happy week and Belle needs that.

'I don't know,' she says, quietly. 'I know how upset Mattia is. He's managed to keep it out of the papers, but this first trip is important. The crossing to New York will establish the brand. It's punishing for him. He was so stressed, he smashed a glass on the balcony this morning.'

I shoot her a look and she shakes her head. 'No, not on purpose!'

But I don't believe her. I don't believe her version of Mattia anymore. Now that I've found out about the affair, how he betrayed his wife, how besotted he is by Belle, I'm fairly convinced he could have killed Viola. If so, then we should all be terrified of him.

I bite back the urge to ask if the focus should still be on the success of the cruise with Bean so ill. But I reframe as I speak.

'Is he not worried about Bean?' I say.

Belle takes a handful of chocolate and crams it into her mouth.

'Of course,' she says, muffled. But she doesn't say anything else.

I wait as she chews and swallows. She takes her time.

There's music coming from a deck bar nearby, and it's playing a tune that spins me back to crewing on the yachts. There was less time to think back then, and certainly no mysteries to uncover. We wanted to discover the world and save some money. We ate up work on the deck like we were starved of jobs, ravenous. Nothing slowed us down.

After Belle's parents' funeral, we'd gone to Santorini on the cheap; downed shots in traveller bars, danced until the sun came up and drunk coffee on the beaches. A beautiful German god called Stefan told me about a job crewing on a boat he was just leaving, and as his tongue slipped in and out of my mouth he said it was departing for a six-week European trip, and if I could make decent eggs for breakfast he could get me an interview.

We both went the next day, Belle and me. I was drunk in lust as Stefan winked at me, golden and shining in the sun. We'd not slept, and I must have still been covered in sand. I didn't think we'd be offered the job. But the fact that we'd both studied languages, and could help out the captain who was struggling with a family who only spoke Italian and had hired the boat for the summer, meant we got in.

I'd had two more days of Stefan showing us the ropes on the boat during the day, and two entirely sleepless nights as Stefan showed off all his other skills, and then he'd waved Belle and me goodbye after we'd cashed in our return flights and phoned Dad to say that we'd decided to work for a few months.

Then a few years.

We'd lived in our cabin, then another cabin, and worked on different routes. I learnt to read Belle like her thoughts were mine. If she was feeling off, I'd take on more. If I was ill, she'd banish me to the bunk bed, re-making the bed for me first, putting water by my side.

It was like blood ran between us.

I knew Dad was having a bad time. It had been around then that his leg had gotten so bad he'd had to take a break from the factory. Debt was crushing him. I'd worried I needed to go back, and Belle started picking up the tab if we hit the beach bars in the evening, picking up the slack so I could send more home.

I would have trusted Belle with my life.

Now it seems she is trusting me with hers.

But she has also lied to me, and our worlds are so far apart. I worry that our history is the only thing binding us together. I can't let that blind me – not if I'm really going to get to the bottom of this. Mattia's influence might be stronger than I know. I don't know where her loyalties lie anymore.

'Oh my God,' she says, staring at her phone.

'What now?' My heart thuds quickly.

'The baby news, it's leaked. It's everywhere.' She looks at me. 'Mattia will go mad.'

28

Belle leaves me to go to see Mattia, who's called the family to his cabin. I walk her part way there, but I don't want to be anywhere near Mattia's anger about the leak while it's still fresh.

'I'm guessing you don't want to come in,' Belle says, as I give her a hug.

'I'll see you in a bit,' I say, thinking no amount of money would be enough to make me walk into that room. 'Let me know how it goes.'

'I don't blame you,' she winces. 'It's going to be hideous. One of the bloody children – I have no idea who's leaking this stuff. My money's on Chloe, but she's the only one not coming now.'

'No?'

'She's the baby.' Belle rolls her eyes. 'Mattia leaves her out of the worst of it. But what if she's capable of harm, despite being the baby?' She shakes her head, then turns.

As I watch Belle leave, I'm reminded that Chloe's the only Scarmardo I haven't really had a one on one with. This is the ideal time. Chloe is an easy one to overlook. She's so young – seemingly so fragile. That doesn't mean she's not capable of terrorising Belle – and me.

I turn down a corridor and pause as I hear the raging of Lila and Jimmi storming past. Jimmi mentions, 'disinheritance', but I can't pick out any of Lila's words. They talk at each other in conflicting monologues and it sounds as though neither listens to the other, like their speaking is simply noise; but I hear Jimmi say, 'I agree,' without taking a break, and feel a surge of jealousy so raw it rips at me.

Siblings work that way. To an outsider it's just meaningless noise, but they communicate through breathing, how they walk. It's what I've lost since the attack – it's what I've lost in Belle.

It's how Belle and I *had* been. And now she's on the inside of this global fallout. Trending on Instagram, locked in a room with a man who has regular dinners with the prime minister. Sits in the Royal Box, moves through the quiet echelons of society that we don't usually see. Some rich parade their money. The real rich hide it. They hide themselves. We see what they want us to see.

That's certainly the case this week.

'Are they all losing it?' Chloe sits up on her bed after letting me in, her face locked into a phone screen so big she props it up on her knees.

'Sounds like it.' I sit by her feet and cross my legs. 'Will you be needed?'

'Oh yeah, in a bit. I'll let Dad burn it off first. I was like, *crap*, when I heard, you know?' She grins. 'He can really lose it. OMFG, like, *reeeaally* bad!' She mimes two fingers slashing at her throat, rolls her eyes and then goes back to the screen.

Her vowels stretch out and she has that mid-Atlantic twang – the ends of her words falling before she can get to the finish, running out of energy and bored with the effort of speaking.

I remember her blotchy face last night. 'You're not worried about Bean?'

Her face is now pointed at her screen. 'Bean's awful when he's ill. So bad.' She rolls her eyes again and throws me a quick imitation of someone dying. 'I went to see him. He was being dramatic, but if he was really, really ill, then we'd know. Like on a scale of one to ten he—' She breaks off and her voice rises in pitch staring at something on her phone. 'No way! Listen to this!'

I'm fiddling with a necklace which hangs low, below my shirt, and I look up. Chloe's face is almost touching the screen now, and she leans back and taps it with her fingers.

'*Belle Scarmardo, the young wife of the billionaire, younger than his eldest three children…*' She glances at me, her eyes alight. 'Burn!' she says. Then continues. '*…is pregnant with Mattia Scarmardo's sixth child. Scarmardo will be eighty-three when his child is eighteen years old.*' She clicks her fingers. 'Such shade!'

Chloe is difficult to dislike, and even though Belle is at the heart of this, I laugh with her. 'Harsh,' I say.

'There's loads of other stuff – loads of memes. Trending big time. But this is like from a real paper!'

I uncurl from the end of the bed and go to her fridge. 'Can I get you a drink?' Somehow lunchtime has been and gone, so I plan to fill up on liquid.

'Is there a kombucha?' she says, scrolling, her finger flicking on her phone screen so quickly it's a blur.

She reads out titbits as she comes across them and I think of Belle. Does Chloe feel lonely? So many eyes on her and so few allies.

'Jimmi said—' But I stop myself short.

'What?' she looks up. 'What did Jimmi say?'

I need to say the next bit carefully. Not look like I'm prying. I think of what I'd heard him say to Lila on his way past, what I'd overheard in the pizza restaurant. 'He said your dad was upset. Is he threatening to disinherit you all?' I laugh, to try to pass it off as a joke, but I have no idea how much of a joke it is when Chloe makes throat slashing gestures about Mattia's anger.

She looks at me, lowering her phone. I remember that Chloe can be clever. And she looks right through me now.

'Are you asking if I'm worried I'll lose my millions?' Her head cocks to the left. 'Nah. Not so much.'

She waits, expecting some kind of response, and I squirm. Then she shrugs. 'I've got my music now. I'm setting up a festival. It will be huge. And I've got my clothing line.'

I nod and decide to probe. 'Jimmi sounded pretty worried.' This isn't exactly true – he'd seemed less worried about the inheritance, more about the fallout from the leak. But Chloe hadn't been there.

She stares again, and takes her time before answering.

'I won't insult you and ask you how much money you have to your name. But imagine growing up and everyone knowing roughly what you're worth, and that's the first thing they find out about you. Imagine if that is the thing that walks before you.' She shrugs, and I can tell she's losing interest in making her point.

'My music, I'm trying to do something real, but people assume I can buy my way into a contract. That my music doesn't count. Imagine never really being able to have a go at something real, because you're always one of the richest people in the room?'

She turns back to her tablet, and her finger goes back to scrolling. She's soon distracted again. 'No way! You'll never guess…'

I listen as she talks, and I look through the glass doors out to the ocean. Do I feel sorry for Chloe Scarmardo? I think of Dad at home, boiling cheap pasta for tea most nights to keep costs low. How can I feel that sorry for Chloe? For any of the Scarmardos?

'This news – how much upset can it cause? It's a good thing, surely. Good news for the family?' I try again.

But Chloe has lost all interest, and doesn't even look up. I'd been trying to find out whether Mattia might really disinherit his children if one of them leaked the news. How much damage has this leak really done? Other than to Belle – who has more eyes on her now than ever.

I suppose what I'm *really* hit with, as I think it through, is that the only person who stands to gain anything from the leaked news about the baby, is Belle herself.

What had she said the other night? I'm sure she had said that Mattia was the one who decided to announce, but then later, she said it had been her. Now this news is leaked, and the children's inheritance is under threat. Belle has eyes on her because of this, but no one is threatening to take anything away from her. Who can touch Belle, harm her, now she is an expectant mother? It would be a masterstroke if Belle had leaked the news herself. It's another wedge between Mattia and his children. Who would wish for that?

Belle. Is she more of a player in this than I know?

29

Heading back to my room for a change of clothes before an early dinner, I see Bean outside. Again.

He can barely walk. He looks weak – exhausted. But still he's made it to my cabin and I have no idea why. I see Mirka come out carrying empty bottles of champagne. I ignore her, and shout, 'Bean!'

Mirka nods as she passes me, the smile fixed and bright.

Bean sees me and falls against the wall. I don't think it's just weakness though – he looks shocked he's been spotted. He's paper white, and I doubt it's down to just the exhaustion of his collapse yesterday. I don't feel any sympathy. Instead, I feel surge of rage.

'What are you doing here?' I don't open the cabin door. Now Mirka has left, there's no one else around. My heart picks up pace.

I don't feel comfortable in a cabin with him alone. I do a quick once over – I could take him if I needed to. Particularly now he's weak. But rule one is don't put yourself in those situations in the first place.

'I was just…' But he falters. He knows there's no reason for him to be at my cabin.

'You were here the other day too. What is it, Bean? What do you want? Why are you hanging around me like some creepy bad fucking smell? And now – when you're supposed to be tucked up in bed after last night?'

He staggers slightly, falling against the wall again. White as a sheet.

'Sit down,' I say.

He slides to the floor.

'Why were you trying to get into my room? What is it? What do you want from me, Bean?' I stand over him, adrenaline racing.

He mumbles something, but I can't make it out.

'What?' My volume rises.

He mumbles again and I take a step back. 'I don't care who you are. You can't stalk me. You can't threaten me.' I'm shouting now but I can't quieten down.

Cryptic notes, being pushed into a cupboard, someone invading my cabin – this is no joke.

His eyes plead up at me, and he takes a huge breath, as though he's about to confess something big. 'Not you,' he says.

'What?'

'It's not you,' he says again. His shoulders sag. 'It's Mirka. I came to see Mirka. She's your butler. I can't get into staff quarters without attracting attention. But I needed to see her. Particularly now, after yesterday. She was all I thought about when I was in bed, when I was sick. It's not you I've been trying to see. It's her.'

I must look confused, because he stares at the floor and elaborates. 'I'm in love with her.'

30

'Talk,' I say.

We're in my cabin and I've made coffee in the fancy machine. I'm an expert now. I'll miss it when I'm back home on the cheap, instant stuff.

'God, I don't know where to start.' His head falls into his hands.

I sip at the coffee. Money can buy you a lot. But not everything.

'OK,' he says, sitting up straighter at seeing the look on my face. 'It started last year sometime. I met Mirka in a bar in New York. She was working there, and auditioning for the theatre – waiting for her big break.'

Of course she's an actress – no one else could pull off such sustained smiling.

'Go on,' I prompt.

'Well, we hit it off. She didn't know who I was. I was having a shit day. It was the first time Dad had reduced my allowance. Told me to get a job. I was sick of being a Scarmardo. I gave her a different name. Ben bloody Smith. She was the bright spot in an otherwise remarkably shit day.' He rubs the heels of his hands against his temples. 'Not unlike today, to be honest.'

'So you're a couple?'

'Were,' he says. 'We were an item, until Xander came along.'

Now the rowing suddenly makes more sense. I remember their words when we'd had the photo taken on the first night. Xander had said to Bean, '*What, you think if I stepped aside then she'd*

153

come running?' I had no idea what they'd meant. Whatever I'd thought, it wasn't about me. It was Mirka.

I sit back. 'Go on,' I say, more gently this time.

'We weren't exclusive. I was wary about making it too serious – I would have to tell her who I was and I was enjoying the anonymity. I don't get recognised as much as the others. I stay off social media. I don't like all the bars. I'm a writer. I've been trying to write for years. I submit under a different name – the one Mirka knew me as.'

Bean as a writer? I hadn't known that. To be honest, I hadn't really thought much beyond the name. I wonder how many people do.

'So what happened with Xander?'

'What usually happens with Xander.' He stares at the floor. 'He'd seen me with her, realised I liked her. She was out with friends in some bar one night, and he recognised her. He swooped in: drinks, backflips on the dance floor. Invited her to a cast party with some amazing director.' He shrugs. 'They had a weekend. Like I said, I'd been clear I didn't want to be exclusive, and she was up front. She told me on the Monday morning. Asked how I felt about it. She said it made her realise what she wanted – me. Where did we stand?' He shakes his head. 'I was so angry it had been Xander – not that she knew about the connection but…I was awful to her. I burned it down, there and then.'

There are tears in his eyes now and he wilts even more than before. 'I called her a—' He stops.

'I've been trying to make it up to her. I pulled some strings and got her this job on the ship – she didn't know it was me. I topped up the salary privately without her knowing. Asked her agent to let her know there were a few theatre directors on the ship. I thought if we were all here, we'd have five nights to…'

I stare at him. 'You bought her time on the ship?'

'I know!' he wails. 'It was stupid. When she realised it was me – who I actually was, she was so angry. She won't talk to me. And Xander keeps mentioning bumping into her. God, I hate him! He loves winding me up – getting one over on me. I wouldn't even be surprised if he'd put something in my drink last night, just to make me look stupid. I wonder how he'd like it if I did it to him. I could kill him!'

I wonder how much of a throwaway comment this is, given Bean's expression. He's been violent already. How far would he go if he were really angry?

31

I stand outside Mattia and Belle's cabin ahead of the gathering before dinner. With the morning meeting behind them, and no resolutions reached, Chloe and I have been summoned too.

Why Mattia wants me here, I have no idea. I don't belong and I'm nervous. I've got nothing to gain by leaking news of the baby to the media, and yet here I am. I've dressed defensively. Some expensive evening dress Belle has given me. Short, strappy, sparkly enough to ward off any Scarmardo rage. At least I hope it is.

Once Bean had apologised and poured his heart out about Mirka, I'd packed him back to his cabin to sort himself out before this meeting. He seemed to be feeling fine. More lovesick and moping than genuinely ill. Whatever had caused the reaction must have been fast acting but also quick to disperse.

The last glass he'd drunk from had been mine. I still don't know what to do with this though. I'm no further forward in working out who is doing what.

I'd been trying to process it all when Belle had called to ask me to come round to the cabin before dinner. It feels like things are coming to a head.

I enter the room as the sun is beginning to set and the orange glow lights up the family, scattered round the huge reception area. The warm light of the sun is in stark contrast to the dark faces in the room, as polished and well turned out as the family are. Mattia and Belle sit on the curved sofa, where Belle and I had drunk champagne on the first day. I try to catch her eye but she stares determinedly down. I settle quietly onto a stool. There are spare seats on the sofa, but all the children either stand or perch elsewhere. There's a ring of space around Mattia. I can't explain why but it gives me the chills.

Very slowly, he holds aloft an iPad. 'This,' he says. That voice. Commanding, distinct. The northern vowels are more pronounced when he's angry I notice.

'Only you lot in this room knew about the baby.' He speaks slowly, staring round the room at each of us in turn. When he locks his gaze on me, my stomach flips. I fight the urge to run back to my cabin, screaming that this is all bollocks as I go. Why am I locked in with his warring children? But I can't say that to Mattia Scarmardo. I'm terrified of him.

'Who did it? Who leaked the news? The last thing Belle needs is press attention on this pregnancy. It's taken her so long to finally conceive. All that effort!' At this spit flies from his mouth and there's fire in his eyes. He throws the iPad down on the coffee table and it lands with a bang. I wince, just as I've winced at all the casual displays of entitled wealth and easy acts of violence so far this week. That iPad is about a week's pay for me.

No one says anything. Chloe is staring at the floor. Xander is drinking again. Lila stands like a statue.

'This isn't the first time it's happened. Belle told me this morning that one of you offered her five million dollars not to marry me!' Mattia is now standing, roaring at the room.

I flinch hard and wish I was anywhere else.

'Which one of you over-privileged, mollycoddled shits did that?'

No one speaks.

I see Xander lift his drink and take another mouthful. Mattia crosses the room without seeming to move and is in front of him, staring up at his son in seconds. He grabs the glass out of his hand and hurls it at the huge doors, which look out to sea. The shattering is loud, and I'm shocked rigid. I look at Belle, but again her eyes are still glued to the floor.

Xander rears back as though he's been slapped.

Still no one speaks.

'Who did it?' Mattia screams, waving his fist round the room at them all.

'*Allora*, this is the game you want to play!' He strides over to the side of the room, where the drinks tray sits near the cocktail glasses.

He grabs a handful of papers and waves them in the air.

'This! This is what will happen!' He throws them, and they lift on the air and float to the floor. 'A new will. With none of you in it. Forget worrying about me delaying retirement, I will cancel your inheritance altogether! This behaviour must stop. Now! Anything else, and I wipe you all out!'

He sags a little, and stares round the room. 'I have tried. Since your mother died, I have tried with you all. I have tried to encourage you more – tried to help you take independent steps. Spent more time with you. I know I was absent when you were small. I left a lot of it to your mother. But I've tried to correct that. And this is the thanks I get!'

I look at the siblings and they look white with shock. No money at all. Can he mean it?

'It stops *now*. Instead of competing with Belle, you can start competing with each other. When I retire, I will no longer divide everything between you all; instead, I will divide it according to how worthy you are. How hard you've tried – to get on with Belle, to stand on your own two feet. Once we arrive in New York, I will see it is done. You behave like spoilt children! *Viziati! Siete bambini viziati!*'

Jimmi takes a step forward. 'Dad, I know you're angry—'

But it isn't Jimmi who finishes the response. Xander is walking backwards, and all eyes swivel to him.

'Take your money!' he shouts. 'Keep it! Mum is dead, and money won't bring her back!' He looks from Mattia to Belle, who appears frightened. But Xander isn't finished. 'Ask her!' He points a finger and Belle blanches. 'Ask her what happened to Mum!'

The sound of the punch lands like a crack. It whips round the room as Mattia flies at Xander and hits him hard across the cheek. Xander stands for a moment and we hold our breath.

Then he is gone.

What happens after is like nothing I've ever known. No one acknowledges Xander's departure. No one acknowledges Mattia's words. He simply says, sounding tired, 'All of you, on the balcony. I have cocktails coming.'

And everyone troops outside, crunching on the broken glass by the doors. I move with them, one of the pack, cursing the day I decided to come. What is wrong with this family?

'Emily!' Belle crosses to me. Her smile is bright but her face is strained. I look round at the others who are quiet.

'Are you OK?' I say.

'It's been crazy,' she says, her fingers tight on my wrist. Her voice drops to a whisper. 'Crazy as fuck.'

The sun is barely visible anymore but the sky is a palette of orange, purple and blues. The moon hovers faintly, waiting to make an entrance when it's her cue.

Belle wears a black dress – short and fitted and she looks beautiful. She has the drop diamond earrings in that Mattia gave her on her wedding day and she shines, despite her exhaustion, despite the strain. We sit on the outdoor sofas, on our own, away from the group. I hear Jimmi talking to Lila and Chloe stood near the balcony, overlooking the sea. He tells some joke, which he follows with a laugh, sounding like he's trying very hard to ease the mood.

'I'm sorry you had to see that. Mattia said you had to be there, as you knew about the pregnancy, and he wanted to warn everyone.' She sounds exhausted. 'I haven't seen you all afternoon; where have you been?' Belle speaks quietly, glancing over her shoulder to make sure we're not overheard.

'I saw Chloe,' I say, but I bring her back to what's just happened. 'Does he mean it? About the will?'

She shakes her head and pours a glass of sparkling water, her shoulders dropping as she kicks off her jewelled flip-flops, lifting her feet to the coffee table. 'Mattia's roasted them all like this before. He's upped his threats more each time, reduced their allowances, but it's just noise. He's trying to get them to take it all seriously, but he doesn't mean it. This isn't the first time I've seen him rage at them like this.' Her hand moves to her stomach as she takes a drink of water.

I pour myself one as I feel sick. If this is Mattia's idea of good parenting then no wonder they're all as dysfunctional as they are.

'The leak must have come from one of them. He's at the end of his tether. He said to me it's time he changed tactics. He's brought them all on here to pull everyone together, but between them, they're pulling us apart. Xander, accusing me of who knows what. Such shots in the dark. And did you see all the headlines earlier?' She puts the heel of her hand to her head and massages her brow.

We get no further as Lila and Jimmi walk from the balcony rails to join us. There are candles on the table and they flicker as they catch the evening breeze.

Belle leans back against the sofa when the other two sit down. No one speaks immediately.

'Nice earrings,' Lila says, taking a drink from a glass rattling with ice cubes. There's an edge to her voice. Her eyes narrow as she stares at Belle.

Something's coming. From the sound of Lila's voice, she

abandoned sobriety a few hours ago. I don't blame her. I'd need a few drinks after Mattia's berating. I imagine he was worse in the meeting earlier today.

Instinctively I look for Mattia to see if he's overheard. He's still in the cabin.

Jimmi looks at Lila and shakes his head. Barely noticeably.

I look to Belle, back to Lila.

I half want to halt whatever is about to happen, but curiosity stops me. What is she going to say? What had Belle said about the earrings? Not just that Mattia had given them to her on their wedding day. She had said something else – that Lila had spent the day staring at them.

'Really pretty,' Lila says. '*Bellisima!*'

Belle turns her head slowly and stares at Lila. 'And what of it?' She speaks quietly.

I squeeze the glass in my hand, my fingers tight on the crystal.

'I thought I recognised them,' Lila continues.

We all look at her. Jimmi closes his eyes.

'They were Mama's. Nonna gave them to her when she died. They came down from her Nonna. They've been in our family for generations.'

Belle's face creases in confusion. 'No. Mattia gave them to me. The morning of our wedding. They're mine.'

'The fuck they are,' Lila says, swigging the contents of her glass. I wonder exactly how much she's had, and also whether she's partly reacting to having seen Xander being hit. It must have upset her – I know how close she is to him. She is far from the calm, collected woman I did yoga with.

I think of Jimmi's Fata Morgana. Am I really watching this? Can today blow up any further?

Belle is still shaking her head.

'They're mine,' she says again, quiet, insistent. But her mouth has drooped and she looks through the window to Mattia. He's lit brightly by the lights in the cabin. The deck has fallen into darkness. He's illuminated.

He must sense something, because as she stares, he looks out at her. He smiles. It's blinding. Diamond bright.

'But—' Belle goes to speak and I look at Jimmi, who is staring down at the wooden deck.

'The fuck they are yours!' Lila waves her glass, drops flying, landing on Belle. She doesn't speak loudly, but she is angry. She rises.

'They belonged to my *mother*! They should never have been yours. If they go to anyone, they go to *me*! How *dare* you take them!' She leans in. 'How dare you take *him*! What gives you the right to think—' She throws her glass down this time. It catches the corner of the table and a shard of glass flies up and hits my cheek.

'Lila.' Jimmi is on his feet and he steps directly in front of her, forcing himself between the women as Lila leans towards Belle. 'Stop. Don't do this. Not tonight. Not on the ship. Not when Dad's already...' He looks over at Mattia, who is leaving the cabin and walking towards us. 'He's coming.'

Lila looks at Jimmi, her head shaking, tears on her cheeks. She whispers, 'Jimmi, I don't think I can. Not anymore.'

'You can,' he says, and he wraps an arm around her waist; he pulls her down to the sofa. He is fierce in his tone, but almost silent. 'You have to.'

Belle is still. Like a statue. One hand on an earring, her eyes fixed on Lila. I can't read her expression.

'What's happening?' Mattia looks from Lila and Jimmi, to Belle. I wonder who he'll ask first.

'Belle, what's going on?'

But she says nothing. Her hand keeps hold of her earring. Mute.

Jimmi releases Lila, and she sinks her head down. He says, 'We're all just upset, Dad. It's been quite a day. We're all upset about the leak. And I think Lila has had too much to drink. I'm going to take her back to her cabin. Enjoy your evening.'

Mattia nods, looking at Lila, but reaching for Belle. He holds her shoulder. She stares down at the coffee table.

Her earrings flash again as the candles flicker.

I touch my cheek, and my fingers come away wet. Blood.

32

My head spins as I chase Belle up to the top deck where the running track sits. She excused herself from the cabin after Lila's accusation, said she was walking me back to mine. Instead, she had run, away from me.

The track deck closes at night. The crew are there, roping off the stairs from the level below. But of course Belle is allowed through.

'Belle!' I say, as the crew member standing guard at the top of the stairs lets me pass when he sees who I am, who I'm following.

'Belle!'

She runs to the front of the ship, and I see her reach the furthest point of the running track, grab the rail and lean out.

'*Belle!*'

I stop next to her, at the corner which turns around the starboard fore of the ship. It's like looking down over a black mirror, the sea still and silent, flat and wide.

'Emily – I can't breathe!' She sobs, and I see the splinters in her. The control that has been so tightly worn at times, slipping only occasionally, comes flooding away.

'Ignore them,' I say, and I grab the rail and lean out with her.

'They're accusing me of stealing earrings now, of stealing *him*. What the fuck? And of being there, when she died? What did Xander mean, about Sicily? Does he really think I was there then? That I had something to do with it?'

It is this moment, I think, in which I betray her for the second time. Because I hesitate. I think of what Xander told me, what Lila told me. And while I don't know if it's true or not, I have doubts about Belle. Had she stayed longer in Sicily than she'd told me? She said she'd left before Viola had arrived. Is Belle still lying to me?

She hears me hesitate.

'Not you, too?' She swivels, and her face has a shield pulled down so tight I wince. Gone is the Belle I recognised when I arrived on the ship.

'No, of course not!'

'Then what?'

She is unflinching. I see a crew member walking up the steps towards us. I take the plunge, get it wrong; it comes out quickly, too fast.

'Well, I suppose it's that Xander thinks you were there. When she – when Viola…' I can't finish. 'They think you were there when she died. I suppose he's just making blind accusations. But I don't get the impression they think her death was an accident, Belle. Not anymore.'

Belle is already stepping back. The crew member walks towards us. 'Can we have some privacy?' she says, and he's gone before I can blink.

She turns back to me, stands tall. 'You know why I didn't invite you to wedding?'

I make my hands into fists and dig my nails deep into my palms. Are we finally going to get into it? I shake my head.

'Really? No idea?'

'Because I ran away?' I can barely hear my own words. I push my nails deeper into my skin and feel them bite. The pressure keeps me standing up. The deck is swaying.

'What? On the boat? No. Who the fuck knows how someone will react when something like that happens. They told me after there are various adrenaline responses. It can make you run or fight. It can also make you freeze. I don't think you get to pick. I've always known that.'

She shakes her head. Stops.

'Belle,' I whisper, but there's nothing to say. I think of sitting on the sofa, drinking a bottle of wine, and watching her on repeat on the hostage programme, alone in the room in the dead of the night. Of her recounting her story on TV: the smell of the men, of her attacker's breath as he dragged her backwards. The blindfold they put on her. The boat hole she was kept in, until the money was paid. 'I remember the feel of the dirt on my feet,' she had said. 'I got a splinter from their crappy boat and my foot stung. I couldn't even wash the blood off me, and at night, there was only a blanket, and...' The only time I could face her. And even then, she had been miles away, on a screen.

The expression she had worn on that programme had been one I hadn't recognised. Gone was the spark, the *rawness* of Belle. She was poised. She was well-presented. She wasn't the Belle I knew.

She was the Belle who stands in front of me now, staring hard as she says, 'No. It wasn't that you ran. It was that you set it up.'

33

I hadn't meant to do what I did, when I woke up that morning. We were crewing like any other day. We drank in a bar that night after docking, like any other night we had off. After the dinner was cooked and the plates were stored, we had a few hours to cut loose on shore.

We were drunk, as usual. Belle was dancing and I was getting drinks. This man got me talking – he was well-dressed, asked which boat we were from. Made some jokes about them and us. *Crewing for the rich, are you? Do you get to unpack their labels in exchange for a few dollars an hour?* He'd paid for the round. He saw how pathetically grateful I'd been to have more to send home, and he'd taken his chance. He'd made me an offer.

Tell me where your boat will be tomorrow, when everyone will be off on some excursion. Tell me where and when it will be empty, and tell me the safe code. I'll pay you ten thousand dollars.

At first, I'd just stared at him. Of course I'd slipped the odd bauble, a sparkly thing in my pocket that had been left behind by passengers with so much they didn't notice what was missing. Whole bottles of perfume tossed in the bin in their cabins. Someone left a Cartier watch once, which I sold for almost a grand. Loose change in the jars on the dressing tables. A cocktail ring with sapphires that I'd got hundreds for. But surely those are just perks of the job? Trinkets they won't miss. In exchange for my whole day and perfect eggs at breakfast.

Who can it really hurt? he'd said. *They won't miss a few bits.*

Dad was really struggling. I knew he'd visited one of those pay-day loan shark people, just to tide him over. He didn't say to start off with, but the stress of the repayments was getting worse, and he'd blurted it out when I'd quizzed him. Physical threats loomed.

One payment would do it. Then it would be over. A straight five thousand for them to leave him alone. The irony of the huge debt was that he'd borrowed less than two thousand originally. Much less than the size of the repayment now owed, much less than most of the jewellery I saw on display every day.

Belle and I had watched the guests on the boat in their glitzy belongings worth hundreds of thousands of pounds. Dresses bought for thousands: Dior, Chanel. Bags that cost more. And they would send back a coffee that had cooled while they chatted; asked for colder champagne, ice cream that didn't melt, the fucking moon made of cheese.

Dad was back at the food banks, too ill to work. Too poor to pay for insurance to cover lack of work. Now drowning in red debt, which kept him up at night and kept him locked in a downward cycle.

There had been a tipping point for Belle and me. I never would have agreed to it without it. A tipping point of seeing such wealth bandied about, money running through fingers like water. More than we'd ever see.

We were reaching saturation point and one of us said that Robin Hood was on to something.

With this money, Dad could afford to recover properly and get back to work for half a watch. It would only take five pairs of sunglasses; one dress.

Would they miss one dress?

We talked about it. How easy it would be. Just to leave one item out of their suitcases when they asked us to do the packing.

But we knew it would come back to us – real theft. We'd get in trouble. And that would be it. The fairy-tale would end.

I looked at the man in the bar.

Well, what do you think? he said. *Just tell me where the boat will be. Give me the code. None of you will be there. It's a victimless crime.*

Belle was still dancing and I drank the cheap beer deeply from the bottle. The night was full of music and mosquitoes.

No one gets hurt. Ten thousand, right now.

Drunk, I'd laughed in his face. I'd told Belle. We'd drank more.

Just before dawn, when we were stumbling back to the yacht, Belle was half unconscious on my arm and he'd appeared again. Two envelopes stuffed with hundred-dollar bills. One for me, the same for Belle.

The four digit code? he'd said. *The next time you're all off the boat?*

The things that you will regret for ever tend to happen quickly. I'd taken the envelopes and said, 9572.

Belle said *tomorrow afternoon – we're at a beach picnic.* Or had I said that part too? Maybe I'd said that. Thinking about it, Belle couldn't even speak.

At my lowest points, I know for certain it had all been me.

I'd stuffed the money in my back pocket. Belle was too drunk so I decided to give it to her later that day, when she'd sobered up. She was angrier than I'd ever seen. Screamed at me for agreeing, for putting us in that position.

But it was done.

Leaving on the excursion, I felt terrified, but when we'd come back from the picnic, and the safe was intact, I'd just felt relief.

They didn't come! I'd whispered to Belle.

Thank fuck, she'd said. *I would never have forgiven you, Em. That's not who we are.*

Instead, they came the next morning. A boat full of pirates with weapons. We never saw the man in the nice suit. We were attacked. I froze. Belle was taken.

The captain was shot dead.

And that was that.

34

The night air is turning colder. The sea is all around us and it's just Belle and me, on the ocean again, but this time we carry the weight of so much.

What am I even doing here? I burnt it all down three years ago. Whoever Belle has become, I have to take some responsibility for. And for the captain. This is what I think of, every single day, the news clipping I'd cut out from a broadsheet report of the piracy:

> Captain Juan Belize, of Spain, was shot when a group of armed pirates raided a yacht off the coast of Sri Lanka. The boat was owned by Sir Mattia Scarmardo, and rented out to friends. Belle Myrtle, a member of the crew, was kidnapped and held for ransom for three days, until recovered. Captain Juan Belize died defending his passengers and one other crew member. His family have asked for privacy at this time. He is survived by a wife and a daughter.

Juan asked a lot of Belle and me, but he was kind. When I'd first heard from Dad about his leg getting worse, how he needed an operation and recovery time, Juan had given me a day off. He'd listened when I'd cried on his shoulder about Dad running out of money. That the sick pay wasn't stretching to cover all the bills.

He knocked some of his tips my way.

When he was shot, right in front of me, it was...

I say it now. I whisper, 'It destroyed me, Belle. Juan dying like that. They may as well have turned the gun on me.' Juan wasn't a rich man. He had a family to support.

She stares at me, says nothing. And I have to apologise for all of it. 'And you. Watching you getting dragged away. Knowing I had given them our location, taken the money – I couldn't move when you banged on the glass. I've never forgiven myself for what I did. And for not being able to face you afterwards, I...'

I stop. Tears cluster in my throat. It's harder to say than I thought.

'Please, Belle.' Her eyes are dark and I can't read them. I say the only thing on my mind in the moment. The thing I've thought of each day since that morning, three years ago. 'I don't envy the rich anymore. I envy the good people. The ones who didn't try to steal and end up giving away more than they had.'

Finally, she shakes her head a little, like she's trying to bring herself back to the present. I wonder if she's half in the attack of three years ago. I am. The smell of the blood from that day is strong in my nostrils.

'You know what it cost me to send you that text? To ask you to come?'

I know she doesn't mean money.

She continues, her voice quiet at first. 'I know how bad you feel. How wracked with guilt you are about what happened. But you never really thought about *me*, did you? You thought about how guilty *you* felt about what had happened to me. You didn't think what you could do next to help me; you just ran home with your tail between your legs to feel sorry for yourself. Going back to the factory? What kind of penance is that, Emily? Did it make you feel better? That you were dutifully curtailing your future and doing the honourable thing, without ever having to do the *right* thing, come and just face me, and say how fucking *sorry* you were, and what could you do to help?'

I listen to the words spilling out, a tide rushing at me. I'd brace myself, but there's nothing to hang on to.

She shakes her head. 'How did it ever help me? What I *needed* was you by my side. To take my calls, not shut me out. To decide whatever guilt you were carrying wasn't going to stop you from being there for me. You've not even asked what happened. For those three days. You've never asked.'

I hang my head. She's so right it hurts.

'Emily, I—' She stops almost as she starts. She looks out over the sea. 'I've been so angry with you. So angry I—' She stops again. Then she turns and looks at me. 'But you came. You came to help me when I asked. And that means something. Can we go forward? I don't know who you are now. Living at home with your dad again – I never thought that would be you. It changed both of us. What happened. I think I'll always be angry. I've done so much *talking* about it. But I'm still angry. I felt worthless. Stripped down. Helpless.'

'I'm so sorry,' I say again.

'I've felt for so long, that you just got off scot free. You were nowhere to be seen. Always the lucky one, Emily. Well. Now we're in this together. This ship. We need to make it work.'

We sit on the deck, under the stars, staring out over the ocean through the rails. This is my chance to make up for what happened. I need to help Belle.

'They've got questions, Belle.' I don't say the siblings because there's just no need. I have questions too. I begin as gently as I can. 'When did you agree to marry him, Belle? Before or after Viola died?' An affair is different to marriage. If Mattia had proposed before Viola was dead, then that speaks volumes about his intentions.

Belle leans forward; she looks at me and her eyes are like green stones. 'When I was safe, I thought, *Why not? Why shouldn't I have something?* I didn't even care what people thought. After what I'd been through, no one had the right to judge me.'

I nod in the dark, the low deck lighting moody, and it feels like it could just be the two of us up here, the only people on the whole ship. Just Belle and me, all over again.

'Don't you think he could have killed her?' I whisper this now. 'He took you there, before their anniversary. He gave you her earrings as a wedding present. He's obsessed with you.' I put my hand on hers. I feel her pull back, and I say it as gently as you can say such a thing. 'Don't you ever worry you've married a murderer?'

Her breathing is loud, although she says nothing. I squeeze my hand on hers, willing her to talk to me. But in trying to confront what I feel is the huge grey elephant on the ship, I have gone too far.

'It's late, Emily. I'm tired.' She stands and walks away from me, without looking back.

I pull my knees up, hug my arms around them, and watch her leave.

I don't know what to do next.

The crew member who was climbing the steps gestures to me. Blank faced. No sign of having heard anything. 'They're going to close the deck, miss. They've asked if you could just step down, if you're finished.'

'I'm finished,' I say. 'I'm completely finished.' I think of something Dad said, when I was at my lowest, crying one morning in the kitchen. He'd put his arm around me and said, 'Maybe it's time to let go, Em. Sometimes, you need to let the past slide away. Not everyone has to die, for there to be an end.'

35

I'm broken as I make my way to my cabin.

I think of Belle's face tonight, how she looked three years ago. I think of Mattia smashing the glass, hitting Xander. Of Xander's face when he talked about his mother. Bean wishing Xander dead. Of being locked in the cupboard, of the notes, the writing on the mirror.

Then tonight. The earrings, catching the candle light.

If Mattia gave away Viola's earrings so easily, how little regard did he have for her possessions – or her life? And if he can kill his first wife, what else is he capable of?

Belle might hate me right now. I hate me right now.

But it doesn't change the fact that she needs me. Even though I worry now I'm the last person she wants to see.

As I enter the cabin, it's dark. I'm desperate for some peace.

I'm so deep in thought – thinking if I could just take Belle and make a run for it – that I don't immediately hear the noise. It's after I've moved to the deepest part of my room. Once I'm inside with no easy exit.

I lurch through the lounge, through the bedroom, into the bathroom. I need to wash my cheek. There's still blood on there, sticky to touch.

I run the tap for cold water. I need to feel fresh. To feel clean.

Then I hear the noise.

It sounds like something falling. A glass, or a mug. It's a dull thud – something landing on carpet.

I'm not alone.

I breathe quickly, and my chest tightens.

I grip the side of the huge sink. The light above the mirror is a pale amber and the glow in the bathroom is Scarmardo green.

Another sound. This time a soft knock against the wall – like someone falling a little to the side.

The bathroom is the furthest room from the door. There's no way to get out without passing through the bedroom, the lounge.

What do I do? I don't know where my phone is. There's no way to contact anyone.

What was I thinking? I got locked in a cupboard. Someone's already been in my room. Two threatening notes, and I'm still here. How much warning do I need?

Another noise.

My head pounds – the sound of my blood in my ears is like someone beating a drum.

I grab the hardest thing I can find – my electric toothbrush – and I run for the door.

I'm so blind with panic I can barely see – everything is distorted.

What I do know is that all the training I've done – the runs, the self-defence classes, the early morning crunches and squats – they all kick in. I run towards the door, but as a figure looms up and in front of me I sweep kick, knocking them flat, then I pause for a second, arms out and sharp, to check there's no retaliation, and then run again.

I'm so focused on the exit, I don't hear my name the first time they say it. I know there's a noise behind me, but panic has me in a tight grip. I don't look back.

The fractions of seconds this takes seems like a lifetime, but the door is open and then I hear it again, only this time it registers: 'Emily!'

Someone shouts my name. Whoever is in the cabin here, shouts again, and all I'm holding is my electric toothbrush. I brandish it outwards, waving it in front of me. Sweat drips in my eye and I can't see clearly, but in my low-lit cabin, light coming in through the open door, a figure rises from behind the circle of sofas in the centre of the room.

'Stay back!' I say – low and firm. *Don't give way to panic.* I raise my arms defensively – ready for a possible attack.

'Emily, it's me! I think you've broken my arm!'

The voice is familiar, but I still can't see properly or place it.

'Who's there?' Even to me my voice sounds alien – high and tense. I know the light switch is behind me but I don't turn around. I hit my hand back to the wall and light floods the cabin.

'Emily, Christ, the pain!' The figure stands, clutching their arm and staggering backwards.

Xander.

36

'What the absolute fuck, Xander! What are you doing here?'

Still cradling his arm, he lowers himself gently to the sofa.

'Emily, really, I think it might be broken.' He speaks as through gritted teeth.

I am still stood brandishing an electric toothbrush like a machete, and Xander looks over at it, raising an eyebrow.

'Death by toothbrush? Really? I don't think you need it. Not with fucking ninja moves like that. What are you? Some kind of undercover SWAT-team member?'

'I was bloody terrified!' I make my way over to him, sit down on the opposite sofa and stare at him. 'I've been attacked before, as you know, and I'm not prepared to go through it again. Surprising me in my cabin? Really?'

What is he doing here?

'I know this looks strange,' he says, and he curses, leaning back against the cushion. He flexes his hand and wiggles his fingers, perking up. 'Oh, hang on. I can feel them again. Maybe it's not broken.'

'Go on. I'm listening.' I reach for the water on the centre of the table and pour two glasses. I neck mine, waiting for him to speak.

'Well,' he looks a little sheepish now. He wears a grey hoodie and black shorts. 'I know Lila told you about Belle being in Sicily when Mum died. I haven't had a chance to talk to you since.

And we've all been so *blah blah blah* about this disinheritance. I know I lost it in there. I mean, what the actual fuck? Belle sat there, like butter wouldn't melt. I just couldn't take it anymore. So once I'd calmed down, I thought, I know, I'll go and see clever Emily, because I see you – you've been taking it all in. So bring me up to date. Where are we? You've had time to digest and speak to Belle. What's the story, morning glory?'

'Xander!' I put the glass down hard on the table. 'I thought I was being attacked! What the fuck? Why can't you just knock, like everybody else?'

'I know, I know.' He lifts his hands, a half apology. 'I tried. The first time I came, bloody Bean was loitering like the lost, sad puppy he is. Then I saw Belle wandering around. I'm already in Dad's bad books.' He touches his cheek where Mattia had hit him, and I wonder if I see a flash of pain in his eyes – how many times has he been hit before?

He carries on, 'I didn't want any reports of fraternising getting back. I thought I better come in by the balcony, so no one saw me.'

He slumps backwards. He's so tall, his legs spill out in front of him, and leaning his head back it lies flat along the top of the cushion.

'Don't get angry. Lila's already torn a strip off me tonight for not playing nice – at least in front of Dad. She's told me to keep it under the radar. So I decided I'd be surreptitious. Such a good word, isn't it? I wore this hoodie, to avoid CCTV, then climbed up over my bannister and dropped to the next deck. Bit more climbing and here I am.' He grins. 'It was a lot of fun actually; I felt like James Bond. Anyway, Dad will never know I came for a Belle conference – a Bellerence, that can be our new code name.' He taps his nose with his finger.

I feel like I might suffocate. These last few days have been too much. 'Like I'd tell you anything! Fuck this, I need air. I'm going to the balcony. Bring some drink.'

I leave Xander and his arm to carry out whatever he can find in my fridge.

The air is fresh but still warm, and there are stars now out over the ocean.

'Here, I've found fizz and tequila.' He carries a tray with glasses and flops down on the outside sofas. 'Sorry again about scaring you.' He sounds contrite.

I feel better out here. It's less claustrophobic.

'Really, I am sorry. I didn't think.' He looks sheepish when he speaks. 'I'll make it up to you.'

He hands me a glass of wine then takes one himself and downs it.

'Go on. Why now? What couldn't wait until tomorrow?' I ask.

'Lila kicked me out. Said I had to go and make it up to Dad – it's one thing apparently to be rude to Belle, but another to do it in front of him. He's in a romantic mood though and I'm not sure I can face it. He's asked the crew to clear a swing for them. Set up some parameters for a bit of privacy. A midnight romantic date with the step-mum of the year. So I thought I'd pop here first – check with you about how upset Belle is.' He stares at me, searching my face. 'Have I pissed them off? I was trying for aggrieved, but Lila said I went in like a brick. I don't want Dad cutting my allowance even more.'

'God, Xander. I don't know! Why would Mattia tell me anything?'

He looks like he's about to ask a question, then catches sight of something behind me. 'Oh brilliant!' He jumps up and heads to the hot tub. 'I didn't know you had one of these. I bloody don't in my cabin. Want a dip before I go and see Papa Bear?'

'Seriously?'

'Come on! I know how to fill them, I think. It can't be all that hard.'

I shake my head. 'Xander, no!'

'Twenty-four-hour service. The boat is good for it – luxury cruise, Emily-on-holiday. You could always call your pretty butler – we could invite her too. There's something I can tell Bean later.'

I stare at him, shake my head.

He's fiddling with buttons and I hear it start to fill.

'It's OK, I've got it! Right, go and get your costume on. I'll bring the drinks.' He's pulling off his top and heading over to the tray. 'I'll get ice.'

I watch him head inside and stare up at the sky. I should kick him out, but maybe I can get some answers. It's well past time for them.

37

'Here.' Xander hands me a drink and I sink down into the water in my black bikini, leaning back up against the bubbles as they pulse out from jets. It's three days since I arrived; three days since Xander looked me up and down and accused me of being on the hunt.

When it comes down to it, I don't trust him, but, he, like all of the Scarmardos, has more to him than first meets the eye.

'You know why I did it, right?' He holds the glass in one hand and the champagne bottle in the other. I'm not attracted to Xander, but there's really no denying his beauty. He is photo-ready – I wonder if I took a picture right now, how much I could sell it for and to how many gossip mags. My phone lies within reach of the hot tub. I lean out and grab it. 'Say cheese!' Never hurts to have a plan-B.

He holds up a peace sign as I click.

'You mean you did it for reasons other than your sizeable ego and desire for drama and attention?' I answer, lowering the phone and then swigging half my glass. I'm drunk enough to want more even though I know I'll regret it tomorrow.

'Ha! Little Emily, coming out of her shell!' Xander laughs and leans forward, filling up my glass. 'Now I'm not propositioning you, but you do look cute as fuck tonight.'

'Not interested.'

'No, it's not the night for it. If I find you in six months after this bloody cruise and I make a pass at you then, when all this shit is out of the way, you'll reconsider, right?'

I kick my foot and splash water at him. The jets are pummelling at my back and I sink deeper into the water; it rises up to my nose and bubbles into my ears.

'I needed to get a rise out of him.' Xander bangs his hand down in the water and it splashes over the edge. 'I have a wild couple of weeks and I get put on a swear warning. Reduced allowance. We find out about that "B" from a necklace in Sicily the weekend Mum died, find out that Belle stayed in Bali before they admitted being together – both of which casts doubt on the death of my mother being accidental – I can't use any of it, not directly, not without alienating Dad completely. Any confrontation needs to be with rock-solid evidence. If there are any doubts, then it would be me, not Belle, who was banished. So instead, I wind him up.' He leans his head back, looks up at the sky, and opens his mouth. He lifts the champagne bottle and tips it down from a height. Some splashes into his mouth, some over his face, in the water.

'Have you told him anything?'

'You think I'm mad? Image is everything to him. I've had this private investigator digging up details for a while. He was the one who found out about your kid – not that I've told anyone. But this PI is on full secrecy pay because if I look like I've peered underneath Dad's perfect charade, then who the fuck knows what he will do. I've always thought I knew where I was with him – distant, but still my dad, as fond as he has become of the odd smack. Since Belle—' He waves a hand at the look on my face. 'Forget that you know her. Just for a second. Just listen to what I'm telling you.' He leans forward so quickly the water sloshes over the side of the tub. I can smell his breath – beer and wine. He sounds as though he's on the brink of something, of tipping over an edge.

'Just hear me out. He's always been the same with us – distant, reliably obsessed with work. When he met Belle, it all changed. I think even Mum knew it. I spoke to her on the phone when she was at the Villa, and she said something. I wish I could remember exactly what. She never bad-mouthed him. Ever. But there was some comment she'd made the evening he arrived for their weekend together. She said something about him bringing someone with him on the boat. She was annoyed. And I know he's dropped the ball at work. The investors for the cruise line were ready to walk, and it was Lila who managed to rescue the money. Even now it's not a cert.'

'Wasn't he stepping down anyway?' I say, trying to make sense of it all. And my brain has latched onto what he said about Mattia – bringing someone with him on the boat. Surely that couldn't have been Belle. She said she'd left before Viola had arrived.

'Yes, but he hadn't stopped caring. Then after this Bali visit, after he'd shacked up with Belle in secret for some dirty sex-fuelled two weeks, Lila had a hard time getting hold of him. He didn't turn up to a few meetings. Jimmi was standing in for him more and more, but even Jimmi didn't know where he was. He's a different man. He just went – "off grid". He forgot Chloe's birthday, said he'd double-booked himself. He's obsessed with Belle! It's like she's cast some kind of fucking voodoo spell over him. He can't get enough of her! Have you seen them together? It's disgusting. I can't even think what she's doing for him, what she—'

'Stop!' I climb out. The heat of the tub disappears quickly and I hug my arms around myself, staring at Xander. I'm angry with him, but I'm also upset at the idea that Belle is still lying to me. I can't shake the image of her arriving on the boat with Mattia. She had made it sound like she'd left Mattia there, and she'd been gone long before Viola arrived.

Instead, I take my anger out on Xander. 'You're painting this out to be Belle's fault. Some kind of bewitching seductress. How outdated is that? *He's* the one who had the affair. Not her! She wasn't letting anyone down – she didn't even know your mum.

It's not just her. It's not *all* her!' I bury my questions about Belle, about how much she has to do with all of this. I can question her, show her I have doubts, but not Xander.

He looks at me, bored, and I realise I need to calm down. 'What evidence is there, anyway? What else did your PI find out?'

He shrugs. 'The affair. He did a lot of digging. He's found photos of them together early on, when it was a secret. He must have trawled through hotel CCTV. Some trips where they're getting off private planes. He was all over it. I paid him enough for him to approach this with a vested interest. I can prove without a doubt they were together long before they said they were. Proving they were both there when Mum died is harder, but the PI has promised me some big deal pictures.'

The mention of pictures reminds me of the memory stick. Are the two linked? Is Blur t-shirt anything to do with this?

Xander slides back in the water and leans against the side of the hot tub. He looks tired. He shakes his head. 'And you're right, it's not all Belle. But she knew she had him. And I hate myself for not protecting Mum. We all watched him start to throw away everything he's worked for – family, the business. All for Belle. And I left Mum on her own. I'm sure Belle was there. They both rocked up and within twenty-four hours she was dead. And if they didn't murder her – why lie about the affair? You know he changed his will after their wedding? Before, it was all divided between Mum and us kids – six ways. Mum insisted. Since the wedding, Belle gets half. Half of everything. That means instead of getting a sixth, we each get a twelfth. I took the family lawyer out for drinks, got him sloshed. I asked him whose idea it was, and he said Belle had said it would make her feel safer. We're already poorer since she came on the scene. And now he's delaying giving up work. And then there's the ship. And now, in this new will he showed us, we'd get nothing. Nothing! Lila won't even be assured of her job at the firm. No more singing for Chloe. Since Belle, Dad's pulled money from everywhere for the ships, and her festival is going to crash and burn because of it. I don't even know what the fuck Bean does.'

Xander slips further into the water, disappearing from view. I'm cold now. A breeze has picked up and I stand in my wet bikini. Goosebumps flair up under my fingers as my hands wrap around my upper arms.

The last thing I hear, before Xander slips out of sight, is his final pronouncement. 'If Belle can convince him to change that, then she's won. And make no mistake, it's a battle, Emily; it's a full-on fucking war.'

38

I can't settle after Xander leaves. So many accusations flying around and I struggle with who to believe. The idea of Belle arriving on a boat with Mattia, when Viola was already there – it would be the second time Belle had lied to me about that weekend.

The night is black – still so hot. I sit out on my balcony under the stars, a t-shirt pulled over my bikini. I notice Xander's phone, fallen on the deck. I pick it up to hand back later. I tap at the screen to see if I can open it. I want to find out anything about the PI, but it won't unlock. I have a stab at the passcode, but I get nowhere.

The wine is open and I pour another glass.

What Xander had said about pictures races round in my mind. The memory stick.

There must be more to it.

I find it, and slide it back in the UBS slot in the media unit in the second reception room, scrolling quickly through the photos. Too quickly.

Forcing myself to take a breath, I start again. I need to be methodical – careful. All the things I don't do well.

The journalist must have given me this for a reason. There must be something on here which tells more of the story. He had said he would find me, but I haven't seen him around. Maybe I could ask Mirka about him? She'd met him that first night.

Xander said he had paid someone to investigate Belle and me.

The idea that occurred to me earlier comes back now – could Blur t-shirt and his investigator be the same person? Looking into the Scarmardo family would definitely appeal to a journalist.

All I see are family photos. Kids on the beach. Bean is in most of them. Mattia pops up occasionally. I continue to scroll through slowly. *What am I meant to be seeing? And how did he get all of these photos of their villa in Sicily?*

There are a few pictures where the children are older, not really children any more. There's one of Jimmi and Chloe, sunbathing. Another of Lila and Xander. More of Bean – sometimes with the others, sometimes on his own.

A few of the whole family.

After what feels like hours of looking, in amongst all the photos, I find it. Taken on the same beach.

Fuck.

My heart races and pin-pricks of light flash in front of my eyes.

No. It can't be.

I blink a few times, then look again.

My insides split in two. I'm utterly divided.

There is a photo of Viola – and Belle.

It looks like they are arguing. Possibly at dawn – the light has that fragile blue quality. The sea is flat.

Belle is on a boat. Viola stands on the beach and her arms are raised as though in anger. It's difficult to make out the details, but I'd know Belle anywhere.

She was there. She'd promised she had been gone long before Viola arrived, but she'd been lying

First, Belle swore she hadn't met Mattia until after Viola's death.

Then she swore she hadn't been to Sicily that weekend at all.

Then her story changed, she said she'd left before Viola arrived, that they'd never met.

She's so convinced that Mattia didn't kill his wife. Maybe it's because…

No.

Could she?

Could Belle have killed Viola?

It's something I could never have imagined her doing. But she's been lying so much.

How far would she go?

Half of me doesn't believe what I'm looking at. Half of me feels like I've known it all along.

39

I dress slowly, pulling on shorts, a cami, shaken by what I've just learnt. I've known Belle since I was three years old, and maybe it's the booze, the late night, the talk of murder – the being outside of myself, outside of my day-to-day life, but I feel like it's crunch time. I'd told Xander, when I kicked him out, to go and sort it out with his dad.

I need to sort it out with Belle.

So much suspicion. I have so many questions, so many doubts. I need answers.

Belle had met and argued with Viola, just before she died. Asked Mattia to change his will. Is possibly leaking media stories. Had she taken the earrings and worn them as a statement – that Belle now occupied Viola's place? Has Belle started a war?

Did she kill Viola?

I'm almost at Belle's cabin when I see her and Mattia much further down the corridor. They disappear right, into the central area near the lifts and stairs. I speed up, not sure what I plan to say, or if I'll dare say anything when Mattia is there. But my blood is racing. Now that I've decided to confront her, I can't back down.

I pick up speed and run down the corridor. I get to the lifts as I see one rising. I've missed them.

I can't go on doubting Belle. I need to know one way or the other.

I take the stairs. I don't know where they're going but they're headed up, so I take a quick tour of the VIP bar, the decks.

Finally, I arrive near the basketball court, lying under the running track that hangs up on its own level over the central part of the deck.

I scan for Belle. There are a few people up here. The heat is intense, even this late. At the back of the ship is the private VIP deck bar, but they aren't there.

Where could they have gone this late?

I hear laughter from the bar. Music thuds out, studding the night with a steady beat and the promise of dancing until dawn.

But there's laughter also from the side of the ship where the swings are – where Lila and I had eaten ice cream looking over the sea.

Of course – the late-night swing.

I head down the side of the ship. A few couples are tucked up in the bucket swings that run down one side of the deck, and I see one swinging out, looking like it hangs out over the ocean, although I know they're firmly tethered to the boat. There are some squeals as the swings go further, the big baskets both intimate and thrilling.

I don't want to intrude so I scan discreetly, searching for Belle. There's one swing right up at the end, slightly separated from the rest. Two security figures stand a little further down. I'm sure they'll let me by. I get the privileges of the Scarmardos this week.

Much closer to the rail on the deck, I hear more laughter.

I can make out just two people in the swing, and the security team let me by. I suppose this is the best time to come to avoid causing a stir. And Mattia had been insistent about doing it, even after the row earlier.

What Mattia wants, he gets.

I walk towards them – steadily, but I feel nerves flare in my stomach. I have some last-minute reservations.

Mainly, after years of being apart, of the friendship lying in the dust – I'm scared I will lose her forever.

But our relationship isn't the same. This glimpse into her life now, the watches, the clothes – the lack of *fear* about living. The easy disregard for the expense of coffees, expensive wines. And yet the terror that it could all vanish – the lengths that these people are prepared to go to in order to sustain such wealth. Our relationship is more unequal than it's ever been.

I worry too this taster of the life Belle lives now has awakened a thirst in me for something easier – for a life that isn't filled with counting the cost of everything, of weighing everything I do. But I'm not the same person I was three years ago. I've confronted the past. I'm not prepared to sacrifice what is right for easy cash. Never again.

I walk more quickly. I need to move while I have strength – not let myself hesitate. I've come to know myself and I am not born with natural courage.

'Emily!' Belle sees me and climbs out of the bucket swing. Her expression is hard to read. I look at her for a moment, silently pleading with her to make this easy. The last time I'd seen her, I'd accused her of having a murderer as a husband. Do we just ignore it? But then with Mattia here, we can hardly pick up where we left off.

Mattia breaks the moment, saying, 'Why did you get out?'

And she laughs in response, saying, 'To push you! Emily can help me.'

Her eyebrows rise, almost in a challenge. She steps to the side to make space for me.

I step alongside, but the dislike I have for her right now is bitter in my mouth. So many lies.

As Mattia swings out towards the edge of the deck, I lift my chin. I need to bide my time until I can speak to her alone. I can't force some huge row here. But I feel sick. I look at her differently. All the glitz she wears – it suddenly seems tasteless and sour. Had Belle had a hand in murder? Is that who she has become?

I grab the edge of the swing. I'm dizzy with the booze and the hot tub, and I say, 'Belle, can we talk?' I stutter a little as I speak, and she stares at me.

There's a shadow on her face. She looks down at the swing as it comes back, and says, 'Let's push him right out!' She returns to laughing, to avoid answering or looking at me too long.

The swing arcs in, and as it lifts towards us, I put both hands on the rope basket edge at the same time as Belle, and we push.

The swing flies up into the black of the night sky. The deck has low green lighting – Scarmardo colours again, as though to remind me who has the upper hand.

'Harder!' Belle cries.

The swing flies back towards us, and I grab it and push. The sky is dark and I'm pleased – I need it to hide my face. My grief for Belle, for what I've made her become, must be shining. And the questions I came to ask, about Viola and Belle – I feel as though they're written on my face.

I channel all of my strength, my anger and confusion, into the next push.

I hear a crack and then a whipping sound.

I turn and look up – the noise had come from above me.

One rope – one of the ropes that anchor the swing to its frame – has split. As the swing pulls out, over the ocean, the basket itself flies much further than it should. Designed to swing with the illusion of lifting up and over the sea, the basket does fly out and this time dangles – split and dangerous.

'Mattia!' Belle screams next to me.

And I can only watch as Mattia falls from the swing, down towards the ocean, one foot catching in the rope of the basket, and the rest of him disappearing out of view, over the edge of the ship.

40

'It was *her*! She cut the rope, she must have done! It's been severed!'

'But she was in the swing too – she wouldn't have done that if—' I say, running after Lila.

'She wasn't in it when it broke! If she's been at the rope, she would know it would break if she pushed hard enough! We're just lucky Dad's foot got caught!' Lila storms down the stairs.

The crew had cut out Mattia and rushed him to the medical deck. Belle had been distraught and I had stayed with her until a team took her for observation. They said to follow. Belle seemed to be suffering from shock.

An alarm had been sounded. Crew had raced from nowhere – I remembered what the captain had said, that a rescue mission could involve an eighty-crew team. They'd all appeared and Belle had screamed as we'd waited for Mattia to be brought up.

There had been a moment when it had seemed as though he'd disappeared out of sight entirely.

I'd felt cold.

'We need to wake Jimmi!' Lila is almost running now, towards his cabin. 'I promised Dad I'd bring Jimmi, and all he could say was that someone needs to look after Belle. It makes me sick! Always Belle – always. Nothing else matters!'

She's crying now as she bangs on Jimmi's door, and I feel a wash of relief as he answers.

He listens to Lila, and is speaking calmly, asking questions as he pulls on a sweatshirt and I stand and shake in his room.

'Here, wear this.' He passes me a top. 'You're freezing. Do you want to go to Belle? She will need someone. I'll get everyone together. Lila, go to Dad now, and we'll find you soon.'

Jimmi's sweatshirt is thick and warm, and I catch the scent of him as I pull it over my head. Lila has already gone by the time my head appears from the top.

'She thinks Belle cut the rope,' I say to Jimmi, without knowing why. I feel lost. I'm out of my depth.

'Go to Belle. She will need someone with her. Lila said she's being checked now?'

I nod.

'Be there for her.'

41

Belle lies on a bed in the medical wing, wrapped in a blanket, her face turned to the wall.

'Belle – Mattia's OK. I've just spoken to the staff.'

She sits up slowly, nodding. I pass her the water sitting by the bed. 'I know, I've seen him. They're just taking an x-ray. He's hurt his leg; I hope it's not broken. They were worried it was dislocated. But he's...' She leans forward over her knees and cries. 'They think I did it! Lila said she knew what I'd done. I can't go on like this. This ship, those people! They think I'm just after his money. It's too much!'

I sit by the bed and put my arm around her as I hear running feet from outside. I wonder if Lila is right, but then I push aside my doubts. I don't believe in her innocence anymore. But it will have to wait.

I'm just about to assure Belle that Mattia will be fine, when I hear a scream. So many screams tonight. But Belle is on her feet, whispering, 'Mattia!' and she runs from the room.

Outside, in the main area of the medical unit, it's impossible to know what is going on. A gurney is being pulled in, and I realise it's Lila who's hysterical. Mattia is not on the gurney – he's in a wheelchair and is white; Jimmi holds Lila back, saying, 'Give them room!'

They're all shouting questions.

One of the medics says something and I look at the gurney, with no idea what I will see.

It's Xander. He's covered in vomit, and is out cold.

'He was unconscious, in Dad's room! Please! Help him!' Jimmi sounds as though he's trying to stay calm, but he's clearly panicking.

'There was spilled whiskey…and he was fitting – even though he was unconscious. I think he—'

But a medic who is bent over Xander, listening to his chest, shouts, 'Defibrillator!' and then people appear from all directions. We are pushed against the wall – Mattia included.

And we watch helpless as Xander's body arcs and falls under the shock of the pads pressed to his chest.

'Again! Stand clear!'

'Xander,' Lila says, and grabs Jimmi's hand. 'Come on, Xander.'

I don't know how long we watch, how many times he is shocked. All I know is that the world spins around me, when I hear the words, 'No, he's gone. I'm sorry.'

DAY FOUR

DAY FOUR

42

The aftermath of Xander's death feels like it happens so quickly I can't make sense of it all.

One minute we're in the medical unit and the shock is like a physical force. Lila falls to the floor, caught by Jimmi.

I freeze – Xander, funny warm Xander. Angry, sweet, rude but charming; kind, who loved his mum. Now just a lifeless body.

I think of him in the hot tub only a couple of hours ago. My teeth chatter. My hands shake. I realise I'm crying when I taste the salt in my mouth. I taste blood too, and later I realise I have bitten into my bottom lip. It's not the first time I've watched someone die, and it all comes flooding back.

I stare at Xander and think *this can't be true.*

And then we move, somehow, to a different room. Not Belle and Mattia's cabin, because a crew member explains, *That is an incident scene now*, but to another room, where the captain sits and talks to us about what will happen next. I listen, but I'm distracted by what I've just seen – the information only arrives in snatches, some of which takes me a moment to process.

The authorities have been alerted. The Bahamas have been told. An unexplained death involves protocol. *The destination authorities have also been alerted.* A helicopter will fly out *as soon as they're able*, but the storm we'd been told about has hit the East Coast badly, right now it's *impossible to fly a helicopter through.*

'So what can we do?' This is Jimmi. He speaks very seriously to the captain, and I wonder if he is the only one who can. Lila is distraught – pale and trembling. Chloe clings to her. Bean is in his cabin – resting. I wonder if anyone has told him yet.

And Mattia, looking frail for the first time. He is in a wheelchair. His leg isn't broken, but his joint has been jarred, and although the x-ray hasn't shown anything serious, it's bruised, inflamed and he can't put any weight on it. His buoyant self has shrunk. He usually looks younger than his years – he looks so much older right now.

Belle sits next to him, fragile and shocked, looking far too young to be his wife, and I realise it's the first time I've thought this. It's the first time it's looked this way.

I'm cold, and I look through the black of the window, to the pale green of the deck lights. The breeze has picked up. The wrapped umbrella I stare at through the window is flapping at the edges. I shiver. I'm not just upset about Xander, but about how real all this has become. Selfishly, I think of what's happened to me so far. How much more real will the threats get? What if I'm next?

The captain is answering Jimmi. 'We can do nothing except carry on sailing. Xander's body will stay in the onboard morgue, ready for autopsy when we arrive. The police will investigate when we dock, or as soon as they are able, weather permitting. I'm assuming you do not want this broadcast?' He looks to Mattia but it's Jimmi who answers.

'No, it must stay out of the public eye. Whatever is going on appears to be contained to our family, so I don't think there's any need for a wider alert. Let the ship sail, the holiday continues.' Jimmi looks to his father as he says this, but Mattia looks back at him and through him all at once. His eyes are watery, and his hands tremble. He opens his mouth to speak, but nothing comes out.

43

We are taken to a big room with sofas and chairs; it must be a private hosting room. I shouldn't be here. This family needs to grieve. The windows look out at the sky, which glows blue-black like ink, and I'm just thinking that I need to get to my cabin, when Mattia says, in a low voice, 'Can someone tell me what the *fuck* is going on?'

Lila stands, pointing a finger, which waves in the air like a flame dancing, flickering – imprecise; it undercuts the confidence that the anger lends to her voice. She says, 'Isn't it obvious? Bean sick, now Xander dead. It must be Belle. She was handing the drinks out at karaoke. The whiskey Xander drunk was in her cabin. She got off the swing before Dad fell! She is trying to kill us. One by—'

Mattia speaks then, raspy, raw. 'No!' The grief is vivid.

I tense, watching the fallout of the accusation. This is the first time Lila has openly accused Belle of anything in front of Mattia.

Chloe begins wailing, shouting 'Oh my God,' over and over, her arms wrapped round her head and her knees rise to the seat. Jimmi stands and puts out his hands, as though this will calm the room, but when he opens his mouth to say, 'Let's not get angry,' he stares at Belle with a look of mistrust. Mattia catches it and shakes his head. His hand goes to Belle and she shrinks into him.

'There's no one else who would want this! Who else stands to gain anything from Xander's death?' Lila swivels to her father.

'Xander had been investigating. He had found out some things about Belle—'

She stops, and I realise it's because it's not just Belle he found things out about. Xander had evidence that Belle and Mattia were together long before Viola's death, and that Belle was there with Mattia when their mother died. This implicates Mattia just as much as Belle. I don't think Lila is ready to accuse her father – so far the aim seems to be to make him doubt Belle. I can only imagine how he would react if he was accused of lies and murder.

Lila stands, staring at them both, her face red and grief-soaked.

'But it was Dad's whiskey,' Jimmi says, slowly. He speaks quietly. He has abandoned standing, has fallen into a chair near Chloe. 'It wasn't Xander's hip flask, it was whiskey from the bottle in Dad's room. No one knew Xander would be there in the cabin.'

'Wait, what?' Chloe looks up. 'I mean, what are you saying?'

'Jimmi,' Lila sounds confused. 'It was Dad's whiskey he drank?'

Jimmi nods and leans his head back against the chair. He looks round the room, but his eyes land on Belle again. 'It was Dad's whiskey, Dad's cabin. It wasn't Xander's hip flask. I don't know why Xander was there. But if someone did put something, whatever it is, into that bottle, it wasn't meant for Xander. It was meant for Dad.'

Lila stares at Belle, cold and hard, but I see she's crying too. 'Are you trying to take everything from us? Did you kill Mum, and now you're trying to kill Dad? You cut the swing, then you put poison in the whiskey in your room – and Xander drank it by mistake. Was that the plan all along? What kind of monster are you?'

As the room goes silent, I see Mattia look at Belle. For the first time, I see the shape of a question in his eyes.

44

Time passes more easily now. When Mattia is away, Marcus is here. He will arrive soon – he offers me the emotional support Mattia is too busy to give.

The two brothers are so different, so entirely separate. And I can't help but want them both.

Mattia was here a few days ago. His hand went straight to my flat stomach, and we were in bed quickly. It never changes, my desire for him. I go back to the beach, to that first night – and he sees that. It's all we're about now. It's all physical intimacy, and then I'm hollow.

But he has gone again, and it's not him I want to see today.

I can't live like this anymore. I can't carry on with empty days and a husband who is only present for the bed.

The doorbell rings.

I've dressed carefully. Not too much make-up, a thin dress. It's warm outside and Marcus said he'd take me sailing. We're taking our boat out, but I said I'd feed him lunch first.

I had rubbed my best lotion all over after my shower. I had someone come round and blow dry my hair.

When you're about to seduce your brother-in-law, you need to be prepared.

Whatever anyone may think, I don't care. If Marcus hadn't been here, I would be downing bottle after bottle of wine by now. I'd have left Mattia, I'd have fled back to Italy with all the shame of a failed marriage, and the shame is more than Mattia would ever forgive me for. Mattia must succeed in all things. He cannot have a wife who leaves him – how would it look? He would destroy me if that happened. He would feel his manhood was questioned, was held up for ridicule. No. I cannot walk away.

Marcus being here has meant I have stayed. And I glow.

The doorbell again. I'm nervous. *Mio dio*. Mattia is the only man I have ever been with.

What if he says no? I will leave. I will have no choice. I've got to a point where I think of him when I make my morning coffee; I think of him when I'm shopping; at meetings for the art gallery; at the opera. I think of him in the bath.

The doorbell, more insistent this time.

'Marcus!' I smile, and he walks in, two kisses as is our custom, and he hands me flowers. I bury my head in them to hide the colour which has rushed to my cheeks at the nearness of him.

'First summer flowers! I'm starving. What's for lunch? It smells good.'

I take his hand, and something around his eyes flickers. I haven't done this before.

'This way!' I say, keeping it light. 'All ready.'

I lead him in and his fingers are like tiny electrodes in mine; all my senses are firing. If he cannot feel it too then I have already lost.

Still holding his hand, I take him into the dining room. It's light and airy, and yet I have lit candles. I gave the staff the day off. Two places are laid. There is wine in the centre of the table.

I pour two glasses and pass him one. I take a gulp.

'Viola, this is beautiful. Is this a special occasion?' He sips at the wine. He is wary. I see it.

I have no time to lose. There is no point beating on the other side of the bush, or however that English phrase goes. Carpe diem.

It is simple. I lust after Mattia – he sets me alight. But I love Marcus. He is who I think of. Who I dream of. Mattia swept me off my feet; he pulled me down to a beach and I burst into life. When I wanted a love story of passion and fire, Mattia was there, and when I wanted to learn who I was, he taught me what my body could give me. He opened my eyes.

Then he went away.

Marcus has gently allowed me to find my feet. I work on a few charity boards now – all voluntary, yes, but still, I do things now. I contribute. I'm taking an art class and I'm doing well.

Marcus has never asked me for anything, and now I do not think of love twinned with death. I think only of a gentle love – but one I can't ignore.

I place my glass on the table, and I lift my dress up and over my head. I wear nothing underneath.

'Viola!' Marcus takes a step backwards. 'Mattia! I can't—'

'Please?' I say. I move towards him. I touch his arm and he jumps. I touch his face, I take his hand and I place it on my cheek.

I can feel him shiver.

'Marcus, it's you. It's just you.'

I stand on my tiptoes, and his mouth is soft. He tastes of coffee and toothpaste, and I feel his head pull away, how he hesitates.

For one crushing second, I wonder if he doesn't feel it too. If it's all been in my head and if all my belief in taking what I want, in making myself whole, is all for nothing.

I kiss him again, and winding my arms around his neck, I step into him.

'Viola,' he says again. Only this time his voice has changed. He breathes my name. 'Are you sure?'

I slide my hand under his t-shirt and lift it over his head. As it falls to the floor, I wrap my arms around his neck again, and the feel of his skin on mine in this sunlit room, which smells of the first flowers of the summer, feels like heaven.

Forget the passion of the gods. I want a gentle human touch. A quiet intimacy.

'Oh, Viola, I've loved you for so long,' he whispers, and he kisses my ear, his hands snake down my back, and he lifts me and wraps my legs around his waist.

It is different. He is less practised, less determined. He is gentle. His kisses are soft, and this time when I cry out, I do not scream, but I pull him towards me, and I know that if I wake tomorrow and he is beside me in bed, he will stay there if I ask. That I will not be alone.

45

We all have choices. It's time I made mine.

I wake in the cabin the next morning and start to pack. I plan to ask Mirka to find me any old cabin, the cheaper the better, out of the way. I can move to it and hide out for the last few days. I stuff clothes in my bag. None of the things Belle gave me. I go back to my cheap clothes, cheap shoes.

I'll drop out of this circus.

What am I even doing here? I burnt it all down three years ago. I didn't get to speak to Belle last night, but she feels too far out of reach. They have their own grief to cope with now. I can't go banging on the door and start quizzing her this morning. Whoever Belle has become – this person who seems incapable of telling me the truth, despite begging me to help her. Well, whoever she is now, I have to take some responsibility for that.

This has to end now. I will go home.

Almost packed, surrounded by piles of clothes and a half-filled suitcase, I find my evening bag from the other night and I upend it; something heavy lands on my bed.

The glass.

When Bean had collapsed on the floor, I had forgotten that before we'd left the karaoke booth, I'd swept up the glass Bean had been drinking from. I'd used the champagne napkin, and I'd wrapped it up and dropped it in my bag.

I don't even know why I did it. But there it is. Lying on my bed.

I lift it with the napkin, and stare at it, thinking again that Bean had drunk from my glass. That whatever had been in there might have been meant for me.

Choices. We all have choices.

There are still so many unanswered questions. Not just about Belle, but about me. Who sent me the notes? Who locked me in a cupboard and scrawled on my mirror? Does one of the family really know that I was responsible for arranging the robbery – for giving out the safe code and our location? And is that same person stirring up trouble for Belle?

Xander and Lila were convinced Belle had been at the beach when Viola died. And she had. They had no proof. But I do.

Now Xander is dead. Maybe he was the person behind the campaign against Belle. What if she thought he had more evidence than he did? What if…

No. Despite everything, I can't believe Belle would be capable of this. Also, the whiskey bottle was Mattia's. Belle would have no way of knowing Xander would go in and pour himself a drink while he waited for his father.

Bean had questioned whether Xander had put something in his glass. Had he retaliated?

But then I'm back to the start, that surely whoever had put something in the whiskey bottle was targeting Mattia. And the children wouldn't do that.

Xander…the whisky…the cut swing…Was *all* that to target Mattia? Nothing makes sense. But here, at least, is something solid: the glass Bean had drunk from before he collapsed. I'd kept the glass, meaning to follow it through. It wasn't a conscious action but now I know why I did it. In case Belle was accused. When we get to New York, they can see if whatever is in the glass matches what's in the whiskey bottle.

What would the old Emily do? Would she have left?

I know the answer: *I'm the lit match*.

So this is what I decide. I put the glass in my cabin fridge and stick a note on it asking for it not to be removed.

Then I slide open the drawer where the video games are kept, and I pull out the silver memory stick.

I have choices, and I choose to stay. No more running. I will get answers to all of this once and for all.

46

There's a knock at the door.

'Jimmi?' I say, stepping back and letting him in. 'What's happening?'

'I told Belle I'd check on you. She's busy with Dad.'

'Is there any news?'

He sits down and puts a coffee on the table. 'I thought you might want this. Cappuccino, right?'

I pick it up and wait. He looks grey this morning.

'No news. We still think it will be about twelve hours until the police arrive. Apparently the storm is bad on the East Coast. We've all been advised to stay in our cabins. The staff are all briefed to bring food. Just let Mirka know what you want.'

I sip at the coffee. I can't think of anything to say. He doesn't seem to want to move. The sun is hot through the glass, though it's started raining. Just lightly.

He sees the suitcase lying open on the floor. 'Going somewhere?'

Shaking my head, I start to invent a lie, but stop myself. I think of Jimmi's phone call in the pizza restaurant, how guarded he's been. He has secrets.

But if I'm going to trust any of the siblings, I think I pick Jimmi.

'I was going to make a run for it. Below deck. Hide out in the cheap seats.'

There's a ghost of a smile there. 'Why didn't you?'

Making a quick decision about what I really think of Jimmi

Scarmardo, taking everything into account, I stand. It might be time for me to gather some help.

'Come and see.'

'Who gave you these?' Jimmi scrolls over the photos, bewildered.

I deliberately skip passed the one with Belle. I haven't decided what to do about that yet.

I fill him in and he sits back. 'And he hasn't come to find you again? But he said he would?'

Nodding, I stare at the screen. 'A lot has happened since. I haven't really been up and around the ship in the same way. Maybe if I did go downstairs, move around, he might find me.

'I also looked up the name on an article I read about Xander, with a photo of him outside a club in LA. The name was Mick Tenor.' It had been the article about the icing sugar he'd bought in the loos for thousands, and I feel a pang for Xander. 'If I'm right, and they're the same person – the journalist and the PI – then that could be his name.'

'Mick Tenor?' Jimmi makes a call and asks for a name check against the passenger list.

I slide the balcony door open, feeling the heat outside. The rain is light on my skin, and the temperature is cooler; it must have dropped a few degrees. I wait for Jimmi to finish on the phone.

'If it's him, he's using a different name on the ship.' He walks out and we sit on the outside sofas. 'Maybe he writes under a different name. His name on the ship would have to be the name on his passport.'

The sea is flat like a pancake, making it hard to imagine a storm beating the East Coast, but the rain has stepped up a little, even in the last few minutes. It's a relief to feel it on my skin after so much heat. The arrival of the police seems days away, not just twelve hours from now.

I can't really believe that Xander is dead. I half expect him to leap up over the balcony rail and to land in my hot tub, dressed in a grey hoodie to avoid CCTV.

CCTV. *Why didn't I think about that sooner?*

'Jimmi,' I say, sitting upright, deciding quickly that I'll never get access to the security systems on the ship without a Scarmardo say so. I've shown him part of what I know – I may as well include Jimmi in almost all of it. 'I have more to tell you.'

47

We stride down the corridor to the security room as fast as we can without running.

'You were locked in a cupboard and you didn't think to tell anyone?'

I shake my head again. It's the third time he's asked.

'But, fuck, Emily. I mean...' He shakes his head this time.

'Look, something's going on. We don't know what happened with your dad and the swing. And Xander.' I stop, because I don't need to say it. 'My point is, there's someone on this boat who is causing trouble, and my problems are the least of it. But we might be able to see who pushed me in the cupboard. And that might tell us who is behind all this crazy stuff. Belle told me she thought someone had tried to kill her. That the wheel on the car she was driving had been loosened back in London.'

'And maybe Belle is playing power games? But you're right. Something's going on,' Jimmi says, his look arched.

We continue running up the stairs towards the bridge, where the security room is. The captain had told us about it the other day. It's bulletproof, locks down quickly. And it covers all the CCTV footage of the ship. There are no cameras in the cabins or on the private balconies, but there are in the corridors.

Once Jimmi has had a quiet word with the security officers, we're sat at the huge screens and someone guides one of them to the date and time I mention.

'This is the hour you need,' the officer says. 'You can just fast forward here.' He points to a button. 'I'll wait until you're done. I'm sorry, but I can't leave you alone with this.'

Jimmi nods a thanks, then sits at the desk, presses the forward button, and we watch.

I don't know who I expect to see. It could be anyone. Even Jimmi. I look at him, his face reflected in the screens in front of us. I don't doubt him any more – I wouldn't have told him half the stuff I have today if I did. Something is going on with him, but I have to believe it's not related to what's happened to me, his father or Xander.

I need allies and I'm not sure I can really trust Belle.

'There's something.' Jimmi leans forward and presses the rewind button.

My heart thuds.

'Here.' Jimmi holds his breath. I hear the quick intake and then nothing.

We watch. I appear on screen. I lean back against a wall. I'm wearing the Prada dress Belle gave me on the first night. Even now I'm taken aback by how different I look to my usual self.

I'm closing my eyes, then I take a lipstick out of my bag and I reapply.

I close my bag, shake my shoulders out, and I set off down the corridor.

A figure comes up behind me quickly, pulls open the cupboard door, and shoves me in fast. They lock the door, pocket the key, and turn. Head down, face away from the camera.

But I don't need a face to know who it is.

That's Chloe's pink hoodie. The CS stitched to the back. Her brand.

'*Chloe* pushed you in?' Jimmi turns to me, and I see the shock on his face.

48

Christmas is only hours away. The tree is up in the hall and Mattia is due soon.

I spin in my bedroom in front of the mirror. I've never loved my body more.

The bump is about six months old and I touch it, feeling it wriggle.

'Not long to go, *bambina*,' I whisper.

'Where is she?' Mattia's voice booms into the house and I laugh. I run down the stairs and he shouts, 'Walk! You must take care!' Mattia comes home early now. He is different – we are different.

When I reach the bottom, he takes my face in his hands and kisses me, deep and long.

'You are beautiful,' he says. '*Bella*.'

I spy the bags behind him. 'What are these? Too early for presents! You have to wait until tomorrow!'

He kisses me one last time. 'No – these aren't Christmas presents. They are baby presents. They are for our bump.'

I kneel and pull out clothes of soft cotton, and a big, fluffy rabbit and I hold it close to my cheek.

'Is Marcus here?' Mattia hands his coat to the housekeeper who takes it and gives him a glass of champagne.

'Not yet,' I say, keeping my face in the rabbit.

When I told Marcus I was pregnant, he looked at me like he didn't recognise me.

'You're still sleeping with him?' he'd said; then he'd sat down hard on the sofa. Mattia had been in China for three weeks.

Nodding, I'd looked at the floor. 'When I see him. I'm still married to him, Marcus. He's my husband. If I said no he'd know straight away there was something going on.'

It was more than that, though. Mattia is a drug I wasn't ready to give up. He irons out life's creases without a thought. Mattia is all of my childish dreams, all of my hopes for how my body can fly.

With Marcus, it is precious, it is special. With Marcus I feel loved and cherished, but with Mattia, I burn.

I have deliberately not questioned this dangerous game I am playing. Two brothers. I ignore any question of how badly this could play out, if there was ever a confrontation.

'You think you can carry on with us both?' Marcus tipped his head one way and looked at me carefully. 'He's my older brother, Viola, how long do you think I can carry on deceiving him like this?'

I tugged at a nail, picked and scratched at it and I didn't want to catch his eye. If I stayed silent then maybe the moment would pass.

'You want me when he's away and him when he's back? Really?'

'He has affairs,' I whispered. 'It's not different.'

I knew he did. It has been six years now since we were married, and there are traces of women on him every time he comes back. The first time I had noticed, I'd confronted him, and I'd wept. I'd screamed.

'Viola,' he'd said, and he'd taken me in his arms. 'Just one night. It meant nothing. I was so tired, so worked up after a deal. You were so far away, and I needed you. I needed you so I closed my eyes. I'm sorry.'

This happened only a few months before I had slept with Marcus, so I reasoned it all balanced out in the end, and it made it all the easier to cling to Marcus whenever I needed to – to fill myself up, make myself whole.

Marcus shrugged. 'He probably does. He always gets everything he wants.' He paused. 'Sometimes everything I want.'

I said nothing.

'But what does that mean, I simply fill in the gaps? You use protection with me and then you sleep with him the rest of the time?'

When I nodded, I could almost hear his heart breaking. All the way across the divide between me in the chair and him on the sofa, and the gap widened with each blink.

'We have to stop, Viola; it has to stop. You need to decide – now there's a baby.'

At the end of the day, it had been an easy choice. Now I was pregnant, Mattia had turned his lights on me like never before. I was lifted and adored. He came home early. He made a nest for us. The tell-tale signs stopped, and if sometimes I long to take Marcus's hand and tell him of a thought, to reach out and touch his cheek and claim him, take his love. Then…

The doorbell.

'Sir, your parents have arrived.'

The Christmas Eve party is beginning.

My life in Newcastle has gathered pace. Now that I am to be a mother, I have an identity here. I am invited along to groups where we all discuss our pregnancies. Mattia is attentive. I am busy creating a nursery, reading about what I will have to do when the baby is born.

We eat and pull crackers. I'm too pregnant to fly, and my parents are too old, so we call them and all crowd round the phone.

Marcus arrives at some point during the meat course, and Mattia berates him for being late. The snow has already started to fall and he dusts flakes from his coat, his hair as he enters, and I feel a pang for this man whom I love, cold and touched with the flakes angels send – what Mama used to tell me when we skied in the Dolomites and I believe it even now.

I linger in the hall as Marcus hands over the gifts to the house keeper and then, for a second, it's just him and me.

'You still have one,' I say. I walk towards him. There's a snowflake on his eyebrow and my hand is halfway out when he closes his eyes and moves back the tiniest of fractions.

'Don't touch me,' he whispers. 'You have no idea how hard it is for me to be here.'

Maybe it's not being able to have him then. Just in that moment. Or maybe it's love. But for a second, my longing for him is all I can think of.

'Marcus,' I say.

The air hangs very still. I look up at him. I think of his hand that lies against his cheek when he sleeps, the way his tongue pokes out when he concentrates, his tiny freckles below his belly button, how he smells when he gets warm, how his hands feel on my body.

'Marcus,' I say again.

The look he gives me sears my chest, and I just take one more. One tiny moment before I give him up forever. I reach up and touch his lips with mine. And the *sweetness*.

'Take your hands off her!'

Marcus flies back as Mattia's voice booms down the hall.

'I was just saying hello!' Marcus speaks quickly, falling over his words, but he is red and flustered, and Mattia strides towards us.

I think of the tell-tale signs of sex with strangers, which I have found more than once, and how easily Mattia had dismissed them like they were nothing, and I find it within myself to smile quickly. 'It was the mistletoe, Mattia. It's Christmas!'

I point upwards at the mistletoe I had hung earlier that day, and I thank God for tradition.

Mattia looks up. He is boiling over.

'Mistletoe or no, she is mine, Marcus. Hands off. Never again.'

Marcus nods, and doesn't look at me.

I think it's finished, but not for Mattia.

With a swift bang against the wall, the champagne glass he had brought for Marcus smashes hard next to his head, and I flinch.

'Never again!' he says as the glass shatters.

I watch a shard fly, and plant itself in Marcus's cheek.

'Oh my god!' I scream.

Blood flows down his face and Mattia is immediately contrite. 'Come, I will take you to the hospital. Viola, summon the car!'

It is stitched up and never spoken of again. But the scar remains. A visible reminder of what I had, and what I have lost.

Afterwards, I am mostly faithful. Once with Rocco, a singer in a band, I stray. What a release! It felt like a holiday. Full of romance, intrigue. Then it was over. Once with Simon, a writer in New York. He was harder work to leave. The romance died at the close of a night in an ER after a reaction he had to something at dinner. Too much vomit. All too real. After getting rid of him, I decided affairs were too much work. He was weak when I left him – empty threats about telling my husband, pleas for me to stay with him. He took it too far once, raising his hand to me in a fit of rage.

I will always put my family first. My vows first.

If Mattia ever knew...I would defend my secrets with my life. And now here we are. Five children. And we are happy.

49

I stand outside the security room and my legs give way beneath me. I grab the wall, and Jimmi reaches out.

The ship spins. If it was Chloe, did she also write the notes? Does that mean she knows what I did? But how? And does she have it in for Belle as well? Did she tamper with the wheel?

Chloe is clever. I have to remember that.

'Emily. You need to sit down.' Jimmi takes my arm but I push him away.

'I can walk on my own,' I say, and I take a breath and stand again, one hand on the wall.

The storm must have gathered pace. The floor moves under my feet. I just need to find my balance.

Knowing it is Chloe who has been threatening me is shocking. It makes the threat feel more real.

But what is the motive? I suppose it could all come down to destroying Belle in Mattia's eyes. The man in the suit gave out two envelopes with money for trading the information on the yacht. To anyone else, it could look as though Belle and I were both responsible. I think I've told myself we *were* both responsible enough times – but I've been avoiding the truth.

Maybe Chloe was going to scare me into a confession, to expose Belle as well. Chloe wasn't to know it was all me. I suppose, if you hung around the bars we'd been drinking in back then – or paid someone to do some digging there – it wouldn't be too hard to find the man in the suit again. The bribe he gave us can't have been a one off.

The world has tipped upside down and once I've got a hold on it, I'll be OK. I'm always OK. I feel my adrenaline steady – anger rising. I'll come out swinging.

Jimmi's phone rings and he checks the ID. He grimaces and looks at me.

'Two minutes?'

I nod. To be honest, I need a few minutes.

I hear him speak. He flips into Italian and takes a few steps away. The same intense tone I'd heard in the pizza restaurant. And I don't mean to listen, but as I cling to the wall and try to make sense of what I've just seen, I hear him say, 'Really? I can't believe it. Thank you for telling me. As before, tell no one. I don't want this getting out. I'll be in touch.'

He rings off quickly, and as he walks back there's a change on his face. I can't tell if it's for the better or the worse.

'A drink?' he says.

'Absolutely,' I say. I need to make a plan for how to confront Chloe but, to do that, I need to steady my nerves.

50

We're on our way to the champagne bar when Jimmi's phone goes again. He answers and, after a few seconds, shakes his head and closes his eyes. 'I have to go,' he says.

'What's wrong?'

'It's Chloe. She's gone on some kind of bender. She's been with Bean most of the afternoon. They're both distraught since Xander died. I mean, we all are, but they've kind of fallen apart. That was him on the phone. She left for some air and didn't come back. He called the crew and she's in the nightclub. They're laying on a set in there because of the storm. She's dancing on her own – well, on her own but with lots of other people watching. She must be drunk. Dad will be furious...I need to get her. I'm sorry.'

'I'll come,' I say.

'You sure? After...' Jimmi hesitates.

'I'm coming,' I say.

I haven't been in the nightclub yet. It's all sparkles at the door, and then a dance floor surrounded by tables and a stage at the back, with an upper level looking down from behind a silver railing. Clusters of passengers are scattered around but what they all have in common is that their eyes are trained on the dance floor where Chloe is putting on a show.

Her latest song plays loudly into the club. We battle our way through phones held aloft, and I wonder how fast Chloe has made it onto social media, how bad this will be for her later.

There's part of me that enjoys the thought of public humiliation for Chloe Scarmardo. Karma appreciation, I guess.

I watch as she spins and dances. It's a fine line between chaotic and graceful. It might not be too bad if she can hold it together, but she looks unsteady.

Jimmi has his cap pulled low over his face, and he pauses at the edge of the floor. I'm still in shorts and a cami, so we don't stand out. He leans close to me, saying, 'Let's wait until this song finishes. It will look terrible for her if we drag her off.'

She's spinning around as some men join her. They begin dancing and one is leering. He looks the type who only really performs for his mates. If he were on his own, he'd never dare approach her – he moves forward two steps then checks behind him to see if they're watching. The weak leading the weaker. They can be the most dangerous.

Jimmi tenses beside me.

'I'll go,' I say.

If Jimmi drags her off it will be trending in seconds. And no matter how much a part of me might enjoy Chloe's humiliation of her drunk dancing being plastered over the internet, I will never enjoy seeing a leering man taking advantage of a drunk woman.

I walk out and Chloe sees me.

'Emily!' she cries and reaches forwards, stumbling at the last moment, but I manage to catch her in a kind of embrace. I throw my arms around her and try to make it seem like we're dancing.

'Time to go,' I say to her, as quietly as I can, but the music is loud and it's more of a shout than anything. Her skin is warm and damp; her thin top clings to her. She wears a kind of playsuit, with zips and buckles.

'Don't leave, Chloe! We love you!' The man who was leering steps forwards, grabs her arm and pulls her back towards him. 'I want to dance some more. Here, smile for my mates back home.'

He pulls out a phone and Chloe automatically smiles, but she looks less certain this time. Her eyes are closing and opening more slowly than usual, and she takes a step back, stumbling again.

'We're finishing up,' I say, smiling as forcibly as I can at the man. He's slick and snide in expensive clothes and a fancy watch, and I can only imagine how much he'd love to tell the story of the night he pulled Chloe Scarmardo. His hands reach for her and I desperately do not want to cause a scene, but I feel my foot rising. As I step forward and slip my arm through Chloe's, I stamp on the inside of his foot.

'What the fuck?' he shouts, stepping back. 'Bitch!'

I flash him another smile, only this time a sweet one. I doubt anyone in the audience was looking where my feet went. I take it up a notch.

'Whoops,' I say, as I lift the glass Chloe holds and fake a stumble. I tip the rest of the drink down the front of the man's trousers as discreetly as I can; when the material is soaked through dark and wet, I pull Chloe away a little, then turn and point.

'Oh my God!' I shout, throwing my hand to my mouth dramatically as I point at the man's trousers. The cameras on us swivel.

'What the fuck?' he says again, and looks down to where I point. I realise he hasn't entirely worked out what's just happened. He sees the stain and lunges at me.

I pull my head down and raise my spare arm as though to protect myself, and the crowd turns on him.

'Easy, mate!' one of his friends says.

'Not worth it.' Another one. 'Time to head off.'

I wrap my arm around Chloe and move as though taking her away from the man, and the crowd part quickly.

'Are you both OK?' Someone steps forward. 'I didn't see what happened – was he aggressive?'

'We're OK. We'll just head back, thank you.'

The crowd follow the lead of the concerned man and only a few people point and mutter.

I just hope that the focus of the story has shifted. If it had been just Chloe drunk in a club on her own, I might have enjoyed it as some kind of penance after what she's put me through. But not Chloe dancing while some sleazebag takes advantage. There's no pleasure in that.

We've almost made it. We're back at the sparkly exit – mirrors, silver lights, the full Scarmardo glitz experience – when I see Jimmi just up ahead, waiting.

Chloe leans on my shoulder, sagging a little, my arm wrapped around her waist to support her. She's half asleep now.

Her tiny frame is heavy, and I'm ready to pass her to Jimmi, when she clutches at my top, eyes only half open. I almost miss her words, they land in a half whisper, dropping just before she passes out.

Her head falls to my shoulder and she collapses against me. Jimmi grabs her before she hits the floor.

I'm so focused on not letting her crash that I only realise what she's said once Jimmi has her steady, her arm around his shoulder, his around her waist. He strides forward, practically carrying her, and we head out of the sparkling nightclub, swaying with the rise and the fall of the ship. The storm is getting closer, even in the last half an hour.

We make it to the lifts without seeing many passengers, and once inside, I lean back against the cold mirror and stare at Chloe, replaying what she said.

'She's a monster.'

51

Jimmi and I sit in a different bar now – a private booth on the VIP deck. There's an umbrella above us and the plush seats are in an array of bright colours. There are booths around us, set out in a way where we feel contained and private, and the low hum of voices competes with the party taking place on the deck below.

It's late afternoon and the rain of the morning has dried up. The air is cooler and there are dark clouds on the horizon. It seems everyone has come outside to enjoy the decks before the storm takes hold. The floor is tipping up and down, but it will get much worse very soon. The captain had announced the outside decks would close in an hour.

I'd taken Chloe to her room and Lila had arrived to look after her. First her mother, now her brother. That's a lot to lose. There was no point in confronting her while she was so drunk. I need to wait.

I suddenly feel alone on this ship without Belle. I need her but I can't face her yet. Not until I've worked out what's going on with Chloe. And also, what Jimmi Scarmardo's secrets are. I feel like I can ask him now.

Jimmi orders drinks and the waiter disappears to get them. On the deck below is the pool from the first night. Hot tubs are laid out around the deck, and the whole place is awash with colour and music. I can feel the beats from the DJ rising up through the seats, and I think of Xander. Of Belle and me years ago.

Is Mick Tenor down there? I look hard and try to pick out his face as the drinks arrive. He is not part of this clamour for inheritance. But he fits in somewhere. I remember his voice being gentle, his cheap clothes. What does he know?

And Jimmi.

'Give,' I say.

'Sorry?' He looks confused.

'Too many secrets this week. Everyone with something to hide. You've been on your phone, switching to Italian the moment you think anyone can hear. I've seen you. Something's going on. If I'm going one more step with you in this, I need you to lay your cards on the table.'

He waves his hand and this family gesture makes me want to scream; he says, 'It's just work.'

'Bullshit.' I pick up my drink and take a gulp. 'Your sister has been lying to me. Don't you start lying too. Tell me, Jimmi.'

He runs his finger around the rim of his glass, and I realise with a start that he's ordered a mojito, the same drink as me. But Jimmi Scarmardo doesn't drink. Hasn't been seen with a drink in his hands since his mum died. It's been water for him this week.

He lifts the glass and takes a long sip.

The music changes tempo and the tune of the summer kicks in. People on the deck below start applauding, more start dancing, twisting in light rain, which must have started again in the last few minutes. Someone jumps into the pool. There's a craziness in the air.

'OK. But only because it's you.' He looks at me levelly and I can't breathe for a moment.

'Ready?' he asks.

I nod. It's going to be big, and I almost regret forcing the issue.

'Just over three years ago, before Mum died, just before the kidnapping, before it all, I had crushing headaches for months. I was drinking a lot – partying. I was basically Xander but wilder.' He shrugs – shaking his head at the mention of his brother and rubbing at his face, where grief rings his eyes. 'You may have seen the press.'

I nod and the band that had wrapped itself around my chest pulls tighter.

'Well, I went for a check-up. I thought they'd tell me to sleep more, to drink more water. I am a Scarmardo – untouchable. Only they hadn't read the memo.' He tries for humour, but doesn't smile. 'A brain tumour. Serious one. They booked me in for surgery, and then chemo. I was terrified. I only had a week before the op. Chances of survival were low. I couldn't process it. I kinda shut down. Told no one. The kidnapping took place a few days after I found out, and Dad asked me to fly over to organise recovery. I was to pay the ransom if they didn't find the boat. I had a few days – and I thought, why not? I was on auto pilot.' He downs the drink and signals for another. 'I haven't drunk in three years. Doesn't taste as good as I remember.'

I say nothing.

'You know most of the next few days.' He stares at me, and I don't look away. 'They found the boat, Belle was free. My job done. So, facing an operation I thought might kill me, I went and got pissed. Really pissed. For the weekend. I met a woman.' At this he pauses, and I feel a thousand things at once.

He continues, 'Then I flew back and instead of killing me, it saved me. I had chemo, changed my lifestyle. I had a check-up last week. This time, the results are all clear. That's what the phone calls have been about. But I've only just found out. I didn't want my family worrying, and I can't tell them what I've been through now. Not with Xander. They have enough to deal with. So I thought I'd take a day off clean living. I think I deserve a drink.'

I stare at him. He looks back at me, with a smile.

'Emily. I thought I recognised you from somewhere. I just didn't realise from where, until about five minutes ago.'

Shit.
Jimmi Scarmardo knows exactly who I am.
So, what happens now?

52

'Jimmi,' I say, and lean forward. 'I'm—'

Then I spot him. Behind Jimmi's head, I see him.

'Mick Tenor,' I say, staring over Jimmi's shoulder. 'That's him. Right there.'

I'm on my feet with Jimmi behind me – our conversation will have to wait – and we weave round the booths. A few people do a double-take. But Jimmi pulls his baseball cap down tighter, pushes his sunglasses higher up on his nose, and he steps up his pace.

Mick Tenor is heading down the steps. It looks like he tried and failed to get into the VIP area. He wears another t-shirt. Not Blur this time, but his signature look is the same – slightly crumpled. Too old for his clothes. He looks like a student who never quite grew up. He wears jeans when it's too hot for them. His hair has outgrown whatever shape his cut had given him. He looks out of place. I run down the steps quickly.

'Hello!' I call.

Jimmi takes longer strides and slides in front of him, but in his cap I don't think Mick recognises him.

'Mick!' I call this time, and he turns his head.

'Emily!' he says. Looking unsure. 'I've been searching for you.'

'Want to talk? We could go to my cabin?' I don't want to frighten him off. He's like a rabbit in headlights.

He nods. 'Or somewhere public?'

'Can I come too?' Jimmi says, from behind Mick.

Mick looks over his shoulder and sees who it is. His face falls as he looks back to me. 'Hang on – I don't think—'

'Mick,' I say. 'This isn't a trick. Please. I don't mind where we talk but we need to hear what you have to say.'

We find a quiet booth in a relatively empty bar. Mick's speech is like him – slightly rumpled, disjointed. He looks over his shoulder every now and again. Starts and stops.

'I don't want trouble,' he says, eyeing Jimmi carefully.

'And neither do we,' I say. 'But I want to understand why you have so many photos of the Scarmardo family. Why you gave them to me.'

He sucks the right side of his cheek in and chews the inside of his mouth, his lips tight and twisted.

'Come on, Mick.'

'OK,' he says, as though he's made a decision, as though he's decided to be brave. 'I'll tell you both. But people know I'm here. If anything happens to me…' He looks at me, then back at Jimmi.

'Go on,' I say. Jimmi hasn't spoken and I don't look at him. If I take my eyes off Mick, he might slip out of my grasp. He looks terrified.

I can feel Jimmi watching me. I'm desperate to talk to him. But it will have to wait.

'I met Xander in a club in LA,' he starts. He speaks slowly, carefully. 'I was outside, taking some photos of celebrities leaving the club. You know.'

He looks at Jimmi again, but seems to gather a bit of strength, his tone becoming a little more confident. 'Well, Xander came out one night, really drunk. I took his photo and he objected.' He pauses and glances down to the right where his fingers fidget. 'He was…angry. Asked me to delete it. Asked me what I thought I was doing, and, you know, I was just making a living. Anyway, we exchanged a few words, and I said I had a photo he might like to see. If he wanted.' Mick half glances at Jimmi. He's still nervous. I wonder what the photo was of, and I'm certain we're getting a cleaner version than what actually happened. I can imagine how Xander may have reacted to paparazzi taking shots of him when he was drunk and stumbling out of a nightclub.

I prompt him. 'And did he? Want to see it?'

Mick nods. 'He did. It was of his dad.' He looks straight at Jimmi at this point. 'It was of your dad and Belle. Before anyone knew they were together.'

Jimmi says nothing but his eyes flick to me and I see a question in them. I remember Lila saying she and Xander hadn't told the others about what they'd learned, as they hadn't wanted them to let it slip to Mattia. This must be a surprise for Jimmi.

Mick carries on. 'He was shocked. I won't bore you with the long version, but after some "discussion"' – he air quotes and I try not to hate him for it – 'we came to an agreement. For a price that would pay for my silence, I would investigate. I wouldn't sell the photos – Xander made it pretty clear what he would do if I made them public.' At this point, he rubs his chin and I wonder how physical the exchange had been.

'So you agreed to investigate Belle and Mattia, and keep all the photos private. How did you get all the early photos that were on the memory stick?' I still don't fully understand this.

'Well, I can't reveal everything. But in investigating them, following them, I had to rely on other sources, who gave me photos of the house in Sicily so that I understood the lay of the land. I set up cameras there. Xander paid me to investigate them. This week he was planning some kind of reveal. When I met you in the bar on that first night, I realised I needed an ally. You were just as much outside the family as I was. What if Xander brushed everything under the carpet and refused to pay me? It's his family, in the end; he might have hushed it up. And what if he thought I needed to be silenced? That's why I gave you the memory stick. I wanted someone else – someone who understood, but wasn't a Scarmardo – to have what I was about to give Xander. As collateral.'

'And did you give them to him?' I ask.

'No – I was due to meet him, but he's vanished. And he's

stopped paying me. I was due a deposit this morning. I wasn't going to give him all the photos until the money came through. I haven't given him all the ones I gave you.' He shoots a look at me, and I know he's talking about the one with Belle. He must have picked that up from one of his sources. I don't fully understand how he got hold of everything and he's not telling me the whole truth – I can feel it. I don't trust him.

He carries on talking. 'You know he asked me to investigate you?' He looks at me. 'There wasn't much to say – I just passed on roughly what you earn, where you live, the fact you have a three-year-old kid. It's part of the reason I knew I could trust you – you seemed honest. Reliable. I thought you'd help me. And now he's gone AWOL.'

I can't breathe suddenly.

He talks as if Xander is still alive.

And I remember that Xander is still the only other person on board who knew about Finn.

Was. Past tense. He's dead.

But now Jimmi knows about my son.

I feel his eyes on me, like hot coals, and I daren't turn round.

53

'You talk to me about secrets!' Jimmi curls his hands into fists as we leave Mick.

My chest is tight. I've been so scared about anyone knowing about Finn. I've always thought if Jimmi found out about him, he could take him. What can I offer Finn when Jimmi has so much? All those custody battles you read about in cheap magazines. I can't put my son through that.

'Emily!' He spins and looks at me.

I could cry. Instead, I swallow it all back. Not in public. I can't do this in public.

'Your cabin? Can we talk there?' I say.

He says nothing, just turns and leads the way to the lift.

Once inside his cabin, he opens the fridge and pulls out some beer and opens one. His room is almost identical to mine, and we sit in the central circle of sofas.

After the noise of the ship – the music, the sunlight, the heat – the air con in here is cold and the silence is oppressive. I know I need to speak.

I play for time, swallowing a mouthful of beer, taking a few breaths.

Jimmi still says nothing. When I still don't begin, he says, 'Emily, you asked me about my secrets and I told you I had cancer. Something I've told no one else. Not a single soul. I don't even know if you understand why I told you – do you? Am I alone in this?'

The ground isn't going to swallow me up. So I begin.

'I thought you didn't recognise me,' I say.

He shakes his head. 'I didn't – not at first. You look different – looked different. I mean...' He shrugs and then stops. Takes another drink. Waits.

'I had short hair; I was covered in that weird glitter face-paint they'd been doing on the beach. I was up for any beach party going. Buckets of moonshine. But I knew it was you. I've known for years. That night...' And I think back to it. I was three days into my drinking binge, stumbling around on a beach. I couldn't have told you which way was up. It was dark – must have been gone midnight, and I can't even remember which part of the country I was in. Columbo? Galle? Batticaloa? Hours on hot buses, moving around the coast. I'd find the nearest beach and drink some more.

I thought of Juan over and over. Could smell his blood. Thought of Belle's face as she was pulled away – the knife against her throat.

I hated myself. I wasn't sure how I would live with it all.

On one of those nights, I'd waded out to sea.

The water was colder the deeper I got. The tug of it as my clothes soaked through – the pull of it. The darkness was intense.

I'd been drinking at a beach bar, and I hadn't thought anyone was watching me, or following me.

The waves were up to my nose, and I could taste salt water at the back of my throat.

I gagged, and pushed out further.

There was a shout. I barely heard it. The alcohol had made me sluggish. I found myself swimming instinctively, kicking my legs, but I was dizzy.

Another shout.

I was so tired. It was so difficult to move my arms.

Then a voice at my ear. A hand on my arm.

After Jimmi had rescued me, we drank and drank. Drank some

more. Had sex. I'd been desperate to feel. So fucking sad. So on the edge...I remember I'd clawed at him, pulled him in.

I'd left as dawn was breaking when he was asleep. Left him on the sand – the man who saved my life.

I collapsed weeks later. Dehydration. And after various tests, and a huge hospital bill, the doctors told me I was pregnant.

I couldn't even pay for a flight home. I'd called Dad, who had been losing his mind. He took out a loan, paid for a flight. Looked after me when I got home. Re-mortgaged the house. Bought a cot. Looked after the three of us.

I'd shut down. Shut everyone out. It was up to me now. I was in charge of protecting us. I'd got a job, got in shape. I'd learnt to defend myself, to protect us. I couldn't face some huge court case about the identity of Finn's father – have it splashed over the press. Or be painted as someone trying to pass my child off as the child of a billionaire. No. I wanted to bring Finn up, to keep him safe.

So it's been work, eat, sleep, repeat. And love my son. For three years.

'You knew who I was? But I didn't tell you my name,' Jimmi says. 'I'm sure I didn't. I was drunk and it was dark. I was so scared about dying, about facing what was coming...I saw you wading out and I knew what you were doing. Mainly because I was thinking of it myself.' He takes another drink. 'I wasn't thinking of sleeping with you. I wasn't really thinking. You initiated it, but you were so drunk. I shouldn't have gone through with it. I'm not sure which one of us was in the worst state.'

I remember it. I remember holding him, hanging on. I clung on to him like there was no other option in the world. 'It was me pushing – don't worry. You didn't take advantage of me.' I suddenly feel like shit. Had I read that moment wrong?

'I don't regret it, Emily.' He speaks quietly. 'I don't make a habit of sleeping with drunk women. But I don't regret what we did for a second.'

'When I woke up, in the light, I recognised you. I hadn't before, not during the night. But I'd been crewing on your dad's boat. You were all over the press after the robbery. I'd seen you on the news when I'd been in a bar that afternoon. They said you were flying over.'

He looks out through the windows. The sky in the distance has clouded over, black. There's a darker grey above us beneath the blue. The storm warnings. It feels right on time.

The captain's announcement rings out, that the outside decks are now closed. The rocking of the ship has become more pronounced.

'You told me everything. That night. I don't really remember it that well, but you told me about losing a friend, someone dying. Over and over.' He looks back at me. 'You'd lost it. I had to fight you to pull you back onto land.'

Had I? I look at him. So self-obsessed with everything happening to me, I don't remember what he said that night. 'Did you tell me about…'

He nods.

'You must have thought I was such a bitch! Not to have asked you this week – how you are.'

'But I didn't recognise you. Occasionally, you seemed familiar, like you reminded me of someone. There was a moment at the pizza restaurant. There was something about you. Then today.' He half smiles. 'Well, I thought maybe you remembered but you just wanted to ignore it – you know, move past it. It meant…it meant something to me. But you were wasted. You were in a bad place. It could have meant nothing to you.'

Now is my opportunity I suppose, to tell him, but he hasn't asked me the one question that matters more than anything, and I know he's going to. The main reason I'd been so scared to come, despite needing to be here for Belle.

'Emily, is it mine? The child? We had a connection that night.

I mean – you were the reason I got on the plane the next day and went back for the op. I was thinking about just staying out there. Ignoring it. Letting nature take its course. But you made me feel like there was something worth fighting for.' He leans forward, his knuckles white on the beer bottle. 'Is it mine? Your child? The timing is right. I doubt we used any protection. Please, Emily. Am I the father?'

Words are too hard; my throat is closed entirely.

All I can do is nod.

54

VIOLA
Three years earlier, Sicily

After our dinner on the beach, I change slowly. I know you have work calls but still, you're so late and this is meant to be a weekend for us. I take off my make-up, brush my teeth. I open the balcony doors and step outside. The night is warm. A wall of air and scent. The plants on the balcony are heady and the ocean stretches long and flat to the moon.

No. I can't wait anymore. I will find you.

I slip on a summer dress, which lies on the back of a chair, and head downstairs.

Not in your office. Not in the kitchen. Not in the house.

I head to the veranda. Nothing.

I glance up at the tiny derelict, haunted shepherds' hut, and not for the first time think I'd be able to see everything from up there, in the light of the moon, if it was possible to climb the rocky path. No one's been up there for years.

You mentioned the boat. You were checking on it, of course. It's moored near our beach, and I think of the first time I walked to the boat with you. The first time I lay on the sand.

The chorus of clicking insects sings to me as I make my way down the steps. It's nice to be reminded I'm not alone. The universe is out here with me.

The lights on the steps are dim as I approach the beach and the moorings. I think I hear your voice.

I speed up, running the last few steps. I could descend these blindfolded.

Your voice again.

But there's another voice, too.

A female one.

Now there's laughter.

I slow. Stepping carefully instead of running. I hold my breath.

Now another laugh, only I know this one. That's your intimate laugh. That's the one I hear when there's no one else around.

Why are you laughing like that, so late at night, when you know I'm waiting for you?

My last few steps are like a sleepwalker's.

You're on our beach.

The beach you bought for me. With another woman.

I turn the last corner, and there's a light – it's just a flicker. A fire? No, a storm candle.

And you lie on the beach. Naked.

You laugh again.

I know you've had affairs before. In far-flung hotels when you've been away on business trips. The odd work colleague who became something more for a short time. I've had affairs too. But here?

Our weekend? Our anniversary?

Our beach?

I don't know what I feel as I watch, standing almost behind the cliff which juts out at the edge of the steps, before they reach the sand.

My skin crawls. I think I'm going to be sick. My head aches and there's a pain between my eyes, short and sharp.

I reach for the stone of the cliff and my fingernails catch a groove and pull.

The flash of a limb on the boat. The lingering look back when you arrived.

This is not just an affair. You would never bring anyone here who was just a fling. To our beach. When I am here.

You are doing this because you can't help yourself. Because you have found someone you have lost yourself in.

So I have just one question.

What happens next?

55

'*This is your captain speaking. A reminder that the outside decks are now closed due to the storm. We advise you to keep balcony doors closed. All the indoor facilities will still run. There is no danger to the ship, but rain and wind will make the decks slippery and you may suffer falls.*'

This time the announcement shocks us both out of the moment. Jimmi stands quickly. 'I better check on Lila and Chloe.' He rubs his brow, looks out of the window, anywhere but at me. 'Can we talk later? I need a...moment.'

I couldn't be happier to run away. I'm at the door before he stops speaking. I don't have a clue what time is it, the dark from the sky is thickening quickly, and I need to leave the room. Leave Jimmi. I can't even look at him.

Once back in my cabin, I stand under the shower, turning it up as hot as it will go until I can't bear it anymore.

I need to go and confront Chloe. I'm so close to working all this out. The revelations with Jimmi have knocked me off track. I can't let that happen.

The enormity of it though. I hadn't wanted to lose Finn. Jimmi's world and my world are more than miles away – more than distance.

If I had acknowledged Jimmi as the father earlier, and he had contested custody, then I just couldn't have competed. I would have lost Finn almost instantly.

I'm a good mum – I really am. He's loved. He's the happiest of boys – now. But if he sees everything he could have, everything his father could give him – over what I can offer. Well, I just can't compete.

When the news about Belle and Mattia getting together had broken, I had been eight-months pregnant and thinking of phoning her. I was ready to face her and I wanted to tell her about Finn. But the moment I heard she was linked with Mattia, that was it. I couldn't risk it. Of all the people she could have ended up with, it was the one family I couldn't see.

Then when Finn was almost three, the cruise invite had come through.

I had told myself I just wouldn't tell anyone about him. I'd focus on helping Belle, making amends for everything I'd done. When Xander sprung it on me at dinner, and Jimmi had been sat beside me, I had thought I might faint.

Even now I'm not sure I'd have come if it hadn't been for the note. I had thought someone was about to spill out the secrets of what Belle and I had done – about the robbery. I'd wondered briefly if the notes could have been about Finn, but no, there's no way anyone could have connected Finn and Jimmi.

I'm the one with information now, though. I have some cards at least. If Chloe locked me in the cupboard, and Chloe sent the notes, then does she know about the robbery, too? Do any of the other siblings know?

Jimmi didn't mention it. I can't have told him three years ago. He was drunk too. And I can't believe Belle would have told anyone.

Maybe Chloe is just taking warning shots to get me to back off so Belle is more vulnerable – making wild accusations to have a clear run at Belle. There's obviously a campaign of some description against her.

But none of it explains who killed Xander.

I'll need to speak to Chloe. Now that Jimmi knows about Finn, I mostly want to run and hide, and wait to see how he will react. But I need to stay for Belle. I think of her hand on her stomach. She has her own child to protect now. It's the least I can do for her. Even if the question of what she may have done on that beach with Viola makes my stomach twist.

None of it makes any sense.

I realise the light in the cabin has almost vanished. The skies out of the window are fierce. Grey cloud fighting with black. The sun has hidden itself away. The storm is upon us.

56

VIOLA
Three years earlier, Sicily

I run back up to the house as fast as I can go, my legs like jelly. By bringing her here, on this weekend, he has put a bullet through us.

I get back to the room and I run my hands through my hair. I can't breathe. The night outside is hot but the air in the room is so cold, it hits my chest like a punch.

All this time.

I need to slow down. I'm not some young girl anymore. I can find a way through this.

Picking up my phone, I flick to a number and hover over it.

I open the balcony doors again, and let the night air in. The scent reminds me of so many nights here. Not just with Mattia. With my children. With Marcus.

Once I was pregnant with Jimmi, Marcus and I stayed apart. Then the twins had been born. Bean came along next.

With a brood to provide for, Mattia was more determined than ever to create a legacy. He worked so hard, and we saw less of him than ever.

The person who came with us for most of the holidays was Marcus. Mattia would arrive for a few days, but Marcus would come and play with the kids. No longer my lover, he was my friend. Their uncle. We worked hard to go back to brother and sister. If there were moments when something like resentment might flare, then we held our breath until it passed.

He taught the children football on the beach, read them stories.

I remember him taking Jimmi, Xander and Lila fishing when I was feeding Bean, and the *glow* on their faces when they came back. It nearly killed me, having Marcus so close, so entwined with the family, but never in my bed. But Marcus was true to his word, though it must have hurt him, too. I saw the way he looked at me, when he thought no one else could see.

Sometimes I wondered if he'd have a breaking point. If it might all be too much. That maybe he'd be angry at me, for being so close, and so far away. That he'd stop seeing us all together.

There were more tell-tale signs from Mattia. There was a pattern to his affairs. If he was away for more than two weeks, it was as though he couldn't go without. And I don't think he ever really looked at it as anything other than sex – like a gym workout.

But over time, the opposite became true for me. Watching Marcus with the children, the feeling that we were all there – even when Mattia was missing. Well.

I sit on the bed, and my finger hovers over his number. I take a breath, and I press it.

'Hello? Is everything OK?' His voice is sleepy on the line, all the way from the other side of the island, where I know he's staying with friends. Mattia is due to join him after our weekend together.

'Marcus, it's me.' I swallow. 'It's time. Will you come? Mattia is leaving me. It's our time.' I know this is madness. That I ask him to come here. But I need support. If Marcus left now, he could get to me. I don't think I can face Mattia when *she* is here too. It's a selfish request, but Mattia has forced this to a head. Tonight, the dice will fall.

'Our time, Viola? What? You mean—'

'It's over. With Mattia. Will you come?'

'I'm not some play thing, Viola. You've taken any chance I had to find another person to love. Don't play with me now.'

'Come now, Marcus. Please. I need you.'

57

I arrange to meet Chloe in two hours. I've checked in on Belle, but she's with Mattia – it's so close to Xander's death, I can't pull her away just yet. For all my doubts about him, Mattia will be grieving. And I can't believe he'd kill his own son.

I stare at the sea, my face pressed up against the glass of my balcony doors, and I hold the handle tight, to stop myself from slipping.

It churns – the ocean is no longer blue. It's grey, dark green, with white, foaming caps, which leap up from the moving hills of water like sea creatures.

The ship rocks. I know we're safe, and the storm offers me solace.

My world is shifted and swaying, in turmoil. Once the weather has passed, then the police will arrive, and they will find answers to what happened to Xander. Right now, nothing is stable or certain.

I hold the back of the sofa as I walk across the cabin to answer a knock on the door.

'Mirka!'

'I've just come to remind you of the massage I booked when you first boarded.'

It feels like weeks ago rather than days. 'I don't think I can go,' I say; it's the last thing I feel like, but the look on her face makes me feel guilty.

'Oh, but Emily, it will do you good.'

I find myself agreeing, if not just to appease her. It will fill the time before I see Chloe.

Although I can't imagine for a second I'll be able to relax, pulling on the white robe when I reach the scented spa, a moment of calm slips over me like a rush of warm water. It's only seven p.m. but the dark skies of outside make it feel much later.

'Hello?' I say as I enter the room the therapist had directed me to, speaking quietly as spas always make people do. No one seems to ever rise above a whisper.

The room is empty, so I climb on the edge of the bed and lie down. The bed is anchored to the floor, and there are rests either side to support me and make sure I don't slip off.

Some kind of water music with pipes is playing, and the room is filled with the scent of infused oils.

It's been a crazy time considering we only got on the ship three days ago. So much has happened. And still so many questions.

I feel nervous. Two nights to go. But in about eight hours, the police should land and some kind of order will be restored.

I hear the door push open, and I smile, ready to say hello.

'Mick!'

His rumpled self is out of place in this room, all about serenity. It's intrusive. I tense; my hackles rise as he raises his hand.

'Now don't scream. I just wanted to get you alone and you've been with the family all afternoon. I followed you here.'

'Why didn't you just come to my room?'

'I didn't know which was yours. I waited for you by the lifts. You were talking to your butler, and I didn't want her to see me, so I came here.'

My blood races. I'm barely dressed and there is only one door, which Mick Tenor is currently blocking. *Check your exits, make a plan.* Self-defence mantras run through my head.

'Look – let me just say what I came to say. I still can't get a hold of Xander.' He takes a step forward and I raise my arm.

'No closer!' I shout.

He looks over his shoulder as though scared. 'Shh, please! I'm not here to hurt you. Xander's just gone quiet on me. I know it looks strange, but Xander asked for a report on Belle and I have it. He's due to pay me. And he needs to clear my bill on this ship – I can't get stuck with it. I can't afford it! Plus there's something I need to tell you.'

His face is red, and I wonder if it's the heat of the candles. He's still in jeans, and the Blur t-shirt is back on, crumpled and with some kind of stain – toothpaste?

Despite the invasion, I want to hear what he has to say. I pull my towel around me, tight. I nod. 'Go on.'

He takes a step towards me, saying, 'It's tricky to start, but Bean—'

He's taken another step. I climb from the table and move back. 'Stay there.'

'I don't want to be overheard,' he says, looking past his shoulder. He steps forward again.

Instead of seeming gentle and vulnerable, he seems creepy. Different to earlier. I don't know what is giving off this vibe but I'm not a fan.

'Just tell me. Come on, just say whatever you wanted to say.' I know I'm impatient but I'm not enjoying this.

'Look, there's no need to get all high-handed,' he says. 'You're not an actual Scarmardo, you know, despite what you might have got used to this week.'

'What?' I'm completely taken aback. He's always been so friendly before. I knew something was off.

His face falls. 'Sorry, I didn't mean it like that. It's just that Xander's ignoring me. He owes me money.'

'Xander's dead.' I can't help myself. I shouldn't really tell him, but I'm angry, making me sharp with him.

'Dead?' He rears back a little. 'No! What happened?'

I shake my head. 'I'm not sure of the details.'

'Well you'll need to find out!' He grabs my arm, pulling it a little. 'Please! He owes me money, I—'

'Take your hand off my arm,' I say, very steadily. I feel my towel slip a little. I repeat, 'Take. Your. Hand. Off. Me.'

'You're not listening!' He raises his voice. 'Look, I have information for Xander!'

I've had enough. I'm being clear and he's not listening. His breath smells stale and I'm getting angrier. 'Get out!' I say.

'Please, listen,' Mick begs now. 'Xander asked me to find out what was going on with Chloe's festival. He said she wouldn't tell them – I got a report through this afternoon. She'd promised a cash injection she hasn't delivered. It's going to crash and the media fallout will be big – it will be embarrassing for her. For the family! But there's more, Bean, look…' He grabs my arm again.

Hanging on to my towel, I push him, hard, away from me and get myself to the door.

'Please, I need to tell you about Bean! I need to talk to you about him. I can't get through and—' He says this from behind me, but I open the door, and shout, 'Hello?'

In this quiet, softly spoken environment, it doesn't take long for my therapist to appear.

Mick Tenor looks left and right.

'I will talk to you,' I say. 'But not here. Not now.'

As the therapist approaches the door, Mick spooks. He takes flight, running past me and I'm knocked to the side. He bumps the white uniformed masseuse and she falls against the door frame, crying out.

I see Mick pelting up the corridor, and the door bangs at the end.

'Miss! Are you all right?' the receptionist asks, running towards us, her hand flying to her face when she sees the therapist righting herself.

'The man who just left. He came into my room, he wouldn't leave. I thought—' I'm not sure what I'm about to say. He was trying to tell me something, but he'd been behaving strangely. He was almost desperate.

Embarrassment takes over, and I start apologising to the staff, but I want to race after him and pin him down.

What was he trying to tell me?

58

I dress in my cabin. I've got twenty minutes until I'm seeing Chloe.

I will go and speak to Mick with Jimmi, I don't want to be with him on my own. It will give him time to calm down.

I leave the curtains open as I dress, watching the waves. I love storms. I love their power. The sea can be as real as it likes and no one judges. Every now and again it reminds you who's really in charge. And tonight, it's putting on a proper display. Lightning cracks the sky open and thick, hard rain lashes against the glass. The boat heaves to the left and I put my palm against the wall.

What am I missing? I head back to the screen in the second reception room to check the memory stick again, slowly. Is there something else on here? Beach shots in Sicily. Family photos. All taken from the same angle. What was Mick trying to say about Bean – can I see it here?

These pictures look like a camera was in a fixed position – they all feature rocks to the right in exactly the same formation. The exact same patch of beach. They've been taken from a height. Does Mick have more of these? Why does he have images from so long ago? Some of them look years old. He said someone gave them to him. But who?

I pause on the photo of Belle arguing with Viola. I stare at it. What has Belle done? The phone proves she lied about not being there, but it's not hard proof of anything else. I still think if anyone killed Viola, it was Mattia. I just can't work everything out: Bean's collapse, the swing, Xander dying. How does it all fit together?

Mick had said he was going to show all of these to Xander once he'd been paid. He can't have shown him the one with Belle on the beach – otherwise Xander would have given it to the police, surely? He would do anything to expose Belle.

Money. It has to be about money. The family are worried they won't inherit – they assume Belle is after Mattia's fortune. Mattia is showing his authority by threatening to withhold their allowance. Belle wears the money on her ears, her wrists, her make-up – she wears it like a prize. Mick dresses in cheap clothes, had said Xander needs to pay off his bill from the ship. He must need money. And Mick was introduced to me at the champagne bar as Emily, Belle's friend; he knew I was with Belle when the boat was attacked.

Mick said he'd wanted someone else other than Xander to see the photos, but what if the reason he showed me the photos was to get Belle to pay him off? Maybe he thought I'd show them to her, and he could take money from Xander *and* Belle?

I look out at the storm. The spray lashes high on my windows, the ship rises and falls.

A lit match. *Think, Emily.*

Xander. He was so keen to get to the bottom of everything, maybe there was more – maybe he had recruited other people. He tried to get me to help, he was paying Mick, it makes sense he might have asked someone else.

The ship lifts again, and I think back to when I had last seen him. In the hot tub.

God – his phone. He'd left his phone.

Rifling through the drawer next to my bed, I find it. I'd put it in here, to give back when I next saw him.

It doesn't open for me – I type 1234 just in case, but no. I try a couple of random combinations, but the phone threatens to lock.

How can I open the phone? There's one obvious way.

No – not that. I can't do that.

I stare back at the storm. The police will arrive soon. With the family accusing Belle of cutting the rope to the swing, and the whiskey being in Belle's cabin; and the look that Mattia gave Belle – I need to get to the bottom of this.

Xander would understand.

The morgue is low down the ship. I check it out from a distance. Luck is on my side, because a cleaner is coming out of there. The bucket props open the door as he swabs the mop. I've got literally seconds. I lift my head as high as it will go, and I stride forwards.

'Hi, excuse me, Sir Mattia Scarmardo was in here recently. He's left his phone. I've been sent to collect it. Are you finished? I'll only be a second.'

The cleaner looks into the morgue then back to me. 'I'm not really supposed to let anyone in. It's kept locked.'

Hating myself, I shrug on entitlement like I'd been dipped in it, and roll my eyes. 'I'll only be a second. Why don't you finish up in the corridor? I'll give you a shout when I'm done.' Then I go for conspiratorial. 'You *know* how he can be. I wouldn't want to be either of us if I have to go up and say no to him!'

The cleaner doesn't look happy.

'Two minutes,' I say, flashing him a big smile. Then he shrugs and leaves the bucket in the door to prop it open.

It's the best I'll get.

I walk in briskly, with purpose. The morgue is small. There is one wall with round doors in two rows. The bodies must be kept in there. It's cold in here and I feel sick. I can't believe what I'm about to do.

One of the round doors has a light on. It has to be him.

I've not got long, and I can only pray the cleaner hasn't followed me in. A quick look behind me. All clear.

I press the green button on the edge of the round door; there's a click. It opens slightly, and I hesitate, then swing it wide. There's a handle in front of me – it's attached to the edge of a long metal tray. And on it, I see Xander.

I pull it gently.

As his body slides out, my stomach takes a blow, like a punch. I catch a sob in my throat and forbid it to escape. I stop sliding as soon as his head and shoulders are exposed. I pull out the phone, hold it above his face.

It opens.

Then I lean forward, kiss his brow and say goodbye.

He didn't deserve this.

I am shaking uncontrollably back in my cabin, curled up on the sofa and scrolling through Xander's emails, when I find something. An unopened message with an attachment. I don't recognise the name at all. It only arrived this morning.

'Hey Xander, not sure why you wanted it, but I managed to remote access the photos from that number you gave me – he had some saved up on his cloud. Sorry it took so long. I saw a couple of your mum, so I didn't look through any more. Sorry, man. Look, I've attached them. Catch up soon, yeah? Sorry for the delay sending. Cheers for the tickets – front row, man. Wild!'

All the same photos that are on the memory stick.

Except one.

There are two adults on the beach, a few steps away from the children. It must be years ago. Bean by the shore in a floppy hat, next to the blond twins.

I zoom in on the adults. There's something about the way he stands.

It's Mick.

And Viola.

Together on the beach in Sicily years ago.

59

I must find Jimmi, and then we'll confront Mick. This photo changes everything. From what I can see, Mick didn't get these photos from anyone else. He's been photographing the beach for years. Why? And how does he know Viola?

I'm just out of my cabin door when I get a text from Belle:

Mattia isn't talking to me. I think he's starting to believe them! What can I do? Please come! I'm desperate!

I pause, imagining the isolation she's feeling. Despite my urgency to work out what is going on, I go to her first.

The door opens slowly. I swallow hard.

'Emily?' Belle stands, hollowed out.

I hug her, but she's brittle in my arms and I know our fight is still hanging over us. All my doubts about her – whatever she thinks of me.

I haven't told her about the photo. We haven't really spoken since the running deck. With Xander dying, it's been brushed to the side, but I have so many questions for her.

'I'm so sorry,' I say, but she's still stiff under my arms.

What do I do?

We've fought before, but this is different. Things I haven't told her, stuff she hasn't told me. The knowledge that she's lied to me stands between us like a wall. That we've lied to each other. But we can get past this. I have to believe it.

When we were about thirteen years old we had the biggest row, or at least that's how it felt at the time. It was one of those arguments that start off small and then suddenly you're screaming at each other, so angry you can't see straight. I think it had started over my hair straighteners. I'd lent them to Belle, and then they'd broken. The comp we'd gone to was a vicious pit of straight hair and foundation. Hair straighteners were uniform.

Belle had left hers at her gran's and we had a birthday disco straight after school. She'd sent a panicked text and I'd run round and given mine to her mum, who answered the door.

Belle said that her mum must have dropped them on the way up the stairs. But I know her mum and she was always careful.

Either way, apparently, they must have been knocked to the floor and when she plugged them in, they weren't working. She even asked if they were working when I gave them to her.

At the time I'd been incensed.

I hadn't used them yet that morning. Belle had netball practice before school, so she'd been going in early.

Cutting to the chase, I couldn't afford new ones, and her mum said they'd replace mine. They said they'd ordered some, but they wouldn't arrive until mid-week. Come Monday, Belle had hers back from her gran's and I had nothing. I asked if I could borrow them, but she didn't see the text until she'd left for netball practice.

I walked around all day feeling naked. Ugly. I'd tried to blow dry it as much as possible, but it wasn't right. I was so angry I couldn't speak to her. I'd spent the whole day feeling cheaper than usual.

Even now, I remember feeling so let down. I would never leave her so open to ridicule. I mean—

Well, I was thirteen. We'd got over that.

But this? If only a trip to Argos could resolve it all now.

'Do you want a drink?' Belle sits on the sofa. 'Mattia is asleep. They gave him some pain relief and it's made him drowsy. The way he's looking at me, Em.' She looks broken.

'Belle, I'm sorry. I should have stood up for you when Lila

was kicking off.' I need to push past this so I launch in. Part of me knows there's more to say, but we don't have long until the police arrive. We need to act now. I need to tell her about the photo of her, of Mick. But I need to start at the beginning.

I start by saying, 'I think Chloe's behind some of this stuff.'

'Chloe?' Belle shakes her head. 'Behind what?' She raises her eyebrows. 'Have you been hanging out with her since I saw you?' Her voice is dry. 'What, drinking with the Scarmardos?'

'Please, Belle.' I try to keep it soft. 'Please, something's going on. Something's happening. And I want to help. You asked me to help. Let me.'

Her eyes close and her head falls back against the cushion of the sofa. 'Look, I meant what I said – about how angry I've been with you.'

Her eyes open but she's not looking at me. She looks at the glass doors to the balcony. The spray of sea from the storm, the black sky. I glance over and see our reflection. A faint outline of our real selves. It's how we've been. Since that day. Just a reflection of who we were.

'I'm sorry, Belle. For everything.' The moment of realisation is sharp and cutting. What she'd said is true. I had run home. I'd avoided her. I'd deliberately not told her about Finn. I'd cut her off when she needed me. But she needs me now.

'Are you?' She looks at me. Leans a fraction closer, but she's still on the opposite sofa. Three feet and two oceans away. 'You don't really do sorry. I used to love how unapologetic you were about what you wanted. Because it was usually what we wanted. But that…that was different. You're just selfish. Something bad happened to me, so you punish yourself rather than checking in.'

Honestly, before she said it all to me, I'd never really looked at it like that before. I walked into the sea that night planning on not coming back. What good would that have done? I think of Finn, of Dad. Of Belle. She's right. These three years have been about refunding Dad for forking out for my flight home when he didn't have the cash, for supporting Finn and me until I could go back to work. And more than financial recompense; I mean paying it back. Proving I was earning my keep.

But I never paid Belle back.

'I really am sorry,' I say. I fight the urge to leave. I'm so tired. I swallow hard to just listen. Not to cry.

Her eyes close again. 'Well, you came this time. And here we are.'

And like a tiny crack in my memory, I remember the day of the straighteners. I'd dropped them on the bathroom tiles the night before. How could I have forgotten that? When Belle had sent a text to say she'd left hers at her gran's, I'd leapt at lending mine to her. So that they'd think she'd broken them and would buy me some new ones. I knew we couldn't afford them. But Belle had two parents, each with a job. So I'd thought...

Like she said.

Here we are.

60

'Look, Belle. I need to tell you what I know. I don't know where to start – with Chloe, a journalist. You already know about some of Xander and Lila's digging.' It's coming out too jumbled.

'Right,' she says, looking exhausted.

There's a sound from the bedroom.

'Christ, that's Mattia. Let me check on him. He's not looked at me properly for hours. Oh, he might be coming through – can you nip to the bathroom for a second? Just in case? Oh, and grab a cardigan. It's late – you look cold.'

I go and wash my face, giving her a minute. I fall against the towel rail as I do; the ship's rocking hasn't abated yet.

As I dry my face I look in the mirror. What do I see? A poor girl on the make. Is that all I'll ever be? Taking cheap shots to make my own way a bit smoother?

I'd promised myself, not anymore. Not after the yacht.

It's one of the reasons I never tried to contact Jimmi about Finn.

A one-night stand and a claim of paternity from a son of one of the richest families in the world? I'd seen those stories in the press. I couldn't put Finn through that.

But maybe Jimmi had deserved to know.

How had I got everything so wrong?

I hear Mattia and Belle talking, and the cabin door closes.

Belle was right; I am cold. The storm outside has made me

want to wrap up. To feel a layer of protection. I slide open her wardrobe and find a cardigan. Cashmere and delicate.

My arms slip into it and I feel instantly better. I won't get over my self-loathing so quickly, but I can be warm while I try. As I close the door, I see a pink sleeve hanging out at the bottom of the pile.

There's something familiar about it.

I kneel and pull it out, smoothing it over my knees. It isn't cashmere, it's a hoody. Pink. With studs on the back. And CS stitched on one shoulder. It's Chloe's sweatshirt, from her CS range. This is what she was wearing when she assaulted me, trapped me.

Entering the cabin reception area, I see Belle on the sofa. I glance at the door. 'Mattia gone out?'

She nods. 'He can't sleep, despite the drugs. He's gone to meet Jimmi. They were just on the phone. Oh my God...If he believes them I stand no chance.'

I sit, holding the pink jacket.

It twists in my fingers and I look at her. Then I lay it on the coffee table, and I watch carefully.

At first, she doesn't look down. She just stares at me, back to looking hollowed out. Beautiful, stunning, all the cheekbones and eyes, but then she sees it.

I watch and wait.

The fraction of change on her face. The tiniest flicker around the mouth – something about the eyes. And I know it was her.

'You locked me in the cupboard? You sent me the notes?' I shake my head. I'm more confused than angry. It makes no sense. 'Why would you send me an invite and then send me a threat, telling me not to come?'

She says nothing.

'What the fuck, Belle?'

'Christ, Emily. You know nothing about yourself, do you? I had to send you both. Can't you see?'

I stare at her, like I've never known her at all.

'Really, Emily? How was I supposed to know you'd come because I asked? You've not spoken to me in three years. When I needed you, you were AWOL, and then afterwards, I was so pissed at you I stopped trying. Someone is definitely out to get me, and I thought, nah, time to call in the chips. This is where I need my bestie, water under the bridge. *Blah blah*. I needed someone. I needed *you*. But how the fuck was I supposed to know you'd actually come?'

'But...' I start and stall.

'You know why you came? Really? I'll tell you. You came because someone threatened to expose your secret. Someone hinted that they knew what we'd done – what *you* did! And you came all fired up, ready to protect yourself.'

'No.' I stand. 'I came because you asked. Because you're my best friend and I'd let you down. I came to make it up to you!'

Thoughts scrabble around in my brain, fighting for a clear route out. But my head's a mess. I have a sudden pain between my eyes and I'm crushingly aware of how late it is.

'But why lock me in a cupboard?'

She waves her hand. That fucking hand wave. 'That was to back up the threats, to convince you something was really going on. Once you were on board, I think something clicked in me, and it was also, a little bit,' her eyes flash, 'it was a bit of payback. I was locked up for three days. I watched you run away when you could have saved me, let me in through the hatch. You put me in there. Don't come crying to me about half an hour in a fucking cupboard. You've no idea.'

'The mirror?'

'Every night I check the room before I sleep! Every single night! Because of you! Maybe you deserve to know how that feels!'

Bean on the floor. Belle had been handing out the drinks.

'My mojito, that Bean drank in the karaoke?' I speak quietly, not daring to hear the answer.

'Chilli oil,' she says, as though suddenly tired. 'I just put chilli oil in there. He over-reacted. How the fuck was I to know he was allergic to peppers? It would have made your mouth burn, your throat. Maybe given you the runs. I was just so angry. But then I saw what happened with Bean and realised…it was too far. I'm sorry about that. But, it's done now. We're even. Tit for tat.' She looks up at me, drained. 'And now with everything else. Can we start again? I've got nothing else. That's it.'

61

The spray of the sea and the rain hits my face like pellets. It's a release. The sky is ink black and lightning flashes, slicing the heavens in a rage. The storm reminds me I can still feel, that I'm not in some crazy dream.

'Miss! You can't be out here!'

I cling to the rail of the running track on the top deck. My fingers are frozen in a tight curl. I just need five minutes. To remind me of who I am, where I am. When Belle told me what she'd done, I just lost it. I couldn't speak. Everything I thought I knew this week was all up in the air. And I still haven't told her about the photo. That I know she'd argued with Viola. Belle is capable of so much more than I ever thought, and I can't find my north. I just don't know what to think anymore.

'I'm sorry,' I shout, but my words fly back at me and a crew member, already drenched from the rain, reaches me, holding the rail.

'Passengers must remain inside!' He's shouting, but I can barely make out his words. Rain runs down his face and I try to pull my hands from the rails but they're fixed there, knuckles locked.

'It's not safe!' he shouts again.

I sob, long and loud, and I feel his hand take my arm.

'Hold the rail, I'll lead you back inside!'

The wind is fierce and the sea, which had been flat and

turquoise this afternoon, now looks like a mountain range that lives – hills which rise and recede in a blink.

'Here! The door! You need to let go of the rail now!'

I'm still wearing shorts, a cami and Belle's cardigan, which clings to me like a second skin.

'Come on!' He's angry now, and with one last scream at the ocean, I let go of the rail and, as he pulls me inside, I slip on the deck and fall. I bang my knee and shoulder hard, and as the ship sways to the left, I slam against the wall, flat in the rain water that streams down the running track like a river.

There's a whack to my cheek, and then his hand pulls hard, and I'm reeled back as the ship rights itself. Before I know it, I'm lying on the floor inside, and the crew member has closed the door.

'You must stay off the deck!' he starts, but I don't get up. I'm exhausted. 'Are you hurt?' He kneels next to me, and he must take pity on me when he looks at my face. I don't know if it's the tears or whatever blossoming bruises he sees, but he sounds suddenly kind. 'I'll take you to medical. You need to be looked at. Come on. Promise me you won't do that again. It's so slippery out there, we could lose you. You're safe inside.'

And I think of what I've already lost, what I've thrown away. I doubt I'm much safer inside than out. But I don't say any of this, because of course it would make no sense, and because I still can't believe where I started and where I've ended up.

62

Shivering, I duck my head as I sit on the sofa by a potted plant and a framed poster of the ship. The crew member left after he'd spoken to the medical staff.

I pull the blanket around me and look at the clock. It's two a.m. and all I want to do is sleep. Putting my hand to my cheek, which burns like someone's set it alight, I feel my skin puffy to the touch. And when I pull my fingers away, there is blood.

I lie my head back against the sofa. No wonder the crew member took pity on me. I must look like I've been hit.

'Hello?' A smartly dressed woman comes walking in briskly, smiling like it's nine in the morning, not the middle of the night, and I think of Mirka and her ever-ready smile. They must pay them extra for all this cheeriness.

'I'm Doctor Cliff. I hear you've taken a blow to the head? Could you come this way?'

The torch flicks on in one eye.

'And open the other eye, please. Any sickness? Dizziness?'

I shake my head, still shivering.

'Your temperature is normal but you better have a warm shower and go and get changed. Any loss of consciousness, then please contact us. Make sure you're not alone.'

At this I wonder who I can ask to sit with me. There's no one.

Doctor Cliff is quick with her smile again. 'I heard you were quite upset. Was that as a result of your injuries?'

Again, I shake my head and tears threaten to rise at the kindness of this doctor who smells of expensive soap and some kind of peach shampoo. 'I was feeling claustrophobic. I know I shouldn't have gone outside.' It's so close to the truth it doesn't feel like a lie, and she looks sympathetic.

'Ships can be like that if you're not used to them. Look, go and get warm. Have a hot drink. Take some paracetamol.' She hands me two in a clear plastic bag.

'Thank yo—'

I'm cut off by a large bang in the reception area. The medical centre is small – the assessment room I'm in is so close I can hear voices.

'She's bleeding!' A shout comes from outside the room.

Doctor Cliff says, 'Stay here. It's a busy night.' She offers a brisk smile and then I'm on my own.

I don't need to be told. It's Jimmi's voice I hear and he sounds angry. I'm frozen to the spot.

'Sir, oh, Mr Scarmardo,' I hear the adjustment in the doctor's voice as she recognises Jimmi, and then the professional tone is back. 'What happened?'

'I found her. In our brother's cabin. Please!'

He sounds so upset I mobilise, and my legs move easily despite me desperately wanting to lie down. But hearing Jimmi sound so…

I feel the kind of pang I get when Finn falls and hurts himself. There's something in their expression that ties them up with each other. It tugs on my heart.

'What happened?'

Jimmi is bending over Chloe. She's conscious, but barely – her eyes open slightly and she looks at me, but I'm not sure she sees me. Blood comes from her head. Much more than from mine. And her lip is split.

'Oh God, Chloe!' I take a step forward.

'Please,' Jimmi is saying. 'Is she OK? I can't find Bean. I ran straight here but I need to—'

'It's OK, I've got her.' Doctor Cliff uses the torch in the same way she had only a few moments ago on me. She takes Chloe's pulse, saying, 'Chloe, can you hear me?'

Jimmi is on the phone, and as he lowers it, he sees the blood on me. 'Emily! What?'

I reach for my head. 'It's nothing. What happened to Chloe?'

'I don't know. I had a missed call from Bean. I was with Dad. By the time I got to his cabin, he was missing, and Chloe...' He looks down at her. I realise he's shaking. 'Who the fuck is doing this?'

63

VIOLA
Three years earlier, Sicily

Marcus is on his way so I won't have to stay long here, on my own. I can't face Mattia yet, but I'll confront him later. It's almost dawn and he's still not back. My anger mounts with each moment. He will assume I am sleeping.

I head down to the front beach – not the small one at the back. Not the one which used to be ours but is now forever soiled.

Sitting in the sand, I wait for the sun to rise. Today will be a new day in all senses. I can be with Marcus now. I have nothing to hold me back. The betrayal of Mattia is sharp, but maybe it's for the best. I have stayed with him for so long for our family – but the children are older now. Even Chloe.

I know that my being with Marcus will hurt Mattia. It will wound him more than a betrayal; it will trigger his competitive side, his possessive nature. He might be violent. But maybe I can enjoy watching him hurt. Like he's hurt me.

Fingers of sunlight poke up above the horizon. I've loved this house, this beach, for so long. But I am ready for something new.

Standing, I see the back of Mattia heading up the stone steps to the house. I've never hated anyone as much.

What does that mean? That *cagna* is still in the cove?

I head towards the rocks. There is a path through, to avoid climbing up to the house and down the steps from the other side. The kids and I found the path when they were small. We used to look at jellyfish caught in the rock pools, find crabs there.

Now I walk over it looking for a different kind of slippery

fish. There's a deep-sea predator, the anglerfish, which lights up to attract prey. Once they mate, they fuse together, becoming one fish. This was supposed to be how Mattia and I were. Once we had children, we'd be one unit. A few affairs but I knew he was mine. But now this girl with the dark ponytail has arrived, and she has all her lights blazing. I am obsolete. I have no doubt. Mattia is as tightly bound to her as he could be – otherwise he would never bring her here, to our beach.

I climb over the rock pools, and I make my way through the sharp rocks to where the boats are moored.

There. I see a flash. Not on *La Piccola*, the boat Mattia sailed over from France, but on a smaller, older one. She must be using it as a getaway. I suppose if the boat Mattia came on vanished, I'd know someone else was here. No one will miss this.

I find myself walking towards it.

Maybe if I just see her, it will make sense. This woman who has usurped me in my own home. Slept with my husband on our beach. Stolen his heart. Taken my place.

A few more steps. The boat is silent, and the sun rises further.

What am I doing?

No. I stop.

This is not what I want. Marcus will be here soon. I can step away quietly. I do not need to look her in the face to accept what has happened.

I imagine Mattia ready to come up to me. Showering first, planning to pretend that he crept in quietly so as not to disturb me late last night. Or maybe he will say he got up early for a morning run. He plays the game he wants to play. He builds the legacy he chooses. If I fight him, he will strip me clean. If I am silent, vaguely wounded, but do not fight, then he will give me everything I need.

This is who he is.

I can step away. Maybe I can finally be happy.

I halt. Move backwards.

Then a head appears on the deck. The anchor is lifting.

I can't help myself. I stand and stare.

Her back is towards me to begin with. Denim shorts, a t-shirt. That ponytail. It swings high, shiny and long.

As she begins to turn, I see how young she is. How fresh.

Oh! It's the girl from the robbery. The one who was taken. She…

There's a catch in my throat.

I didn't know Mattia had met her. I saw the documentary they made and I had liked her – she was brave. She was vulnerable.

The deal is done. I will gain nothing from this. But still, I stand and stare.

She is pulling ropes, readying the boat. It is then she sees me.

'Viola!' Her voice comes out in a squeak.

A confrontation. How does this end?

64

No matter what I think of Belle, she is bound to be suspected for some or all of this. I need to find her. I'm almost at her cabin when I crash into someone. 'Mirka! I'm so sorry, I was—'

Stopping, I realise she looks different. She's not smiling. But it's more than that. The usual glow isn't there – her face looks raw, as though something has scoured the life out of it.

'Are you OK?'

She sits up, touching her elbow. 'I banged it, I think, on the way down.'

'No, I don't mean that. You look…upset.'

She says nothing, and I realise she isn't in her crew uniform, and I don't really know her at all. I sit back on my heels, holding the wall as the ship leans to the left. 'I'm sorry, it's none of my business.'

This time she looks at me, and I can't read her expression, but I'm sure there are questions there.

I'm desperate to get to Belle, but I feel torn – it would be rude to run off but equally rude to intrude. I try one more time. 'Mirka, can I help? Has something happened?'

At this her eyebrows rise and she says, 'Something happened? Don't pretend you don't know. You know all of it! All of you bloody Scarmardo group. Secrets close to your chest, building walls to keep everyone else out. The fortress family! And Xander dead. And now I've heard from the crew that Bean is missing!' With this she bursts into tears, and her head falls to her knees.

'Mirka, I'm so sorry. I should have thought.' Of course she will be upset. 'Would you like to come and see the family?'

She shakes her head. 'Of course not! That bloody family. Bean was different before. When it was just him and me, and I didn't know who he was. Here, he's part of them. He keeps apologising, but I didn't see how I could forgive him for lying. Now he's missing – I wish I'd just...I wish I'd said...Oh, Bean...'

I put my arms around her.

'We will find him. You know the ship, Mirka. You and the crew know it better than any of us. You can help by looking for him. Jimmi is speaking to the captain now. They'll need help.'

She's already standing, nodding. 'I'll start now. I'll get the other staff to help. I've been pushing him away. But the moment I thought he might be in danger – well, it clarifies a lot.'

I hug her. 'We'll find him. He'll be OK.'

'Belle?' I bang on the door; there's no answer. I call her phone, no answer.

In the end, I head to the bridge to find Jimmi. This time the captain isn't smiling. The huge viewing windows look out onto the black sky, the black sea. It's so late now.

The dark is like tar, and the storm is raging.

I hover at the edges. Mattia looks washed out and even older than the last time I saw him. He sits with a walking stick.

Jimmi is talking to the captain and I hear the tail end: '...we can't find your brother anywhere. If he was as upset as you say, could he have hurt your sister, or himself? How distressed was he?'

Jimmi shakes his head. 'No. He wouldn't hurt Chloe. He's been devastated. We all have. He seems to feel responsible in some way. He and Chloe both. Chloe's sleeping now. She said she had no idea what happened. She was in the room, there was a knock at the door that Bean went to answer, and the next thing she knew, he was gone and she was waking up in the medical unit. We're looking for Lila too. She's nowhere to be found.' Jimmi looks at Mattia.

'Or Belle,' I say.

They all look at me. 'I've just tried her cabin, her phone. Nothing. I think she's missing too.'

The captain looks shell-shocked. 'Well the crew are still searching and—'

'Captain!' A woman at a desk calls out. 'One of the lifeboats has been activated. It's descending.'

'Can you stop it?' The captain is on his feet and moving quickly towards a control panel.

I move beside him, looking at the lights flashing. The crew work quickly and urgently. An alarm sounds steadily. I see Jimmi touch his father's arm.

The storm is vivid through the glass. It's hard to tell the black of the sky from the black of the sea, but I gasp as, in the distance, lightning hits the water, and for a second the whole world lights up like day, and the line of the strike falls straight into the ocean.

There's no power like it. I turn to Jimmi.

'He'll be OK,' I whisper, as the sky falls to black again, like the curtain has fallen.

'If the lifeboat hits the water now, won't whoever is in there be in danger?' Jimmi says. 'The storm…'

'Yes. We can't leave a boat adrift,' the captain says.

'I can't stop the lifeboat! It's going to hit the water,' an officer says. 'It's been switched to manual. Someone is releasing it.'

'Get the crew down there!'

The officer moves at the captain's command, and without any obvious signal, two other officers on the bridge follow.

'Stop the ship,' the captain says. 'I need a complete halt. If anyone is on that lifeboat, then we'll need to pick them up.'

Jimmi moves beside me, looking at the screen even though there's little to see, but he swings round as there's a whimper behind us.

'What's happening?' Mattia says. He reaches out and takes my arm. '*Mia famiglia. Mio dio.*'

'We'll save them,' I say. And then I sprint after the crew who are heading for the lifeboat, with Jimmi only seconds behind.

65

It's still raining as I head to the door, which opens to the lowest deck. We're back close to where we boarded on that first day. Crew are searching from all viewpoints of the ship for the missing lifeboat. We've followed one officer here. I figure we need to get as close to water as possible. The ship has a search light which scans the sea, and it flashes in front of us, lighting up the waves briefly.

'Stay here – inside,' the officer says, then heads out into the rain.

I hook the door open against the wall, so we can hear what he's saying.

My shorts, cami top and Belle's cardigan are wet again quickly as the storm blows back at us through the open door.

Jimmi stands next to me, shouting, 'Anything?'

But the officer shakes his head, looking out at the sea. 'There's a platform which opens lower down. Once the rescue raft has the lifeboat, they'll enter through there. They haven't found it yet.' He's practically shouting over the wind.

Jimmi looks so frightened that without worrying about it, or thinking of the consequences, I take his hand, and I hang on to it. Trying to offer up as much support as I can.

'Where are they?' he says, barely registering me, looking out at the sea. But I feel his hand tight on mine.

'I can see the rescue raft the crew released. They look like they've spotted something!' the officer shouts.

I watch as the ship's light does another sweep.

'I can see it!' the officer shouts. 'I think they've almost got to it!'

I step to the window, and press against it, looking out at the sea. The light from the ship has found the lifeboat. I see it lift and fall on the waves.

'It's so small,' I say.

'Don't worry, they'll bring it back in!' The officer's voice comes in with a blast of rain. Jimmi's hand is still on mine, and we watch the lifeboat, with no idea who may be on board, or why it's been released.

The lights of the boats bob closer to the ship. Two boats – one pulls the other.

The officer comes back in and closes the door, rain streaming off him, and the sudden stillness inside as the wind is locked out, makes the room seem silent.

He speaks on a radio. 'Anyone on board?'

There's some static crackle, and I can't really see boats now, as they're so close the ship. They must be lifting the passengers through the platform the officer spoke of.

More crackle.

Jimmi's hand tightens again on mine, and I step closer to him.

'There's one person aboard.'

'Fuck,' I whisper. *What now?*

'Who is it?' Jimmi shouts.

'It's Lila Scarmardo!' the voice crackles over the radio. 'But she's not conscious. I need to check her for signs of life.'

66

My chest is tight as I race down the steps to the lower decks. The external rescue platform has been closed and I see Lila on a stretcher, unconscious, being checked. Jimmi and I follow the officer, not wanting to get in their way.

'Don't move her!' someone shouts.

'Wait for medical!'

I feel a wave of sympathy for Jimmi. His face as he waits for news of Lila – he is crushed.

Jimmi Scarmardo. I've been tied to him for three years. I see his face in Finn every day. What we did has bound us forever. I've been frightened of the consequences of him finding out, and yet here he is, lost and afraid. I see Finn in him now. Without thinking, I wrap my arm round his waist, and try to help him stay strong.

The ship is still rocking, and I grab the wall as it rolls to the right.

After what seems like a lifetime, there's a shout. 'She's alive!'

The collective gasp is like a breeze.

I don't linger. There are enough people here to look after Lila, enough people looking for Bean. There's one person I need to find.

'Jimmi,' I say, 'I need to find Belle.'

67

I run round the decks, checking all the bars. Most people are in bed now. It's almost four a.m., but those passengers drinking hold on to their glasses, don't leave bottles on the tables to slide off. The ship is still in the grip of the storm.

Belle is nowhere.

I try up on the running track, the swings. I go outside, holding the rail tightly, the rain lashing. 'Belle!' I scream into the wind.

Where is she?

I check the pool. The water sloshes and slaps, but still, no Belle.

Nothing.

I'm shivering, and I'm almost done. I ache from my fall earlier – everything throbs. But if Lila was pushed out to sea, I need to make sure Belle is safe. I can't just leave her.

The crew are searching for her and Bean. The whole ship is being covered, but I can't rest.

No matter what she's done.

I can't think about the worst possibility – that Belle has anything to do with Chloe being hurt. Lila in the lifeboat. Bean missing. Xander dead. Viola dying. I focus on the photo with Mick on the beach with Viola. That must be where the truth lies. There's more to uncover, and we're still thrashing about in the dark. I can't jump to conclusions.

Xander and Lila may have been rooting into Belle's secrets, may have been trying to expose her. But surely she wouldn't go this far. She was so calculated in getting me to come that I'm sure she's stirring up trouble with the family in some ways. But I have to believe she's not capable of hurting them. Not the Belle I grew up with. And if Belle has changed, it's because of me, what I put her through.

Belle's no killer. She may fight to secure her position with Mattia, but no way would she murder.

She must be in danger. She's a Scarmardo, a target for whoever is doing all of this.

Someone must have taken her. Mick has to be involved.

But where do you hide someone on a ship?

I think back to the first night. She could be trapped somewhere, like the store cupboard. But that doesn't feel right.

I think of the one place that is capable of being left behind at sea. Where Lila was found tonight. Adrift.

What if Belle's in a lifeboat too? If it is Mick doing this, then he doesn't strike me as someone with the most imagination.

I can't face the worst possibility. That somehow the ship security system has not registered the lowering of another boat. That she's already at sea.

No, this ship is too good for that. If she's in a lifeboat, then I can find her.

I race around the deck where I remember all the lifeboats are hanging – half out over the water, half over the deck. I know modern lifeboats can hold at least one hundred and fifty people. If not more on a ship of this size. That's certainly enough space in which to hide someone.

Stopping, feeling suddenly overwhelmed, I think back to the first night. I remember the boat's champagne bar had them hanging over the edge of the deck. I run.

There's no one here. Those passengers still up appear to have flocked to the club and the bars near the front of the ship. I check the doors to the terrace area, expecting them to be locked.

They open.

The deck here has lifeboats positioned over the rail to the deck. There are four. Steps lead up to the entrance, and they are big, with hard tops – not open like in old movies, but like mini arcs, so that in a storm they are completely safe and watertight. They have about seven windows, and a door for access.

I race to the first. My fingers slip on the rails as I climb up to get into the boat. I fall on the deck and there's a stab in my ankle. I'm moving too quickly, and I bang my cheek again. My face is on fire.

I start again. The door is shut firmly. I run to the next one, ignoring the pain in my ankle, and as I start to climb the rails, wet – rain soaking me through – I hear a noise. Not this one. Further up.

There's noise coming from the third one.

My chest tightens, and I just know.

A lit match? I'm terrified. The bitter taste is back in my mouth and I'm dizzy.

I shout, 'Belle?'

Come on, I will myself, and rush to the boat.

I will not leave her again.

68

Lightning flashes as I climb the ladder up to the boat. It seems further away now. I hope this means the storm will pass soon.

The lifeboats hang, ready to swing out and lower to sea. I look down at the swirling waters. I'm just guessing, but we must be about twenty to thirty feet from the sea.

The ship doesn't feel as though it's moving since rescuing Lila. I suppose until Bean and Belle are found, the captain might not want to move away.

The door to the lifeboat has been opened, and not fully closed. I edge my way inside, half out and half in.

I can sense people in here, but it takes a second for my eyes to adjust. They must be a few metres away from me.

There's a shout.

I'd know that voice anywhere.

'Belle!' I say, and I slip in the boat, as I try to race towards her. I fall to the floor.

My ankle, already hurt, crunches beneath me and pain makes my head spin for a second.

A voice brings me back to myself.

'Emily Mason.' It's Mick Tenor.

His face slides into a grimace. My eyes have adjusted and the lights from the ship glow in the lifeboat, through the windows. 'Almost got me locked up for the rest of the trip after that stunt you pulled in the spa.'

I look from him to Belle. She is shaking in the half light.

He has his hand tight around the back of her neck. I can't see his other hand, but I dread finding out what he's holding.

They are only a few feet away from me but I'm nervous about surprising him, and what he'd do.

'Maybe I overreacted,' I say, carefully. My heart is thudding fast. I can smell the blood from the boat three years ago; I need to stay very calm.

'You think?' he says. 'Come along now to fuck this up too?'

'What are you doing, Mick?' I take a step closer.

He shakes his head and tightens his hold on Belle. 'One more step and this ends fast. I'm only taking what is rightfully mine. A life for a life and all that. You must have found the photo of her on the beach with Viola by now. Took you long enough. I thought for sure you would have mentioned it earlier, and you and your little friend here would have sought me out and offered me money to stay silent! Too busy enjoying all this fancy living?'

I curse myself for being distracted by everything else.

He carries on. 'This little bitch here basically killed Viola!' With this, he gives Belle a shake and her eyes widen in fear. 'She took her away from me! And I loved her...Viola.'

I glance at Belle – her head shakes a little, as much as his hold will allow.

I don't know what to believe, but I know who I have to protect.

'Let her go, Mick.'

He snarls – a proper snarl – and I'm frightened of him like I'd be of an angry dog. He's all teeth and menace. How did I not see this before?

'You say you loved Viola?' I ask, playing for time.

'Haven't you worked it out yet?' He stares at me, and something around his face looks too clever, too amused. 'You think I'm someone unimportant – nothing to do with this great and illustrious family. Like I told you, I wanted someone else to have the photo, before I'd shown it to Xander. The lovely Belle here is going to be blamed for Viola's death. I wouldn't have minded some money to pay for my silence along the way, but in the end, I needed that photo to come to light. But not through me. You can't trace me on this ship. You don't even know my real name. All you have is proof that this one was with Viola the day she died.'

Now he growls.

Belle's face tightens in pain.

I'm frantically trying to work how to signal for help without alerting Mick.

He's still talking, but as he does so, he pushes Belle to the ground, places his knee in her back and starts tying her hands behind her.

I almost leap at him, but I see the knife he is holding, tight in his teeth. If I moved, he could still hurt her. And it takes me back to the yacht three years ago, all the knives carried by the attackers.

Christ, what do I do? Can I tackle him? I can't risk Belle being hurt. Shit.

Think.

I tune back in to what Mick is saying. Why is it that men like this are always so *proud* of the evil they do, can wax lyrical about all the ways they are superior? I suffer from shame – stall my life and bury myself away – and yet here he is sounding all clever and resourceful, like he's cured fucking cancer.

'I'm so tightly bound up in this family, it would blow apart if they discovered the truth. Or should I say *when* they discover. Which they will, once this new bitch is out of the way, once everyone sees what she's done. I've set it up so everyone will believe that she is responsible for all of this.'

Belle is shaking violently now. Tears stream down her face.

'Mick, tell me, what is it you're going to tell the Scarmardos?' I inch closer, relying on the fact that he will be so distracted by his own brilliance he won't notice. I need to get in and kick away the knife. Then I'll push Belle out of reach, I'll get between them.

And we'll fight. I flex my fingers, ready. I could probably grab him now if I leapt.

As plans go, I've had better. But I'm out of options. I take one more step. 'Tell me what you've done that's so clever. How are you connected to the family?'

'Well for starters, Bean is my fucking son, not Mattia's.'

At this, I stare at him. Is this just bullshit?

Mick carries on, and I inch closer still.

'Where is he then?' I say, taking the tiniest of steps again towards him.

'He's safe. I've left him locked in a room next to her cabin.' He shakes Belle and tears stream down her cheeks. 'It will all point to her – she had access to the whiskey, she pushed the swing. I left her earring by Lila when I hit her. Bean is unharmed. I wouldn't touch a hair on his head.'

He waves the knife at me. 'Stop moving, Emily. Don't think I don't see you. You can't stop this. I was going to tell Bean when he inherited. But it all changed. Killing Mattia seemed the easiest way. But he wouldn't fucking die. Not in his car with a loose wheel, not on the broken swing, not drinking poisoned whiskey.'

'Mick, it's not too late to stop this. You can tell Bean. Mattia doesn't have to die!'

'I need money, you fucking bitch. You wouldn't understand. You can't stop this.'

'Stop what?' I take one more step.

'This.' He moves so quickly I'm not sure what happens.

One minute, Belle is trapped by him, shaking on the lifeboat floor. Then he opens the door on the other side of the lifeboat. He pulls Belle up, and as I blink and run forward, he lifts Belle and pushes her hard. I scream as she falls backwards into the water below.

'Belle!'

In answer, there's a trace of sound, like an echo from far away; I hear her cry out.

She is gone. I run at the open door to jump and follow her, but

Mick sweeps my feet and my ankle screams as I land hard on the floor of the boat.

He kicks me and my vision lights up with pin pricks of pain. Bright dots flash everywhere and my head spins.

Mick waves the knife around and is still talking. 'I fucking loved Viola, but she was so angry that day – after her row with Belle. She was so angry I didn't have a choice but to do what I did. And Belle drove me to that! Belle forced me!'

All I can think about is Belle in the water. Would she even survive the fall? She's a strong swimmer, and used to the sea. But she's pregnant, and her hands are tied. My heart races and my chest feels as though it could explode. I climb to my knees. The door is open. I just need to dive through it.

But he grabs me. Holds firm.

'You fucking psycho!' I scream again.

'Not so fast, Emily Mason. Don't think you're getting to her any time soon. I need to deal with you.' He lifts the knife. It catches the green glow of light coming from the ship. It glints. I think of the captain, of Belle, and of when I ran away.

He waves the knife closer. 'They'll believe you and Belle died together. They'll believe what they want to. They'll find the memory stick in your cabin. They'll never know about me.' And he raises the knife.

I came on this ship for this. For this moment. I take a breath as the knife plunges towards me, and I spin, throwing my leg high in the air.

He anticipates it, and catches my foot.

'Not this time,' he snarls.

But I'm better. I've trained. I've pushed myself further in the last three years than I had ever thought possible. I grab the side of the lifeboat, and I lift the other leg. I throw my weight up, and I feel my foot connect with his jaw. There's a clattering as the knife falls to the floor.

I have no time. I feel him fall, and I don't look back. There's a lifejacket hanging on the side of the boat, and I grab it. Then

I hold the frame of the door, hanging over the water. Rain hits my face; the drop down is bigger than any dive I've ever done. Belle might be dead already, and the fall could kill me, but I have no choice. I'm the lit match. I send a prayer to Finn. *I love you.*

I must try to save her.

I close my eyes, take a breath, and then I jump, into the air, into the nothingness, heading towards the water.

69

The dark of night is thick, and I kick out through the churning ocean.

It's icy, but I've broken through that point where the cold makes your limbs ache and sting. I know if I don't keep going, then Belle will sink. I will sink.

I can see her in glimpses, up ahead. The light from the ship is sweeping the sea again. I can only hope the alarms are ringing and the crew are coming to save us.

The salt is sharp and I have to force my eyes open; I can't make out much. There's a new sound from behind me, and I hope it's the sound of the rescue boats.

I push out further.

I try to listen again, but the sea is so cold, my senses are dimming. Now, all I can hear is the lap of water in my ears, my own eardrum, my heart thudding.

The lifejacket holds me up, and I see her again. I can do this.

There she is – floating up ahead. Water and darkness obscure everything. She's just a few strokes away.

I break through the waves and my chest is so airless and tight from the cold, I can't call out her name. The light is too sparse to make out much. This week could still kill us both.

Wealth is a drug. To the rich it's as invisible to them as air, as water from a tap. As fluid and as constant. But threaten to take it away and they'll fight you like they're fighting for their life. Mick will kill for it.

That's what this week has been about.

And looking back. Confronting what we've done. What we didn't do. *Should* have done.

What Belle's done – what she *might* have done. I think of her on the beach with Viola. I know that no matter what, I'm here for her. Whatever has happened.

I strike out in front crawl, cutting through the inky sea and I brush her arm with my fingertips. I grasp the cloth of her top, and reach for her head, face down in the salty water.

If Belle dies, then half of me dies.

'Belle!'

I have so much to say sorry for, to make up for. Five nights would never be long enough. I just need the chance.

'Belle!'

She's not breathing. My legs are tired and the numbness that comes as a relief when your limbs stop aching with the cold has become a kind of dragging weight. I feel dizzy; lights flash around me from the ship.

Paddling pools, school holidays, growing up together, side by side.

There isn't very long. Not long at all.

'Belle, come on!' I grab the back of her head with one hand and slide my other hand under her chest, lifting her face upwards for air. 'Come on!'

I shiver, and all I can think of is Belle holding me when Mum died, and promising that she would always be there.

And now Belle will be a mother – I need to save them both.

'Belle,' I whisper.

I've loved her all along.

It's crystal clear. Even when I've been so jealous of her it tasted like hate. A best friend. A sister, really. All that time wasted.

Now there's barely any time left.

I start to fade. The world falls in on itself. My life is compressed into a series of images: Finn, fat fist in the air, asleep in his baby salute; Dad, younger, running beside me in the park when I ride a bike; Mum, in hospital, her hand soft when I held it.

I've been the richest one all along; it's just taken me a while to realise.

I can't feel Belle anymore. I can't feel the water.

I fade.

Then there's a voice.

'Emily! Grab my hand!'

It sounds too far away, and I'm so tired.

A splash. Lights flash.

Then I'm lifted.

Another voice. 'Let go of her! Emily, you have to let Belle go.'

It's then that I feel her, cold, in my arms.

DAY SIX

70

Noises are coming from somewhere, and I don't want to open my eyes. I'm so sound asleep, it feels too early to wake.

The noises become voices, then the voices become words. I hear her name. 'Belle.'

The water, the storm. Belle missing.

Dizzy, with a crushing headache, I sit up. The room spins, but I open my eyes.

'Emily! She's awake!'

Lila sits at the edge of the bed I'm in and throws her arms around me. 'Oh God, Emily, they said you were OK, but I didn't believe it. You've slept for so long.'

Lila's cheek is damp against mine. She has a dressing on the side of her head, and a black eye.

'How are you? How is Belle? The baby?' I manage, looking round the room. Chloe sits in a chair at the corner of the room, balled up with her arms around her knees, looking about twelve. She is bruised, and a plaster covers what must be a cut on her head.

'They think she'll be OK. She vomited water but started breathing on the lifeboat. She's being looked after. The baby's heartbeat is strong.' Lila tells me this, but her voice is hard as stone. 'It's more than she deserves.'

There's a clock on the wall by Chloe, and it's reading almost six a.m.; time is a jumble to me, I can't think straight. I must only have been asleep for an hour or so.

'Mick…Is Bean…? Lila, the lifeboat…'

'Bean's OK. Mirka found him.' Lila closes her eyes briefly. 'The police arrived yesterday. They managed to land the helicopter once dawn broke. Bean was in a state. He's been talking to them – it's been…'

'What?' I look at Chloe. She peers at me over her knees.

What had Lila said? I say slowly, 'The police arrived yesterday? But – what time is it?'

'You've been asleep for almost a day,' Lila says, gently. 'You've been on this drip – totally out of it. Chloe came and sat with you.'

Chloe. 'Thank you,' I manage. I'm glad it wasn't her sending me threatening notes in the end. I like her. I'm pleased I don't have to resent her.

My head hurts so much. I try again. 'Mick, somewhere on the ship. It was Mick. Blur. I…'

What had Mick said? I feel like my head is still underwater.

'Chloe?' Lila looks over at Chloe, who rocks slowly now. 'Do you want to tell Emily?'

But Chloe looks at me, under a bleached fringe, her eyes dark and heavy. She looks as scared as I've seen anyone.

Whatever she's about to say is going to cost her.

Chloe rubs her eyes with her knuckles, and lifts her head again. Her voice is so quiet I can barely hear her.

'We didn't mean to make her this angry. We just wanted to frighten her away. I saw the test and took it – I knew what it meant. I knew she was planning a child to use like a weapon. The money, the rock didn't work. But now she's gone crazy.'

I think back to Belle telling me she thought someone had taken the pregnancy test. It feels so long ago. But this can come later; they need to know about Mick, to stop him. My teeth are chattering and I try again. 'Mick,' I say, but I'm not sure they hear. Chloe is still talking.

'When Belle wore Mum's earrings at the wedding, and Mum always said they'd go to Lila, I was so angry. She must have talked Dad into it, like she talked him into everything else.'

She drops her legs down and crosses them under her, sitting up straighter. 'She's taken so much from us already. I've been keeping tabs on what else she's stolen.'

My head is still aching and my mouth is dry. I reach for the water by the bed. It's one of those hospital beds in the medical deck, and the room is small. Belle must be nearby.

'What has she stolen?'

'Everything!'

'Shhh,' Lila says, slumping in the other chair; she looks exhausted. Chloe continues.

'And now.' Chloe's voice chokes up. 'Lila told me she was in Sicily when Mum died. I knew she was bad to start with. But I didn't know about Mum. I mean, I've leaked photos of her – spending our money. We paid some kids to chuck a rock through the window when she was home on her own. Just to frighten her off. Bean offered her money through his lawyer to get rid of her, to leave Dad.' She speaks quietly. 'I would never have *hurt* her. But Bean and I have been trying to push her away... Now Xander is dead. She's tried to kill Dad. I think we pushed her too far.'

Everything is happening quickly. Too quickly. I'm still trying to tell them about Mick, but my head is spinning. Chloe is still talking when the door opens and a tall man, accompanied by a member of the crew, pokes his head in and announces he's with the police.

'I'm sorry, is this a good time to speak to Ms Mason? We heard you were awake.' His accent is American and there's clear deference in there. He glances only briefly round the room and to give him credit, he doesn't linger or stare at the Scarmardos.

I, however, can't take my eyes from Chloe – I want her to shut up so they listen to me. I try again, 'It's not Belle,' I say. But Chloe just looks at me sadly, like she thinks I'm deluded.

It's not a good time, I think as I look at the officer. I lie back down, my head spinning. I'm going to be sick. 'Mick Tenor is to blame,' I say.

But the officer has already started talking, 'Can I ask you about the evening of the incident?'

I start to repeat what I've said, when there's shouting. Bean comes crashing into the room.

'Have you charged her?' he says to the officer. 'Have you charged Belle for all this?'

I take a deep breath, and I shout, as loudly as I can. 'It's not Belle!' This time they all look at me, including the officer.

'It's not Belle, it's Mick Tenor, and if you're trying to charge her, it means he hasn't been found.'

'Who?' Lila says

'He said he was Bean's real father! I know it's crazy. He said he had an affair with Viola and it was him who threw Belle over the side of the lifeboat.'

'What?' Bean is white.

Chloe looks confused as she looks to Bean, to me. She speaks first. 'She fell? We assumed she had jumped; that once she realised Lila had been found, she was trying to escape on the lifeboat with you and fell out.'

'No – he was in there. With us.'

'They found one of Belle's earrings in my cabin, where I was knocked out. It must have been Belle who hit me and put me on the lifeboat,' Lila says. She looks at me strangely. 'Didn't you know? I was ambushed in my cabin, from behind. Whoever it was hit Chloe too, but we didn't see anything. Her earring was on the floor where I'd been standing in my cabin. Chloe's right, she's behind it all. She killed Xander, tried to kill Dad. She'll get half of it all. We'll be ruined. She needs to be arrested. She can't win.'

ean looks at me. 'What do you mean, *my father*?'

'Mick Tenor. A journalist. Jimmi's met him. He's on board and he says he's your father.' I realise the full enormity of what I'm saying, but there's no time for niceties. I also realise that if they've found the memory stick, they'll have found the photo of Belle. The photo of Mick is on Xander's phone, and no one will have seen that – it will have locked again.

Mick's dangerous. We need to act now.

Bean shakes his head. 'My father? But—'

I interrupt. 'It doesn't matter if it's true. He believes it. And there's a photo of him on the beach, too. I found it on Xander's phone – no one else has seen it yet. He was with your mother years ago. I think he killed her.' I shake my head. 'I know it doesn't make sense, the affair, his claim, but what does make sense is that he tried to set Belle up. He said he tried to kill Mattia – and that the poison Xander drank was put there by him. He's on the ship! We need to find him.'

There's a stunned silence in the room.

I need them to move. I could cry with frustration, so I shout this time. 'He was the one who threw Belle off the lifeboat! She didn't jump; she was pushed!'

Chloe looks unconvinced. She speaks to me calmly, like I'm confused. 'It was Belle, Emily. It was all her. I've never heard of this Mick Tenor. I know you're trying to defend her. But now's not the time.'

'I think it's time the room was cleared. Let's give Ms Mason a moment.' The officer says this. I must look desperate – beaten up by Mick and the sea. But I feel so helpless.

It isn't until they've all left, including the officer, and I realise how crazy I sounded, that the door opens again and Jimmi comes in.

'Lila just told me what you said. They think you're confused – but we can prove it. I believe you. Where is he now?' Jimmi asks.

All I can do is shake my head again. 'I don't know. We need to find him.'

Jimmi and I run, limping, as quickly as I can up the steps to the top deck. Everything hurts, I feel my arm stabbing like I've wrenched something. I don't know what I'm doing to my ankle moving like this, but I can't focus on that now.

Dawn has almost cracked its way through the entire sky; the earlier splinters of light through the dark clouds are now bright. The sea is flat and already I feel the heat beginning to dry up the water lying in puddles on the deck.

'What else did he say, Emily?'

I think. 'He said he'd made it seem like Belle had pushed Lila out in the lifeboat. He did it. Everything. He tried to stab me – to kill me – and said it would seem that Belle had done that. He's setting her up. He also said Belle killed Viola, but—'

'Maybe he did that too.' Jimmi's face is dark. 'Come on.'

72

Three years earlier, Sicily

'I thought—' The girl looks to the steps which lead up to the house.

'You thought I was asleep. That makes it OK, *certo*?'

'I'm...'

I'd feel sorry for her, if it wasn't my beach, my husband. My life. She looks so young. She must be about Bean's age. Not quite as old as Lila.

I see red and black. I feel my veins run hot like lava. 'How dare you!'

She glances right and left again. She takes a step backwards.

'What gives you the right to think you can take him? A cheap thief! That's all you are. Ignoring the number of his age to see the numbers of his bank balance?'

Even as I say this, I know Mattia is no one's loot. No one could take him. He is not that kind of man. If he has chosen this girl, then he has made a deliberate choice. But I want to hurt her, I want my words to make her skin sting, and I want them to bury themselves inside her head, so that sleep is out of reach. So that self-respect is gone.

I want her to feel like I feel. Everything I have lost. I have been overlooked. Cast aside.

I stop. Her face already carries the wounds of my words. Even looking me in the face – it is costing her. And I don't want to be a pawn. I'm a grown woman. I have choices. Those stories of romance, the love affairs of the gods; those stories are not for adults – the gods play like children.

I remember what happened to her on our boat – she was held for ransom, and she already knows that she has a price. Some day it will not be high enough. Society watches women grow and cheapens them accordingly. Some day she will lose.

I have Marcus. Marcus is coming.

A man like Mattia sees the price of everything. The value of legacy. Up to this point, I have been part of that. He now craves this girl. But that never lasts. When he wakes up one day, and realises his legacy is tarnished, his family divided, he will realise the real price of this union. And I believe he will decide it was too much.

There are tears on her cheeks, and I stand back.

'Take him then,' I say. I want to wound her. I want her to know the truth. What she faces. What I've put up with. 'You'll need to give him a child!'

She looks at me. She is white, like a ghost.

'He will only stay with you if you give him a child. He lives for his legacy. But he can't have children. I've never told him. He doesn't know. You either emasculate him by telling him the truth, or you betray him with an affair, and get pregnant some other way. If I had told him the only way was IVF because he couldn't father them without it, he'd have hated me for telling him he wasn't a man – it's how he would see it. None of the children are his. All fathered by different men. So you are faced with what I faced. How to keep him, but also keep him from the truth!' I don't have time to wonder if I've gone too far.

I watch as she fumbles with ropes, pulls up the anchor. The tide is high enough, and I watch her sail out of the cove, as though she was never here.

I need to go and unpick the pieces of my broken life. I need to assemble them into something new. Marcus will help me with that.

The children will remake their idea of family, of Christmas and birthdays, and I will not make it difficult. I will not fight him.

The slip of a shoe on the step behind me.

Has Marcus arrived already?

73

There are already passengers out enjoying the sun. People must feel they have spent long enough inside their cabins because of the storm. The decks will be busier than usual today. We arrive in New York this evening.

We head towards the cabin Mirka had suggested. She met him on the first night, and she'd been my only shot at finding him.

'We're lucky,' Jimmi says. 'We don't even know his real name. I guess he was going to hide out in his cabin. We would have only been able to hope we'd catch him as he disembarked.'

Jimmi is right. I have to pause for a second, and hold the rail; my ankle burns. I look out and see the outline of land. We will be there soon enough.

It's almost seven a.m. now. Guests are making their way out for an early breakfast; sweaty runners are heading back for showers. We weave through them all. A few point and stare, recognising Jimmi.

'Should we call the police? Let them know?' I say as we approach the cabin. 'He's dangerous, Jimmi.'

'Definitely, but not yet. Let's just make sure it's really him. Remember we have no evidence he even exists. Everything points to Belle. The police could think we made up someone else to pin this all on.'

We race to the cabin and my heart is like a drum in my chest as we arrive at the door. Jimmi seems nervous, and we exchange a look as he prepares to knock. 'Ready?'

My hands close into fists and my adrenaline is sky high. I nod. Jimmi adopts an almost falsetto tone. 'Sir, just to confirm disembarking details. Do you have a moment, please?'

74

The door opens a crack and Jimmi puts out his foot. I see Mick Tenor's face briefly, before he sees me, and I manage to dive into the room, just as Mick hurls his weight forward to shut us out.

Jimmi falls back, hit by the slamming door.

But I scramble up, seeing Mick turn and run.

'Call for the police!' I shout through the door as I hear Jimmi banging. There's no time for me to turn back; I'll lose Mick.

I run into the room, my ankle stabbing. I pause for a second as the pain recedes. I think of Xander and Bean fighting in the lift, and I scan around, in case he grabs me from behind.

Instead, I see him by the balcony doors. He's through them, and is locking them from the outside.

He gives me one very brief look – it's him, but it doesn't look like him. Instead of grey, his hair is now black – he must have dyed it. Instead of an old t-shirt, he wears a crisp pink linen shirt, and chino-style shorts. He doesn't really look like him at all. That's how he was going to get off the ship. Walk off, like he didn't have a care in the world.

'Jimmi! He's outside!'

I run to the door and manage to loosen the catch. Mick's already over his balcony, and dropping down to the cabin below.

I can't let him escape. I can't let him run.

I grab the balcony rail, and peer over. It looks like I'll fall straight into the sea again. I have to trust I can do this. I can't let him go.

Holding the balcony firmly, I swing my legs up then under me, turning at the last minute so that I aim for the hammock on the deck beneath this one.

Crashing on the netting, my ankle pulled up high to save it as much as possible, I hear a scream from the cabin, and look up to see Mick running at top speed through the occupied room and opening the door.

Limping forwards, I shout a, 'Sorry', to the guests, and then when I'm out in the corridor, I look left and right. Which way did he go?

I pull my leg towards the lifts. Sweat from pain drips in my eyes. My breath is tight in my chest. Surely the police are close by? Someone must have alerted them. Does he have his passport with him? He must need to return to his cabin.

I can't let him go. He's the only one who can clear Belle. And even if she managed to avoid a charge, who's to say he wouldn't come for her again? Or me? Or Finn? He seems to *blame* her for Viola's death. He's the only one who can say what really happened.

Running as fast as my ankle will allow, I make for the lift and the stairs.

Almost there, I turn my head briefly to see if Jimmi is behind me, and then someone grabs my neck, and yanks me backwards.

The world goes black. I fall to the floor, and I realise I've been pulled into one of the side cupboards. There's a bucket and a mop in here, but of more concern, is the hand on my mouth, and the sharp knife I feel cutting into the outer layer of my skin.

'We'll stay here, Emily. We'll stay right here until it's time for me to get off. Any screaming from you, and I cut you deep. You get it? Let your fancy friends run around the ship looking for us. We'll be right here. Quiet. Like mice.'

75

The sound on the steps isn't Marcus.

Simon. But how can it be?

'Viola, it's been years.'

I open my mouth to speak. I feel myself take a step back, and I don't know why, but I'm afraid. 'What are you doing here? How did you even get here?' I look up at the house, and whereas a moment ago I was thinking of how much I was dreading seeing Mattia, I wish he'd come running down the steps right now. Mattia would never hurt me. Physically at least. He'd never hurt a woman. He'd defend his family until his eyes bled.

I don't trust this man.

'The shepherds' hut.' He gestures to the building that sits up on the cliffs. 'I own it. I've been watching, and I saw Belle Myrtle come and go. I thought now was the time for us to come clean. Now that we're free to be together.'

What he says makes no sense, but I start with the shepherds' hut. 'But no one owns that. It's been deserted for years.'

He shakes his head and takes a step towards me. That shiver I felt when Mattia had arrived the other night is back. Love and death. Is that what tonight is about?

I take another step back. I feel my feet get wet. I am in the sea. The dawn is breaking and I think of Helios launching his chariot across the sky. Will he be on my side?

'I bought it after our affair. After I was *dismissed*. I saw you pregnant afterwards, and I could never even get close. He's mine, isn't he, Viola? Bean. He's mine.'

Shaking my head is such a reflex. They're all Mattia's, of course they are. If not in blood, then in everything else.

I have never told Marcus that the first baby is his. I was married to Mattia; once I was pregnant I had to make it work. At the end of the day, vows are vows.

After all the fertility treatments and testing, a doctor told me one day that it was Mattia who would never be able to conceive a baby naturally, without IVF.

I knew this would kill him. So, I pretended it was me who had the problems. And when I was sleeping with Marcus, I stabbed every condom with pins.

I was in love with Marcus, and it all fitted perfectly. I knew it would mean the babies would look like Mattia. By sleeping with his brother, I had managed to give Mattia everything he had wanted.

After Jimmi was born, Marcus wouldn't have me anymore. He believed Jimmi was Mattia's. It broke my heart, but I did what was best for my family nonetheless. When it was time for the next child, I dressed up. I bought a wig, I went to a bar. I was Viola no more, and I found someone beautiful. Rocco, a tall musician with bright blond hair.

Our affair was brief. I told him I was a photographer from the south. I only left him when I knew I was pregnant.

After Lila and Xander were born, I thought that would be enough. But in New York one night, I met a writer, just after Mattia was saying it might be time for another. I wouldn't have chosen him, but he was easy. I've always been attracted to penniless writers – the romance of it all. Another few weeks, and I left. Simon.

Only this time, Simon didn't disappear as easily as Xander and Lila's father had. Simon clung on with nails like steel. He followed me. He researched me, and once he discovered the truth of who I was, he confronted me.

I paid him in the end. He had threatened to tell Mattia of our affair so I paid him and then I threatened him. I do not live in Sicily without knowing how its history has evolved. I have seen my father do business many a time. And I would protect my family with my life.

The shepherds' hut. Surely no one lives there? I look up at it again. The odd flash of light – haunted, we had joked. All those times on the beach, here. All my privacy, invaded. Who is this man? What else is he capable of?

'I knew you came here for the summer, so a week or so each year, I come and camp out in the hut. It belongs to me now – and its tiny patch of land. I have a camera fixed up there to take photos at intervals – it's been snapping for the last few hours. And over the years. I wanted to see my son grow up. I have pictures of you and I talking on this beach years ago. I have proof. I looked through the lens tonight – I see Mattia has found a new woman. She is not like the others. You must know that. Viola, this is our time! I've always loved you. We can be a proper family now. You can leave him. If you need proof, come and see the photos I took of them a few hours ago. He seems to like her *a lot.*'

He took photos of Mattia and her, on our beach? How low can this man go?

'What do you want, Simon?' I take another step back. The water is up to my knees now.

'What do any of us want? Bean is mine. He even looks like me. And I have nothing. The money you gave me years ago lasted me a while, but it's gone now. I have nothing. No son, no wife, no money. Come and live with me. Let's tell Bean, after he's inherited from Mattia. We can be happy. We can be rich. I want my life to feel…' He gestures round at the cove, then up to the house. 'You have all this. I have nothing. You can't refuse me, Viola. I have too much evidence, I have my DNA. You need to say yes this time.'

The water is up to my thighs. Our boat – *La Piccola* – bobs behind me. It's light, easy to handle. It moves quickly, even without too much wind. I need to get this man off my beach, away from here. Before Mattia arrives. Before Marcus. Neither of them can know what I've done. Minutes ago, I wanted Mattia to come chase Simon away. Now I know they can never meet.

'Come for a sail, and we'll discuss it?' I say.

Hesitation streaks across his face, so I don't wait. I grab the edge of *La Piccola* and I lift myself up. I'm used to it, but it will be harder for him, so I toss the rope ladder over the side, and I ready the boat. Mattia hadn't put a tarpaulin over it, so it's all ready for a sail. I raise the anchor and pull over the tiller.

'There's no need...' he starts. Then I hear his feet in the water. 'OK, fine. Let's go. I guess you're worried your *husband* and his *mistress* will come and find your grubby little secret.'

We head out into the cove. I look out across the sea for any sign of her – see if she has decided to return. But no, she is gone.

I had locked a world of steel around my family.

One night, years ago, when Mattia suggested we had one more, I let myself return to Marcus. I invited him out here. Only him and me. I lied to him, told him Mattia would come then said he'd been held up for work.

I dismissed the staff, and after dinner, I suggested we went swimming in the sea.

He'd had wine, and although I could tell he was pulling away, I slipped out of my dress and walked into the water, calling him.

After four babies, I had less faith in my ability to convince him. But Marcus and I have always been about more than that. I turned and called his name, splashing water at him, lying back and kicking the sea up at the stars. 'Come for a dip! Only a bit of fun. It's so hot.'

His arms had slipped around me like they belonged there. His breath was familiar, the tightness of his legs, muscles in his thighs. I had clung on tight to him that night, knowing I'd only have one shot.

Chloe was born nine months later. If Marcus had ever

questioned it, he'd never let on. Jimmi and Chloe are both his. The image of him and Mattia. Lila and Xander belong to the blond musician, and Bean to this man. I look at him now. There are rocks over by the edge of the cove, before it opens to the sea.

Simon is still talking, and each word is a hammer to my heart. 'Once Bean inherits, then tell Mattia. Tell him Bean is mine. Tell him you're leaving him. If you don't, then I will.'

I think of what Mattia would do to me if he realised my betrayal. His legacy, his children. If he realised they weren't his. He would destroy me. He may destroy them. I can't let that happen.

My hands tremble, and I look again at the rocks.

If I come about quickly, swing the boom, can I knock him off? He would fall, and then if I left him out here – in the half light of a blue dawn…

Can I do this?

'If you don't leave him, you will ruin me, Viola. I can't let you do that.'

What does he mean? I look at him. His face is twisted. The early light of the day makes him look uglier than I have ever seen anyone look – so much hate. I think this man could kill me. And it makes what I do next all the easier.

I look at him quickly. 'You can't tell Mattia.'

'He is my son. Not Mattia's.'

I close my eyes. I can do this. I turn *La Piccola* a little against the breeze. Again, I only get one shot.

'OK then,' I say.

'Really?' He looks up at me in surprise, and as he does so, I push the tiller hard, let go the main sheet and the boom swings out, hard and fast.

It catches him full in the chest, and one minute he is on the boat, the next he is gone, tipping backwards over the side.

My hands shake and my heart pounds.

I can do this. I can do this. All I need to do now is to head back to shore. It's deep out here, and the tide will take him into the rocks.

I realise I'm crying as I turn the boat again. 'Good girl,' I say softly. She'd never let me down.

Despite myself, I turn to look for him in the sea. The tide is strong now. Even if he was a capable swimmer, he'd never be able to pull himself out. His fate is sealed.

I can't see him anywhere.

'*Andiamo*,' I whisper to *La Piccola*. Let's go. Let's get away.

'Viola?'

I turn, a cold feeling sweeping over me, and I see him rise. He must have caught hold of the boat as he fell. The rope ladder – I didn't pull it up.

'Simon!' I shout. I lift my arm in the air instinctively. I defend myself as he climbs onto the boat.

He takes hold of me, and screams, 'Bitch!' in my face. 'If it were not for that little whore being here! She has stirred you up – she has twisted this! If you were not already angry, then you could think calmly about what I've said! Now, we are fighting, and that little bitch has driven us to this! How could you let her do this?'

I feel his hands take hold, and I think of my children. Of Marcus on his way to the beach. At least Mattia will have someone with him when I am lost.

I remember them all when they were tiny, and I offer a prayer of apology that I couldn't save them one last time. Whatever this man will do, I hope he puts his son first. I hope Bean isn't crushed by the weight of this beast – his anger, his greed.

From love to death.

I am out of time.

76

He has me by the throat. Blur t-shirt man. Mick. Whatever his real name is.

'You have been a thorn in my side, Emily Mason. You were supposed to help Belle try to cover up her lies. Why did you not do that? But you will not come between me and what is mine. I will get off this boat, clean and clear. They will not recognise me. No one but you has any evidence against me. Then I will get the money owed to me. Why is it right that so few have so much, and so many have so little?'

His hands tighten on my throat.

I kick my legs up against the door, and it opens a crack. It's not locked. I need to fight, despite the pain in my ankle.

Mick reaches out and pulls it closed again. 'Bitch!' he whispers, fierce and hushed. I feel something sharp against my skin, and I remember the knife. I am terrified.

But this is my moment. I can do it. I elbow him in the stomach, sharp, and as he bends slightly, winded, I bite his hand hard.

He screams, and whacks me across the cheek.

I fade. But just before it all turns to black, I reach for the mop handle and I pull it hard, down on his head.

Then the world disappears. And I feel nothing.

77

'Emily!'

I open my eyes to a familiar voice. I have no idea where I am, what's happening.

Jimmi's face. Jimmi's arms.

I am safe.

'Oh my lordy, what have we here! Oh gosh, she's hurt!' The sound of running footsteps and a woman's voice. I know her.

'Please go and get help. And here, give me that drink, it will help bring her round!' Jimmi's voice – and other footsteps. Someone else runs slowly, with an uneven gait.

Everything is hazy, and then I taste the tang of Coke from a bottle.

I open my eyes to a big, blue hat, and a woman with hoop earrings, shiny red lipstick and the kindest face.

'It's Emily! Emily from the first day. Oh, my dear. What has happened to you? We've got you now. My husband's gone for help.'

The lady from the queue is stood up over me.

But I feel Jimmi's arms, and when he leans forwards, he's all I can see.

I don't know where Mick Tenor went. I don't know much at all.

'Please don't leave me,' I manage. 'Where is Mick? Did they catch him?'

'I'm staying right here.' His voice is soft. 'Yes. It's OK.'

I feel my eyes closing, and I want to speak, but the throb in my head is too much. I try to move my legs, but I can't lift them very far – they feel too heavy.

'I'm right here, Emily. You're safe now.'

EPILOGUE

The sun is hot on the streets of New York. I've been in hospital for a few days. Long enough for Dad and Finn to fly out.

Belle has been calling, but I asked to be left alone. Dad and Finn have been with me, and they're all I've wanted. They've kept everyone away.

I've not seen any of the Scarmardos since the ship. I haven't seen Belle since the water, when I wasn't sure if she was alive or dead.

I've not had a chance to discuss Mick Tenor. Or Simon Cartwright, as the police said was his real name. He'd been caught very quickly. He managed to get out of the storeroom he'd trapped me in, but I'd hit him well with the broom, and he collapsed only a few metres away.

The police told me he was in custody. They searched his cabin and his luggage and found traces of a poison. Once the analysis was done, it matched the poison found in Xander's blood. They found a receiver in Simon's bag, and a bug in Belle's make-up case. Simon had planted a listening device, and heard all her and Mattia's plans.

The officer who spoke to me said, once they confronted him with all this, he crumbled pretty quickly. He really did seem to believe he was in love with Viola – though how he could go on to kill her is a mystery. I suppose there's not much point in staying quiet about the rest, once you're charged with murder. He'd known Mattia was planning to go for the midnight swing, and he'd cut through the rope. He hadn't cared if he'd killed Belle too. He was relying on Belle to take the fall for the crime, and then he'd get off scott free. And he'd confessed to loosening the wheel on their car, as he had to me. The siblings released a few stories about Belle, offered her money to leave Mattia, had a brick thrown through her window, but they'd never tried to kill her. It had all been him. There was no way out for him. Not now.

My phone beeps.

Nearly here? I've got a table at the back.

I spot Belle tucked away as the waiter leads me through the spacious fancy New York restaurant that even I've read about.

She rises as she sees me, hesitant. Gone is the imperious Belle, but also gone is the old one I knew. This one looks both wiser and also less secure.

'Emily?' She opens her arms, and I step into them briefly. Then we sit.

'I'm sorry about it all,' she says, looking at her menu before she looks at me.

I nod. 'So am I.' I lift the water the waiter pours, then I watch as he leaves. 'How is everyone?'

'So so,' she says. 'The funeral is in a week. Jimmi is organising it.'

At the mention of his name she looks at me quickly, but says nothing else.

'And how is Bean? Was it true, that he's not Mattia's son?'

Belle nods. 'It was a huge shock. There's been a lot of discussion. A lot of tears. But I think they'll be fine, I *think*. Mattia was devastated, but he's been really trying – he's seen him every day since the ship. He's trying with them all. I think he realised how much him and me—' She stops. 'Bean's writing. He's taking it all very seriously. And dating Mirka – again, taking that seriously as well. He's a changed man. He's a broken man, but he seems to be making an effort to build himself back up.'

'Did you tell them? About the earrings?'

She looks at me quickly.

'Belle, come on. You took them, didn't you? You banked on Mattia not realising which ones they were. You flaunted them in front of his children. It was you who asked Mattia to tell them about the baby on the ship, to stir it up. It was you who leaked the news of the pregnancy to the media, then blamed the Scarmardos. Was it you who suggested he threaten to disinherit them all? What was it you said to me – *it would do them good, to make it on their own?*'

Her head disappears back into her menu, but I hear her say very quietly, 'I told him most of it. But Bean and Chloe also told him what they'd been doing. We've all said sorry. I was so frightened he'd pick them over me, I pushed them away as hard as I could.'

I wonder how it can go from here. Can they ever really mend the fractures in the family?

'And Viola's death?' I ask.

She looks surprised. 'Oh, didn't you know? They went through the photos they found in Simon's apartment. There were loads of the day she died. It was very clear that he was there. And there was some footage from another yacht, of me sailing away. I'm in the clear. He's confessed to killing her – but he said it was self-defence with Viola.' She shrugs. 'He's been charged.'

Once we've ordered, the food's been eaten, and we've passed pleasantries, I show her photos of Finn. Jimmi and I haven't told anyone yet that he's Finn's father. Finn has to know first. And Dad – she asks about Dad. She tells me the ship made enough money on the voyage to secure the funding Lila had been pursuing. The ship is assured financial security for now. There had been some negative PR after the search and rescue incidents. But the company had managed to blame it mostly on the storm, and had offered up compensation and cheap return cruises to appease passengers.

I ask how the pregnancy is going. It had been a huge relief to

RACHEL WOLF

hear Belle hadn't lost the baby after the fall from the ship. Thank God for all the diving from yachts Belle and I had done. We both knew how to hit the water. She had been badly bruised, and had been watched carefully, but it could have been so much worse.

I think about the IVF. Had it really been Belle who couldn't conceive? I wonder if she'd been so set on having a child to keep Mattia that she pretended she'd had issues so that Mattia would agree to it. But I realise I don't care. Belle can keep her secrets. Viola can take hers to her grave. It's time to leave.

'Where are we, Emily? Can we be friends?'

I look at her – good dress, diamonds at her neck. Her hair has been recently blow-dried and I wonder how much it's really cost her.

'You know, years ago, when I accused you of breaking my hair straighteners, it was me. I broke them, then lied so your mum would buy me a new pair,' I say, and I don't know why this is the time, but it feels as though we need to start with a clean slate. 'I was always jealous of what you had.'

'Oh!' She laughs. 'We knew! Emily, do you think we didn't want to help? You've fought from the very start. Even with nothing, you fought harder than anyone I've ever met. You made me apply to uni, when I didn't think I stood a chance. You made me go for that interview in Santorini – you were the one who talked us onto that boat.'

'I was the one who arranged for us to take that money, when the boat was attacked.' I say this bit quietly.

'Neither of us got it all right,' she says. 'But, Emily, why do you think I asked you to come? I'd be dead without you. Or in jail. You're a fighter. And I love you.'

She puts her hand on mine. 'Don't judge me too much,' she says. 'It's just a story you've heard before. Don't look at me like that!' She half smiles. 'We've all read fairy tales. It's the reason people buy lottery tickets! Just the same old story.' She shrugs.

I had taken my fair share. I think of Juan. I think of Dad, of foodbanks. Reasoning it out doesn't make it right.

'I think we were richer than we ever knew, before all of this,' I say.

I stand. Then I hold my arms wide. 'No creases,' I whisper, and she laughs.

We'll be OK. It will just take time.

But I've loved her all along.

Heat swells up from the pavement in New York in the summer like they put heaters under the sidewalk. The sun bounces from the tall buildings as I head to Central Park. Dad and Finn are waiting for me. They have ice creams. We're staying in a cheap hotel nearby. Mattia and Belle sent an offer of a room at the Plaza, sent clothes. I returned it all. I'll put in some overtime when I get back.

'Pretzels?' A shout from a nearby seller, and I buy three. Huge, and coated in lumps of salt so big they look like crystals.

I can see them up ahead.

'Emily?' A shout from behind me.

I'm still nervy, and I jump a little.

'Sorry.' It's Jimmi. He stops, looks contrite. 'I didn't mean to scare you. I hope you don't mind. Belle told me about your lunch. I just missed you at the restaurant, but I saw you head this way.'

Neither of us speak for a minute, and I remember all the thoughts I'd had in hospital. I'd played this out so many times. I need to get it right. But I can't help myself. I start hard and say, 'Finn is mine.'

He nods. Slowly.

I wait. I need him not to fight me on this.

'Of course,' he says. Then he takes a breath. 'Can I meet him?' He smiles. 'On your terms?'

The sun is so bright, I can't really make out the expression in his eyes. I can't read his face. I think of his stare when I saw him on that first day in Portsmouth. When I thought Jimmi Scarmardo didn't know who I was. That had changed. So much has changed.

'Emily.' He steps forward, and this time I smile. 'You know, if you ever wanted to visit Milan, you have an open invite. Can I say the same about a certain English seaside town? We met on a beach. I'd like to see how we manage on the British sand. Less alcohol, maybe. What can go wrong?'

I laugh, and watch his face crack open. I've envisioned that face many times since Finn was born. And he's been there for me. I'm not sure I would have survived the last few days without Jimmi. I can't forget the time we met – he was the one who held me when I needed someone.

'You know it's much colder than Italy. And you'd never get a job in the factory. You're too soft,' I say.

He takes one more step forward. He lifts the pretzels out of my hand. 'I'll carry these. Can you buy me one? If I'm going to be part of the family – however you'll have me – the least you can do is put some bread on the table.'

I buy another and we head to the park. The sun is in my eyes again, and the figures of Finn and Dad are hazy – shimmering up ahead like a melting horizon. Can I see a future with Jimmi in it? I glance at him.

'I'm nervous,' he says, and I hear it in his voice.

'Come on,' I say. 'Come and meet your son.'

ACKNOWLEDGEMENTS

A huge thank you to my fantastic agent, Eve White, and also Ludo Cinelli and Steven Evans.

Thanks also to the incredible team at Head of Zeus for all that they do. I benefitted from a brilliant editorial team: Laura Palmer, Bethan Jones and also Peyton Stableford, and the book is all the better for them. From cover designer to copyeditor – I am very grateful.

A particular mention should go to the impressive work done by Hostage International. Belle was held for a fictional three days, but the many real stories of hostages freed or still in captivity are heart-breaking and deserve to be heard. Thanks to Nicole Moody for checking my Italian so carefully and not minding all the texts.

I'm grateful to all crew (and the Captain!) who answered questions tirelessly about cruise ships. Particular thanks to Nirmal Saverimuttu and Tom McAlpin. And also thanks to Victoria and Matt Quinney, and Geraldine Gardener, who took to the seas with me for the purposes of research.

I'm indebted to those who read the novel and offered advice: Ella Berman, Kate Simants and Dominic Nolan. And many thanks to my CBC writing group and to my criminally minded author friends; you make a dream job even better.

As always, love to my endlessly supportive parents, sister and children. And to Rob.

ABOUT THE AUTHOR

RACHEL WOLF grew up in the north of England and studied at Durham University. Before turning to writing, she worked for a holiday company and travelled widely. *Five Nights* takes inspiration from some of those travels.